Alison,
Thank you so much
for your support & I
hope you enjoy!

Smoke & Mirrorz

D1522743

Cynthia Lucas

Lucas, Cynthia
Smoke and MirrorZ
ISBN : ISBN-13: 978-1491034798

Cover art: Amygdala Design
www.amygdala.net

THE JINN

There are many legends surrounding the Jinn, as they are known throughout Arabic myths. The word *'genie'* in English is derived from the Latin 'genius', which originally came from the Arabic 'Jinn' or 'Jinni'. And although its most ancient meanings are lost now to most modern students, and the word 'genius' is used to denote unusual intellect, the original etymology of the word meant a sort of tutelary or guardian spirit with great wisdom...a twin soul, who remains hidden in the space between matter, assigned to each person at their birth and who may guide and inspire the person to the answers they seek outside of human perceptions.

The Jinn reside in a parallel realm to that of humankind and there are several different types. The Marid, the Shaitan, the Angels, and the Ifrit. The Ifrit (pronounced 'eefreet') when in their native state are made of what is described in legends as a smokeless fire; a heat energy with the power of creation. The Ifrit can be good, wielding their great power for noble intent, or evil....a devastating and destructive force to be reckoned with... or of neutral benevolence.

The Ifrit are the most powerful of the Jinn. Sometimes they come forth into the world of humans when called upon, or even during the hot, swirling siroccos that cross the desert sands as they blow in from the sea. They are sometimes, although not always, as arrogant as they are powerful and attributed with granting wishes to humans, if somehow imprisoned and ordered to do so.

Unlike the Angels, who take their orders from God or Allah...the Jinn, like humans, are beings of free will and curiosity.

Humankind's frail earthly weapons hold no power over a Jinn...however, *magic* does.

And love is perhaps the greatest magic of all.

ACKNOWLEDGEMENTS:

When I first began this journey of a writing career, little did I know the twists and turns that awaited me, nor did I know where it would lead me. Three years, an Amazon #1 Best Seller, a Top 20 and all of my books being Top 100 Best Sellers later, here I am. And I did not arrive here on my own!

First off…as always, to my family and my husband, who stand by me and support my long hours of writing and editing…the late nights and the hectic deadlines; you have my deepest love and appreciation for putting up with me so I can follow this wonderful dream.

To my beautiful friends at I Heart Books who've supported my work from day one…Jeannette Medina and her team, my love to you always. You're the best!

To my friends who've read and shared my books…and to my beautiful readers who've read and enjoyed my stories, you're the reason I'm here.

To the spirit of Scheharazade, who walks beside me and breathes inside me the stories in my mind's eye….

And to the Jinn, Azizi ab'd al Jadu: thank you for the inspiration. Your wish was my command! ;)

SOME FACTS:

One in every four women will experience domestic violence in her lifetime.

An estimated 1.3 million women are victims of physical assault by an intimate partner each year.

85% of domestic violence victims are women.

Historically, females have been most often victimized by someone they knew.

Females who are 20 - 24 years of age are at the greatest risk of nonfatal intimate partner violence.

Most cases of domestic violence are never reported to the police

Witnessing violence between one's parents or caretakers is the strongest risk factor of transmitting violent behavior from one generation to the next.

Boys who witness domestic violence are twice as likely to abuse their own partners and children when they become adults.

30% to 60% of perpetrators of intimate partner violence also abuse children in the household.

****

The crimes in this story are fictitious, but every year millions of women and children suffer very real injuries, both physical and sexual, at the hands of an abuser.

If you or someone you know is in danger or has been the victim of abuse, please contact the numbers below.

THE NATIONAL DOMESTIC VIOLENCE HOTLINE:
1-800-799-7233

THE NATIONAL SEXUAL ASSAULT HOTLINE:
1-800-656-4673

NO woman or child (or anyone) should ever have to suffer at the hands of those who would be so heartless, OR who've been victims themselves and who have been so damaged themselves that they then propagate it and harm others in this way. It all stops with you, with me…with US working together.

If someone you know needs help, BE that angel that offers the hand that picks them up off the ground, helps them seek justice and by doing so gives them the greatest gift of all: being a survivor.

Dedicated to the memory of Giorgio aka 'George'

For 15 years, you were the King of Cats.
You are loved forever, and remembered with
great fondness....

CHAPTER ONE

"Step right up, ladies and gentlemen and be amazed by the sights you are about to witness; a magic carpet ride that will blow your mind and leave you breathless!"

The tall man in a top hat and tuxedo tails stood in front of the large carnival tent, with the words, 'Smoke & MirrorZ' emblazoned across the side, his announcement booming through a PA system from the small stage platform that stood by the entry. His long hair hung down his back like a cape of black silk, his beard was trimmed into a neat goatee and his kohl-liner rimmed eyes widened with all the drama expected of a barker as he half spoke and almost sang his well-rehearsed patter.

Scheri Bloom eyed him warily as she stood in line waiting to get in, marveling at how much he looked as though he could have stepped from an old sepia photograph from bygone days.

Well…almost. Except for the Rolling Stones t-shirt peeking out from the top of his jacket and sleeves that were rolled up to his elbows, exposing forearms covered heavily in tattoos of every color. A mixture of vintage finesse with modern day biker chic would be a more accurate description.

As the line moved forward and she came to a stop right in front of the platform, he eyed her with admiration, noting her long black hair and hazel-green eyes.

Her jaw tightened as she tucked her hands deeper into the pockets of her jacket, wishing she could wrap it tighter around her body, shielding her from his gaze.

Men. She hated all of them right now!

She winced slightly as her hand dug into a large bruise on her hip as her fingers pushed deeper into the pocket of her coat. The faded purple mark, along with several others were harsh reminders of the cruel bastard of a husband she'd run away from, and as the carny's eyes lingered on her for a

1

moment longer she suddenly felt self-conscious as her mind traveled back in time over the events of the past few months in an instant.

She tried to move by quickly without making eye contact and instinctively, her hand came out of its warm cocoon and her fingers traced the curve of her cheek near her left eye. She hoped the swelling was down and the discoloration covered well enough by her make-up. It had been a couple of weeks now and it had turned from a deep purple to a lighter shade of greenish yellow.

Her husband Derek Worley was a wealthy lawyer....handsome, educated and seemingly the perfect catch. She had been working as a copywriter at an advertising agency in the office building where his law firm was located, when they'd met. From all appearances he seemed taken with the fact that she was bright and ambitious and was impressed with not only her outward appearance, but her gift for creative writing as well. Not just advertising copy, but short stories and longer works that she dreamed of adapting to movie screenplays.

He also seemed appreciative of her donating her time helping with fundraisers for a local nursing home and the SPCA. She'd lost her mother some months earlier and spending her free time helping others eased the pain and kept her mind and body busy as she worked through her grief.

She hadn't been looking to find anyone when she'd met Derek...but he'd come into her life at just the right time to help her get past the grief and move on to better days.

They began dating and had allowed the relationship to move slowly...taking their time to get to know each other over intimate dinner dates, long walks, movies and quality time. When they'd finally ended up in bed, she certainly had no complaints about his skills as a lover or the raw attraction to him that she felt. He was tall, well-built, handsome and elegant with his sun streaked hair and blue eyes that sparkled with intelligence. He knew how to rock a business suit like a runway model, could wrap you around his finger with engaging conversation and there was something positively magnetic about him. She often wondered what it was he saw in her, when he could probably have almost any woman he wanted...another lawyer or a doctor maybe. But he seemed more than content and just as attracted to her as she was to him.

As their relationship progressed to the next level and they'd moved in together, he'd began talking about investing in helping her start up a small publishing company that would get some of her own work out there, but also that of other writers.

With each passing day she was more certain he was 'the one' but never pushed for any kind of commitment. They were happy living together and she didn't want to seem over-eager or make him wonder if she were latching on to him because he was wealthy and seemed to be interested in helping her pursue a writing career that she'd always dreamed of. She wanted him to know that she really loved him. She was happy with things just as they were. But to her surprise, exactly one year after they'd begun dating he decided to propose on New Year's Eve.

He'd given her a stunning 3 carat diamond and she thought her heart would burst with love and excitement at the thought that she was going to spend the rest of her life with this incredible man. Their engagement had lasted for about six months and although she'd felt a little twinge of something or another when he'd brought out a pre-nup for them to sign, being in the business of law, she knew it was certainly nothing personal and all about being sensible and protecting one's assets.

Their wedding night had been absolutely beautiful...perfect in every way and for several weeks afterward life had been everything she'd ever dreamed it could be. Like a fairy tale come true.

3

And then one day shortly thereafter, the magic carpet ride in the clouds became more like getting the rug pulled out from under you and falling out of the sky.

One evening he'd come home from work and she was cooking dinner when she accidentally dropped a glass on the floor. He stared at her for a moment with a strange look in his eye and as she reached for the broom to sweep up the mess, he'd walked over and grabbed her arms to stop her. He backed her up against the counter and stared at her menacingly for a moment. At first she thought maybe he was joking or wanted to do a little 'role playing' when he began to squeeze her wrist and said, "You have a lot of nerve breaking one of *my* glasses, missy."

She'd smiled at him, and said, "What do you mean *your* glasses, mister!" waiting for him to smile back and then give her a kiss or something. But instead he said, "What the hell are you smiling about. Wipe it off now, or I'll slap it off for you."

Her expression quickly grew to fear as he grabbed a handful of her hair and bent her backwards over the counter, his face just inches from her own. His fingers dug into her neck and she felt the blood pressure building up in her head as she grew lightheaded and started to pass out.

"Clean this shit up…now. And then you'd better have dinner on the table by the time I get back downstairs."

She looked up at him as he spat out the words. His eyes…those baby blues that she'd once admired for their depth and warmth, now seemed like pieces of ice cold slate; the sparkle gone, replaced by a flat, almost reptilian emptiness..

He let go of her as she gasped for air, holding the counter to keep he legs from buckling underneath her. He didn't say another word as he headed up the stairs, taking them two at a time. She started to grab her purse and run out the back door, as his voice rang out from the top of the landing, "Don't even think about running. Because I will be on your ass in one minute flat and when I catch you, you will regret the day you were ever born."

"I'm calling the police," she said defiantly.

He laughed. "Go ahead. Call 'em. I see these guys in court every day of the week. I defend the innocent and help punish the guilty. You know damned well how close I am with the Attorney General...or did you forget that? I'm one of the 'good guys' and all I have to do is tell them you're just another gold digger...a starving writer who married into money and now you're crying abuse so you can try to break the pre-nup and cash in on a divorce. I know plenty of shitbags who can easily be paid off to say that you hired them to rough you up to make it look real, too. They get paid to do what they're told and keep their mouths shut. So if you think anyone's going to take you seriously you're out of your fucking mind."

He walked over to the phone, picked it up off the ringer and tossed it down the stairs to her.

"Go ahead and call," he sneered. "When they get here you can tell them all about it and I will have someone over here in five minutes to show up acting like a boyfriend on the side. And I dare you to run, you little bitch."

She'd quickly put down her purse and began to shake all over. Would anyone believe her if she told them he had threatened her and actually already laid a hand on her? What the hell was going on and why was he acting like this? Was he drunk or on drugs?

She walked back into the kitchen and quietly finished cooking dinner and tried to calm herself so that maybe she could talk rationally with him and try to understand. Maybe he was overworked to the point of snapping and needed therapy or something? She'd heard of people in high powered jobs having nervous breakdowns or going psycho.

She sat at the far end of the table in silence watching him wolf down his food, as if he'd never said the things that had come out of his mouth just minutes earlier.

5

"Derek, listen. Is there something going on at work? Are you being put under some kind of pressure and you just snapped? I know this isn't the guy I married. Maybe you need a doctor."

"Doctor?" He laughed out loud. "Honey, this is exactly who you married, and I don't need a fucking doctor. I just need you and all of your kind...you little people, to shut your goddamned mouths and do as you're told."

"Why are you doing this?" Her voice was barely a whisper and her eyes welled with tears.

He stopped chewing for a moment and smiled.

"Because I can."

The soulless, almost inhuman expression that crossed his features as he spoke the words chilled her to the bone.

In the weeks to come, she'd tried several times to escape while he was asleep or out of the house, but every single time the bastard either woke up, or tracked her down somehow and forced her back home at gun point. And no matter how careful she was in her attempts he always found her...as though he had some kind of crystal ball and could see her every move. He had no doubt hired someone to watch her.

And then came the brutal beatings she'd suffered at his hand afterward. He would usually try to not leave any evidence of his psychotic rages on her face, but sometimes a split lip or a black eye would have to be covered with extra layers of make up or darker shades of lipstick. One time, they'd had to attend a dinner party and she was forced tell people that she'd gotten lip injections trying to get that 'bee stung look'.

Since most of the other law partners' wives were all about boob jobs and Botox they nodded and smiled knowingly...all the while oblivious of the truth of her pain and suffering at the hands of the monster they all viewed as a 'pillar of the community'.

6

Perhaps the most disturbing incident though, had come one night when instead of his usual physically abusive onslaught, he'd forced her to drink a cup of thick, metallic tasting red liquid that she was sure was blood and she'd passed out shortly thereafter, only to wake up the next day with no memory of anything that had happened.

Her only visible evidence had been a tiny slice in the wrist of her left hand and residual soreness and blood between her legs which made her more than a little certain he'd had some rough sex with her while she was out cold. She didn't want to imagine the possibility that he may have invited some of his disgusting, sleazy friends in for the 'party' as well....maybe even the thugs he'd hired to keep tabs on her.

She'd struggled to remember what happened but no matter how hard she tried to get a picture....*any* picture...nothing would come to the surface.

After that, she realized that she didn't care anymore if she lost her life in the process of escaping because living the way she was wasn't living at all. And somehow she knew that if she didn't get away, she would die by Derek Worley's hand someday anyway.

And so she'd waited for her moment, knowing she was going to have to plan everything down to the last letter, because he would have traces on every credit card, bank card, her cell phone. Everything. And if he did have someone watching her and tailing her every move, she was going to have to be very resourceful in coming up with some way to leave without being seen.

And even if she was able to make her initial escape and lose whoever he'd paid to keep tabs on her, he still had access to what he needed through a few detective friends who were apparently just as scummy as he, and if he wanted her found, she would be if she left any kind of paper trail or electronic transactions anywhere behind her.

It was unsettling, but she was going to have to try to live off the grid for awhile and she would have to stay moving.

So, she'd bided her time, put up with the rages and the beatings as she'd managed to hide away small amounts of cash a little at a time until she had enough to make a run for it.

He'd gotten lazy in the last couple of months because she'd been playing the part so well of the cowering, obedient wife, acting completely beaten down and never giving him any reason to believe that she would dare to try to run anymore. He'd even gotten lax in the severity of his abuse. She would take a couple of hard slaps to the face, beg his forgiveness for whatever she'd done to upset him and then would quietly excuse herself to go clean up and get ready for bed.

And on those nights when he would come to bed ready for sex she would close her eyes and simply allow her mind to drift away to someplace else so she wouldn't have to confront him touching her body or that she was being forced to touch him. She wanted to ask him why he bothered with her, when she knew he had plenty of women on the side, but she knew it would be just one more reason to set him off. So she left it alone. If she could endure it for just a little longer, she would be free..

Then one night, he'd gone out drinking and gambling on a boxing match with a friend of his from the Attorney General's office and he'd lost a pretty decent amount of money, and come home and taken it out on her.

He'd split her lip with a punch to the face, blackened her eye and thrown her down on the floor so hard she slammed into the wall on the other side of the kitchen. She lay there gasping for breath, because it felt like one of her ribs was broken and her hip hurt so bad she could barely move.

He saw her lying there in agony and she became aware of just how sadistic he was, because he became

8

aroused at the level of pain she was in and raped her right there on the floor, purposely putting pressure on her injured rib and as she stifled her sobs of pain, seeming to enjoy it even more.

She lay there unable to move and trying to send her mind off into another place to escape the pain and humiliation until he was through. It wasn't difficult because she hurt so much she felt like she would pass out.

When he was finished and had walked away, she somehow managed to pick herself up off the floor and stagger to the bathroom to clean up.

As she stood there looking in the mirror at the bleeding gash in her lip and the welts on her side, she decided…no more. She was going to have to make do with whatever she had saved up and get out of there or die trying.

In the past he'd never drunk to any degree that would hinder his reflexes in case she ran, but that night, fate…and his complacency were on her side. She waited until she was sure he was really passed out asleep, and then quietly gathered up the few belongings and the pile of cash she'd carefully hidden aside.

She took the Emergency Exit stairs out of the building they lived in and after carefully cracking the door to make sure no one was there, she'd slipped out the back service entrance where there was no security or doorman. She then headed down the back alleyway to the nearest hedge, which she ducked behind and ran along, hidden from view behind it until she hit open pavement again one block ahead, never looking behind her once. Her injured rib was killing her but she knew this was it…there was no looking back. No going back.

She also knew that one of the security cameras had caught her leaving the building but she could only hope that she would have until Derek woke up and reported her missing before anyone played anything back and started looking for her. It was hours til dawn…a good head start.

But she was still on foot and had limited cash. She was going to have to plan transportation carefully and make sure it couldn't' be traced. She would be limited to riding the bus but no way could she risk reserving a ticket. She'd have to just walk up to the counter and pay right there, and pay with cash. In the cities she could take a taxi as well because that was not traceable either, but it was more expensive.

It was going to be a challenge. No car. No credit cards. No cell phone other than a cheap no-contract one with prepaid cards. No trails of any kind. She had no family...her mother had died of cancer three years ago and her father had never been a part of her life from day one. She didn't even know his name, because her mother had bore her out of wedlock after having a fling with a less than honorable man who had taken off without a trace. She'd tried to track him down more than once over the years, but apparently he hadn't even been using his real name when he was with her mother and there didn't seem to be any name associated with the social security number or other personal information she'd been given.

So...she was completely on her own. No danger of Derek tracking her through phone calls to family members, and she had few friends since she'd gotten involved with him. He'd seen to alienating all of hers, and insisting they only hang out in his wealthy circles.

Now here she was two states and hundreds of miles away from the life she left behind, and she could only pray that this time he wouldn't find her. She'd been gone for almost two weeks, never staying in one place for too long as her body and spirit slowly began to heal; left with the memories and lessons learned. The marks would fade away quickly, but the emotional scars would take much longer.

It would take time, but somehow she was going to get through this, and eventually find a way to live a normal life again...get back to her writing and find a permanent home. For now though, it was one day at a time.

She was snapped back to the present as the line heading into the carnival tent moved forward a few more feet and she heaved a sigh of relief that she was finally inside, and could find a seat and become invisible amid the crowd.

She walked down the large aisle between rows and moved in several seats before plunking down in one of the folding chairs in front of the large stage.

As the area quickly filled, most of the seats were soon taken and she felt much safer. She was just another face in a huge sea of people.

The lights dimmed down and the boom of the speakers thundered as the opening music of the show began.

Mist clouds began to pour out along the floor of the stage and two ghostly looking assistants that looked like they were coming from a movie projector were pushing a large platform on wheels that held a free-standing floor mirror. They pushed the platform to the center of the stage so everyone could see the large reflective surface, and then they rotated the entire platform 90 degrees until it was facing sideways.

Then as larger billows of smoke began to pour from either side of the stage and an array of lights rolled down like lasers across the stage, the music grew louder and all of a sudden a man's leg appeared from 'inside the mirror'. The leg came forth, and then an arm, and then finally his head and body stepped through his 'portal' and he turned to face the crowd. The audience went absolutely wild at the brilliant illusion as he stood there before them smiling.

Scheri gasped out loud at the incredible sight, wondering how the hell he'd done it. It was better than anything she'd ever seen on any magic show on television or in Vegas!

And her breath caught in her throat just a little more when she realized how handsome the man the announcer had just called 'Z' was, standing there on the stage.

He was over six feet tall, with long hair that hung to his shoulders...as black as a raven's wing, broad shoulders accentuated by the tight sleeveless shirt he was wearing, and a body carved out with well-defined muscle. His skin was like coffee with cream, and there was a large multi-colored dragon tattooed across his left shoulder; its tail draped down his arm and curled along his thick bicep almost to the elbow.

From a distance and in the changing lights it was hard to tell what color his eyes were, but they didn't appear to be black or brown beneath his thick but well-groomed brows. They were light colored and his teeth were straight and white and stood out in bright contrast to his dusky skin.

He looked like some kind of beautiful Arabian Knight come-to-life and she could feel her heart pounding in her throat. The world stopped moving for just a moment and there was no sound, no crowd, no anything else but the picture of him standing there.

He was at a very safe distance, yards away up on the stage completely unaware that she was even there in the sea of bodies watching the show, and yet as she was suddenly jolted back to reality, she felt as though he could somehow sense what had just happened to her.

Livid at herself for allowing her treacherous hormones to betray her in any way, she forced her eyes to look away and reminded herself of the suffering she'd endured at the hands of a man. And not one of them was ever going to touch her...or hurt her again.

She dragged in a deep breath, composed herself and focused on what would come next up on the stage. She was, after all, supposed to be here to try to enjoy the show....although the real reason she'd come here was to see if there might be any job openings where she might pick up a few bucks under the table for a few days working as a ride operator or selling food at one of the concession stands.

Carnies came and went with little notice and often no paper trails as their road show moved from town to town. No one kept an eye on them and it would be an easy place to hide out, while saving up a few dollars under the radar. This would be the last place on earth Derek would ever come looking for her!

The show proceeded and Z performed several illusions that had the crowd whooping their approval, including making the two holographic looking assistants that had pushed his platform out onto the stage crackle and fade out. She wondered how they 'moved' along right beside his platform to have it look like the two ghostlike apparitions were pushing it along…he must have some kind of track in the stage or a pre-programmed pattern that it rolled so the two holograms could also be programmed to move along side of it. It was a cool effect regardless of how it was done.

Somewhere in the middle of the show, he'd closed his eyes, and as a misty smoke began to fill the air above their heads he floated out above the crowd, landing in one of the aisles. Walking past the rows of people he reached out, shaking their hands and greeting them personally with a smile as they looked for the wires attached to him and found…none. Somehow the smoky haze surrounding him must have disguised them?

She watched as he neared the row where she sat, thinking he was either really incredibly nice to want to reach out to his audience in that way…or he was a conceited ass who just wanted additional attention. Hard to know since he was simply being a showman and at a distance like that how could anyone read his expression.

Without warning he suddenly announced, "Okay people….it seems my assistants disappeared on me. I guess I have that effect on women?"

Several enthusiastic girls in the audience yelled "NOOOO!!" as he smiled and shook his head and motioned for them to settle down.

He laughed out loud. "I need someone to come up here and help me out."

The group of girls who'd been yelling a few moments ago was standing up making noise and jumping up and down trying to get his attention, but he only offered them a smile and a wink as he walked right by them.

She inched down in her seat as his gaze scoured the crowd for the person who would become his on-stage helper for the next illusion. She even went so far as to reach down and pretend she was picking something up from the floor so her head would be below the level of the seats and she wouldn't be a part of his equation.

When a 'safe' amount of time had passed she sat back up figuring he'd surely passed by. But instead she found he was walking directly to the row where she sat and his expression changed for just a moment as he spotted her sitting five or six seats in.

He stared at her for a moment and then without warning, he motioned for the people in the row to stand and move out, which they gladly did, and he walked into the row and approached her where she sat.

Utter and complete panic overtook her, when she realized what was happening! Not only because she didn't want him coming anywhere near her, but even more so because she needed to be as invisible as possible! She tried to stand up too, praying that maybe he was eyeing someone else further in and he would walk right by, but she soon realized that was not the case, when he stopped right in front of her and offered her his hand.

She looked around at the enthusiastically cheering audience and shook her head 'NO!' in adamant protest but he smiled as he took her hand in his own. His expression took on a look of concern for a split second when he made contact with her skin, but he immediately regained his composure and smiled again before the crowd noticed anything.

He nodded toward the stage, leaned in close to her ear and whispered, "C'mon. You're safe. I promise."

She stared at him for a moment a little taken aback. He'd just promised her she'd be *safe.* And there was no mistaking the way he'd said it. Did he sense something about her life? Was that even possible?

She shook off the feeling. It was ridiculous! The guy was a carnival magician for God's sake!

What was more disturbing was realization that she was *not* going to get out of following him up on the stage, as the crowd cheered loudly.

She felt his hand tighten around hers and he guided her out of the row of people and toward the brightly lit stage. Her knees began to shake and she could feel her heart pounding in her chest as she climbed the stairs and turned around to face the sea of people enthusiastically waiting to see what Z was about to do.

She looked over at him and he nodded as he pulled a chair out from behind the platform and then motioned for her to sit down. He then pulled out a blindfold and a second later, she was engulfed in blackness as the light was blocked out. It didn't matter...she could still feel the hundreds of pairs of eyes that were watching every move.

Goosebumps broke out on her skin as she felt his warm breath against the side of her neck.

"Just stay perfectly still."

"What are you going to do?" she said quietly.

"It's probably better if you don't know 'til after. *Don't* move."

He laughed and a moment later she felt her feet lift from the floor and she could tell that she was floating up off the ground. Despite being blindfolded....and wondering how far above the ground they were since she was more than a little afraid of heights, she couldn't help but wonder how the hell he was doing it!

There had been no visible wires or any kind of see-through platform under the chair as she'd walked up to it on the stage. Not to mention the fact she could feel her feet dangling in thin air! There was *nothing* underneath her. So how?

The crowd gasped as he stood beside the chair and both of them levitated up into the air about twenty feet off the floor. He took a large hoop and passed it over them to show there was nothing holding the chair up. A second later, the chair turned 45 degrees and appeared to be on its side as it continued to float in the air before suddenly righting itself.

Wild applause and whistles thundered through the air and a second later Z reached over and untied the blindfold as he held her shoulder with his other hand to keep her from being startled when she saw they were actually up off the ground. He tried to keep an even expression himself, because he was quite frankly startled, that when he'd had a fleeting thought of how cool it would be if he could rotate the chair 45 degrees, it had seemed to do exactly that, as though it had a mind of its own! His powers had limits and he had no earthly or unearthly idea what the hell was going on but he was determined to find out.

Her breath caught in her throat and she grabbed the seat of the chair holding it tight. She'd felt the shift in position a few moments ago but refrained from screaming.

She looked over at him. "Put me down. Now!" She looked out at the cheering crowd, and continued smiling as she spat the words through clenched teeth.

For a second she was taken aback at the bravado of her own demand. If she'd have said anything like that to Derek, he would backhand her so hard her teeth would rattle in her skull and so she'd taken on a quiet, mousy persona out of necessity during the last several months. But this wasn't Derek...and for the first time in a very long time she felt empowered enough to speak her mind. This daredevil idiot hovering her how many feet off the floor without even asking her permission was a good place to start!

The chair slowly descended to the ground. He helped her to her feet and they walked to the edge of the stage where he took a bow and motioned for the crowd to give his 'assistant' her due applause.

He walked her to the bottom of the stairs and then bounded back up as the ending music of the show began to thunder through the speakers and a moment later he walked back over to the mirror still standing on the platform and stepped 'into' it as his exit mirrored his entrance at the beginning of the show. A moment later he was gone and the stage went black. The music continued to thunder as the audience cheered.

The lights came back up inside the tent and the crowd stood to leave, forming neat lines up the aisles leading out to the exit. She stood, taking her place in the line behind an elderly man and his wife who were still trying to figure out how Z had done it.

They turned to her as the woman, asked, "Oh, my goodness… weren't you scared being turned over so high in the air. And how did he do it?!"

She shrugged. "I wish I knew. And no…I didn't know beforehand, thank God, or I probably would have had a heart attack."

The old lady patted her shoulder and chuckled lightly, "Well, you did a wonderful job up there, dear."

She forced a polite smile and sighed. "Thanks."

The crowd formed two neat lines leading to the exit of the tent and all she could think of was escape. She needed to get out of here, away from all these people who now knew her face and away from this carnival. It was a shame because she'd really hoped this would be her opportunity to find some work for a week or two. *Thanks a lot, Z,* she thought to herself.

A few moments later she noticed that he had appeared from behind the curtains on the stage and was now standing at the exit to the tent shaking hands with his audience as they left.

She scanned the area to see if there was some other way out because the last thing she wanted right now was to talk to him. He was, after all, the cause of her missed opportunity after making a spectacle of her...not to mention he made her feel uncomfortable. He was too self-assured, a little bit smart-assed from what she could tell, and good-looking enough to get away with both. It was the same deadly combination of traits that had attracted her to Derek....not that she would ever be remotely interested in him. But, she'd learned her lesson the hard way, of what kind of demons people carried within, and there was no way in hell she wanted to speak with him...not even for a 'thank you' for being his unwilling assistant.

Luckily he was busy with the dozens of people waiting to say hello and shake his hand. She had to get out of here and get safely on the road again...now.

She spotted a large flap that looked it might be a way out of the tent that was in the opposite direction that the line was moving and immediately headed towards it.

CHAPTER TWO

Azizi ab'd al Jadu...otherwise known to his audiences as 'Z', watched as the woman he'd called up on stage with him scanned the area for her escape route. He didn't know much on first contact, but once he'd touched her skin, he'd seen enough about her recent past to know that she was on the run from someone who'd beaten the shit out of her.

He stared down at his hands still reveling in the jolt of power he'd felt as she'd been sitting in the chair, and still couldn't believe that he'd had enough power to actually turn the chair over with her sitting in it...because although he was able to levitate objects and dematerialize himself and those things he'd conjured, he usually did not have quite enough power to carry extra weight....or turn it with such ease. And usually a fleeting thought was not nearly enough energy flow to make matter move. Hell, some nights he worried whether his power would work at all....particularly if he'd had a couple shots of tequila and his senses were dulled.

Being a Jinn, such limitations were frustrating to the point of insanity sometimes, but he'd come to grudgingly accept it since he'd broken The Law and came here to this realm of his own choosing instead of being called forth to serve.

Oh, this place had been all fun and games when he first arrived; being able to experience all the sensations of the physical world. But that had worn off all too quickly. Now? All we was left with was the remnants of his once vast powers and the title of 'carnival magician' to add to his resume.

Humans called his kind 'genies' and they were attributed in ancient Persian and Arabian legends with everything from ghostly apparitions and rattling the windows at night, to the bad luck or perhaps sometimes good luck that came from nowhere.

Most Jinn activity was simply ghost-like apparitions, and supernatural phenomenon and that's where it ended. They kept to their own realm pretty much. Thankfully, there were a very few humans who'd ever figured out how to call forth a Jinn and in modern times when the old ways and magic had been pushed aside in favor of technology, no one bothered because they didn't believe it was possible anyway. Nowadays it was all 'legend' and that was probably a good thing because in the hands of the selfishness of mankind, nothing but destruction would come of it.

The word 'genius' in the language of man had come from the word 'Jinni' because although genies were often implicated in some of the more spine tingling supernatural phenomena, they were also attributed with influencing the brilliant ideas that would suddenly come from nowhere bringing new wisdom and inventions. But many Jinn…and particularly the Ifrit, were mischievous to say the least…most were downright spiteful. Here and there, a benevolent one would come into being, but it was not often.

Being that he was an Ifrit, he never kidded himself about his selfish nature….but something inside him wanted to believe that he had a soft spot for humankind buried away somewhere inside of him in a little corner of his soul. He'd come here long ago… and it was no more than a distant memory.

He was born out of the forbidden love of one of those rare benevolent Jinn, his mother Soheila, who'd come to walk among mankind herself, and one of Allah's Watchers; an Angel named Morad who'd fallen from grace after defying orders from above to be with her.

He had grown up never knowing his father, other than the stories his mother would tell him because he had left her side soon after his birth to 'ascend' to some higher level after being accepted back into the Order.

He'd never forgiven his father for abandoning him and his mother, because in his estimation the only purpose it could serve was to show that he didn't care enough about them to stick around. Forbidden love or not.

As for his Jinn side, Ifrit were born in fire…not the fire of physical love, but of spirit. But he was not typical had been actually born to his mother in while she was in her human form. She had lost her power because she had broken The Law, and taken human form of her own free will.

To come into human form of one's free will was strictly forbidden because most Ifrit had quite the level of magical power, but little responsibility or benevolence to use it wisely. Giving humans three wishes was also just as dangerous but there were rules about that too.

The Law was like an insurance policy of sorts, and the basic rules were simple. A Jinn's energy would change and become 'impure' and polluted here in this place. Their power didn't work here in the human realm unless he or she were serving a master, and only three wishes could be granted, just like the books said. But since so few humans had ever done such a thing, if ever, it was all legend anyway.No one had any proof that it had ever happened except in story books.

A Jinn had power in their own realm and influenced humans from a distance. Their power simply didn't work if they came here because what was considered 'normal' in their own realm, would be 'magic' here. As an added bonus, if you could call it that; apparently if a Jinn came here and their powers were working, they couldn't use them for serving themselves.

He often wondered why he himself had not completely lost all of his powers since he had come here by his own hand, just as his mother had. Maybe it was purely luck…or maybe because he was half Angel.

His father Morad had met his mother here and felt sorry for her and after he had healed her energy, she'd been

21

able to change back to her native state and her powers were returned to her. She'd dematerialized them both and spirited them both back to the Jinn realm where she raised him on her own.

Although she grieved over the loss of her Angel lover, his mother had never spoken badly of him for leaving and in fact just the opposite. She had said that he'd told her that someday she would understand exactly why he'd left…and that were he not to leave, the lessons needed would never be learned. His mother had never fallen in love again after that but instead stayed happily by herself.

There was, however, a Jinn who'd been watching her intently with lustful intention for a very long time. His name was Abdul al Leil, which meant 'Servant of Night' and there was something dark and secretive about him that matched his name. He constantly pursued Soheila with gifts, and overt gestures, which she politely refused without being rude.

He did not like or trust Abdul….or the way he looked at his mother. Not because he was filled with bitterness over his father's abandonment and did not want to share her…but because he could just tell that Abdul's intentions were not good.

He'd known a happy upbringing with Soheila, although he knew he would never fit in as a true Ifrit and so at her urging he'd looked at the possibility of developing his Angel side.

Perhaps it was his defiant nature that drove him, but he quickly discovered that he couldn't bring himself to bow down and follow the orders of what he felt were no more than the Angels high and mighty whims. Soheila had tried to explain to him the levels of compassion, selflessness and courage that it took to follow through on a mission or help an earthly being in need of a lesson or assistance, but he found that he had no interest in being anyone's savior. From what he could tell…most humans were even more selfish and destructive than the average malevolent Jinn!

There was no way he could bring himself to waste his time as some pious doormat for the sinners of the world to walk all over as they committed their destructive acts toward one another and then begged for forgiveness after the fact. Why commit a perfectly good sin and then beg for forgiveness for it afterward? It was the most ridiculous thing he'd ever heard of!

He'd also found that in many respects the Angels were sometimes no better than humans either. Look at his own father...who'd abandoned his lover and the child she bore him in the name of some 'noble purpose'.

Noble purpose? He'd learned what that meant, and the last thing he would ever do is swear his fealty to them or anyone else. Much the same way he would never give his heart to anyone, because what did love bring in the end? Not much if his mother's life were any example.

He'd never had any love for following rules; in fact just the opposite. And so, despite knowing The Law and the accompanying threat of losing his power, he found himself unable to resist his hedonistic impulse to cross over into the material realm and take human form to see what it felt like. He figured if he got stuck, Sohelia would probably come to his aid. In his estimation, it had been worth the risk at the time.

There was an old magician who regularly practiced his craft and whose mirror was the perfect doorway into the world. The old guy was fairly senile and never even knew he'd come to visit!

Once he'd done so, he quickly discovered that for whatever reason, he had not completely lost all his powers and he could return to the Jinn realm if he wanted to. And of course, the sheer joy of breaking The Law was enough to make him want to do it again and again.

The human realm was full of many vices...booze, women and pleasures of a physical nature that one could only experience while in a body and he sure as hell didn't plan on missing out on any of them! However what he didn't know at that time was that as time passed, his powers would wane with the 'pollution' of the material world. It was a place of distraction designed to dull the spirit and tantalize the physical senses.

It came as no surprise soon after he arrived, that word had gotten around of what he'd done, thanks to Abdul and he soon found his existence in danger. Perhaps the Jinn elders were jealous or just plain pissed off because he'd broken their stupid law; but either way, they wanted him dead and gone and he could no longer safely keep going back to the Jinn world...it was only a matter of time before they caught up with him, trapped him and dispursed his energy out into the cosmos. And so, after bidding his mother goodbye, he had come back to the human world to stay for good.

Through some act of God or maybe just chance, the old magician had happened to be trying to conjure up some magic on the human side of the mirror that night and instead of being sound asleep with his wine cup in his hand as usual, and he'd been wide awake as he'd come through the looking glass. He then suffered a heart attack and died upon seeing a real genie emerge from the shiny surface...apparently he wasn't much of a *real* wizard or magician after all, to be so frightened by the appearance of a supernatural entity.

He had little care for petty human foibles, but he remembered the moment well as he'd bent over to check for a pulse, and was surprised to find that he felt a little bit bad that his coming here had caused the old man's demise. It was the first time he'd ever felt even a smidgeon of compassion for a human...and at the time, he had hoped it would be the last. He'd come here to escape and hopefully have some fun...not sit around feeling sorry for himself or anyone else.

He tried to revive the old man, but nothing he did was able to bring him back to life, and he was soon to learn the limitations of Jinn power in the human world.

Since there was little else he could do, and there was now a position to be filled, he decided to take on the old man's job as a magician, working in the king's court and even at his worst, he was better at it than the human had been.

That tenure had lasted for some time, until he realized his body did not age at any sort of normal rate and he couldn't stay in one place too long. So he'd moved on and lived as a traveling jester and mage among the Gypsies utilizing his power for entertainment.

But he also had to be careful because any form of magical entertainment that seemed too real, wasn't something that humans were ready for. During barbaric times in the past, he'd had to go into hiding and lost his home more than a few times because he couldn't exactly stick around once someone was onto something being 'off' about him. Not because of any fear of physical harm...human weapons had little or no effect him because he could dematerialize. *Magic* however was another story.

Not the everyday parlor tricks or illusions of the average human magician or psychic or whatever they called themselves, but real magic, practiced by those well-schooled in the occult. They were few and far between here in this place both in past times and present.

Oh, sure, there were plenty of wanna-be vampires, wiccan chanters, and those who walked around in their 'I-am-a-child-of-the-night-capes and robes'. It was quite laughable actually. And they had no idea what other realms, and there were many, that lay just outside of their perception in this atomic-particle marvel of a dimension that consumed the mind and the senses once you were trapped in it.

One thing he did know was that at least according to legend, if a Jinn were to be called out, he could be trapped and ordered to serve by granting three wishes. It wasn't much...but in the right hands, it could do quite an amount of destruction, despite the Laws of Jinn Magic.

As for his being here...well, he did have limits to what he could do. He could see things about people if he touched their skin long enough, although not every detail. Dates and times were vague. And he could create illusions of smoke, levitate his own human body, materialize and de-materialize it and other small items which he'd conjured but unfortunately, since they were not composed of the exact same atomic energy, once they were here, they didn't stay solid for long....long enough to do a magic show or maybe a few days. Then abracadabra and poof! They would start to de-materialize. He constantly had to keep creating new props to work with and other things he'd made.

Creating money wasn't going to happen either, because it was 'using magic to serve himself, and being that it was Law, his magic simply wouldn't work to do it.'

The only way to 'cheat' the system and use magic to serve himself was by using it to work a human job...as a carnival 'magician' and earn his money fair and square. In past decades he'd had the good sense to hoard up plenty of old coins, silver and antiques as the decades and centuries had gone by that he could sell to collectors and dealers.

Money was a system of control here in the modern material universe, just as it had been back then, but he didn't really give a shit, because as with almost every other obstacle, he'd found a way around it.

There were other basic rules that were 'givens' as well. For instance, when a Jinn came into the human world, there would be an object that served as a portal. Usually a mirror or a lamp....that had a history of magic in its past. In his case it was the ancient mirror that belonged to the old magician.

From the human side it was no more than a solid object, but from the Other Side it was like looking at the human world through a large window with a view. Since he did not live in the Jinn world anymore, the in-between place just on the other side, served as a retreat where he could go for privacy and solitude away from human eyes, and Jinn too, since it wasn't a part of either world.

And although it was a place to just 'get away from it all'...he could not just stay there indefinitely because it was a sort of limbo between realms. After awhile his energy would need to be settled in one place or the other...Jinn or human. He couldn't go back to his own realm and so he was forced to materialize and take human form at least once every 24 hours or so and vice versa because his human form would begin to lose its solidity, since it was yet another 'object he'd created.

Teleporting to other locations any further than a few yards away was yet another power that had waned away to nothing over time...he could dematerialize and go to the other side of his mirror but that was it. He was pretty much stuck right here where he was until he moved himself the good old-fashioned way.

He grudgingly put up with his limits because he had no choice in the matter. That is until tonight when he'd touched the girl and his powers had seemingly increased enough to lift both her and the chair high into the air.

He'd come out after the show just as he always did to shake hands with the crowd as they left, but this time he found himself unable to take his mind off of finding and speaking with woman he'd gotten up on stage with him.

He wasn't sure why he even gave her passing glance other than wondering why he'd been able to levitate her so easily. He'd known many relationships, with human females over the centuries and they had all been for pleasure alone because if for no other reason, it was too dangerous to disclose the truth of his nature to anyone. Love was out of the question...and he'd had no need or interest in it anyway. There was no shortage of women falling at his feet. So why settle for just one? Booze, women....all night parties...a seemingly endless trail of pretty bodies to take his mind off the reality of his situation. It was a lifestyle he'd come to enjoy.

27

As for this one...yeah...she was pretty, with that cascade of black curls and those green eyes of hers, although it was hard to tell what kind of body she was rocking under the baggy jacket.

And he hadn't touched her long enough to see more of her past. That could only happen if he were able to make contact with her skin long enough or if he were observing her through the portal from the Other Side, as some Jinn did when they'd found a human who they had their eye on for whatever reason. But he could still tell from the few moments he'd held her hand that she'd been through some pretty rough handling in recent days and that she was afraid; of people in general...and of him.

He sure as hell wasn't looking to be anyone's savior now or ever. That was more along the interests of his father and their kind. But to his own annoyance he still found himself unable to take his eyes or his mind off her as she made her escape.

He saw her as she turned away from the line and started to head in the other direction toward a tent exit that was currently closed off to the public. He smiled graciously and shook the hand of the woman standing in front of him, and then waved to everyone before excusing himself and walking back behind the curtain onstage.

Meanwhile, she had managed to make her way to the hidden exit by that time and began to undo the heavy canvas ties that held the flap door shut and stepped outside into the late afternoon sunlight. She carefully closed the flap behind her and when she turned to walk away from the tent her breath caught with a start as he appeared seemingly from nowhere.

He was standing right in front of her and she found herself staring up at him, unable to ignore the color of his eyes, which she'd been wondering about even as she'd sat in the audience. They were an unusual shade of hazel with golden flecks. He was taller than he'd seemed on stage when she'd been up there, and the muscles of his shoulders and arms filled his shirt sleeves.

"How did you....?" Her voice trailed off as she pointed back to the tent.

He shrugged. "Magic."

She dragged in an annoyed breath. *Okay idiot...so you think you're the next Criss Angel.* She wanted to say it out loud but decided he'd probably take it as a compliment.

"You had me hanging upside down in a chair how many feet in the air without my permission? What if I'd fallen?"

He stared at her for a moment.

She'd kept an almost even tone, but there was no mistaking the *'I'm going to be a complete bitch so you'll just go away'* expression he'd seen so many times on human females. He'd observed it on many occasions in bars and nightclubs, and never directed at him, but usually at some balding, middle-aged, married guy named 'Herb' or 'Harry' who's on a business trip and trying to get laid because 'his wife just doesn't understand him'.

He turned around and looked behind him. Nope. No Herbs or Harrys anywhere in sight. 'The look' was directed at him. He smiled politely, pretending that an imaginary Herb was there after all, and that she were giving the look to that guy instead.

"You weren't upside down, and you weren't in any danger. Believe me."

He sounded almost humored by her concerns although he had to admit she was probably right. He hadn't had enough power to levitate a chair with someone in it for a very long time. He hadn't even been sure it would work! Ah, well...she'd never know. And yep, her attitude was shitty...though he had to admit from what he'd seen when he touched her skin, he couldn't exactly blame her.

"Look...I need to go," she said firmly.

29

She averted her gaze, not wanting to look at him for too long because he made her nervous and she somehow knew he was picking up on it.

"What's your hurry?"

"No hurry. I just need to get going," she lied.

He eyed her suspiciously for a moment and then without warning he reached out and touched the place near her eye where the faded green bruise lay hidden under her make-up. He flinched and drew back quickly as if he'd been burned as his fingers made contact with her skin and the image of the impact she'd taken appeared in his mind...the pain and fear as a man's fist had connected with bone and flesh.

"Who hurt you?"

"I don't know what you're talking about."

She stepped back from him, out of reach.

He shook his head and smiled. "You're a worse liar than you are a stage assistant."

"I never asked to be your assistant!" she shot back defiantly.

"What's your name?"

She stared at him in silence.

"Well? I'm not a mind-reader," he said, matter of factly. He'd been able to detect her physical pain in the brief moment he'd held her hand, but not her name or where she'd come from.

"It's Scheri," she said quietly and yet still managing to sound more than a little aggravated.

"Pretty." He stared at her for a minute. "I'm starving....you wanna go get something to eat?"

"I already told you...I have to go."

"Back to whoever did that to you?" He nodded toward her eye.

"I'd rather die first! Not that it's really any of your business,"

Her hand drifted up to the side of her face as she brushed him aside and started walking across the huge lot toward the exit of the carnival.

He wasn't letting her ditch him that easily, though he still wasn't sure why. She had made it more than clear that she didn't want to have anything to do with him.

"So...why are you here?"

He tried to sound genuinely interested, although he wasn't so sure if he was anymore. Maybe it was just his ego. It *was* actually bothering him that she viewed him as a 'Herb'.

She dug her hands deep into her pockets as she looked over at him while they walked. She shrugged. "Why does anyone come to a carnival?"

"My point exactly...they come to have fun, and that's sure as hell not what you're doing, from what I can tell."

"You don't know anything about me."

"Maybe I'd like to get to know more."

She rolled her eyes. "Great pick up line. Look...Z. I don't want to be rude or anything. But you really should just go hang out with your fans, and those screaming girls that were dying to meet you, and let me be on my way. I didn't ask you to get me up on stage or to follow me."

He sped up and got in front of her, walking backwards so he could face her as he spoke.

"Sometimes the things we don't ask for are the things we need the most."

He almost smiled to himself at the bittersweet humor in the words...since they were after all, coming from a genie. A being whose legendary job is to grant wishes and give people exactly what they ask for....at least that was how it went in the storybooks. Here in real life in *this* place, the 'your wish is my command' shit only happened on I Dream of Jeannie.

As for the words, they had been the last his mother had ever said to him when he'd left her that night to come here, knowing he may never see her again.

He turned back around and trudged on in silence for a few moments next to his unwilling companion until she finally sighed heavily and stopped dead in her tracks.

"Will you please just leave me alone? Do I have to call security…or whoever they have around here to get rid of you?"

He sighed and shook his head in exasperation. This one was a real pain in the ass and he should be walking as fast as possible in the other direction, but something made his feet keep moving along side of hers of their own accord. At this point, he figured maybe it was just his inner Jinn wanting to argue, even if only for the sake of pushing her buttons a little…but he knew that was a lie. He wanted to know what the hell had caused the power surge. He needed more time…he had to keep her around for at least a little while, maybe touch her again to see if the same sensation turned on.

"I'll make you a bet. And if I lose, I'll leave you alone."

Her brows knit together. "What kind of bet?"

"If I can tell you three personal things about yourself, you agree to walk with me and go get something to eat. If I get them wrong, then you walk away alone. Deal?"

"Yeah, right! You already know my name and somehow or another you figured out about the bruise. I'm sure it's showing through my make-up."

"Fair enough. So how about if it's things you haven't told me?"

She eyed him suspiciously and then her expression softened just a little and she wanted to kick herself because she had to admit she found his smile disarming.

"Excuse me…but you're a magician! I have a feeling I'm about to be taken."

He laughed out loud. "Well, then you know the risk."

32

She stood there in silence and he could tell she was torn by her desire to run, and her intrigue.

"C'mon. What's the worst that can happen? Fifteen or twenty minutes of boring conversation and some good old-fashioned, artery-clogging carnival cuisine?"

She struggled to maintain an even expression and he could tell she was warming up regardless of her determination not to show it. She finally nodded in agreement as she held out her hand for him to shake it, sealing their 'deal'.

"So if I do this, do you promise you'll just leave me alone?"

"No. Only if I don't tell you three accurate things about you."

He smiled as she reached out to him, because he knew that once her skin came into contact with his again, just as it had when he'd walked her up to the stage, he would be able to see more things about this woman named Scheri.

She started to withdraw after half a second, but he stopped her. "I need to hold on to your hand for a minute...kind of like a palm reading."

She nodded and as he held her hand in his own, he could feel the tingle of energy flowing through him as the pictures in her mind began to materialize in his. The brutal beatings she'd suffered in recent months, the death of her mother, an office building with a desk and computer...stories.

She was a writer. She was 33 years old and she'd never known her father. And he could clearly see the face of the man from whom she now ran. Her name...'Scheri', was an abbreviation and he suppressed a laugh as he realized the campy humor in his being drawn to her.

Here was a storyteller named Scheharazade. She was living day by day, in fear of a husband who had threatened to take her life, just as that legendary weaver of tall tales from 1,001 Nights had been, and the most laughable part was that she was sitting here with a modern day version of 'Aladdin's genie'. Step right up, folks! It was like some bad comic book version of Arabian Nights.

He was expecting some miraculous revelation would come flooding into his mind about why he'd had the extra jolt of power, but to his surprise....nada. Just a strange buzzing sensation in his chest and instead of the pictures fading as fast as they normally did, the impressions lingered. Almost like they were his own memories. For a split second he felt something else but he couldn't quite put his finger on it.

He was jolted out of his reverie as she abruptly pulled her hand from his, and a little disappointed that he hadn't felt the exact same surge of power he'd felt on stage. Maybe it was a fluke.

"Okay...that's long enough," she said warily.

She stared at him in silence for a moment and then raised a brow. "Well? What are you smiling at?"

He quickly pushed aside the humor of the situation, knowing that she probably wouldn't find it funny, even if he could tell her.

"You're running from someone," he said quietly.

She pointed to her eye. "Well, duh. That's not very hard to figure out. Strike one."

"We agreed it only had to be something personal that you haven't told me."

"Yeah, but that was not very hard to figure out. It doesn't count."

He sighed. "I can see you're trying to make this as difficult as possible. But don't you think it's going to freak you out just a little if I go ahead and tell you what I've seen about you?"

She smiled sarcastically. "No. Because I don't think you can do it."

"Really, now? Okay...well, whether you like it or not, you running from someone counts as number one. Number two: you have black hair and hazel green eyes." He

34

laughed as she gave him look of utter disdain. "Both answers are personal and you didn't tell me either of them."

"You're completely cheating!" She sighed. "Just like I said, you can't do it. But that doesn't mean you won't win, because obviously you're a lawyer when it comes to loopholes."

He looked at her for a moment and found himself resisting the urge to stare at her lips, which were full and beautiful...and for a split second he wondered what they would taste like. He also knew the likelihood of him ever finding out was zero to none. They probably tasted as vinegary as her words anyway.

She sat there smugly after dismissing him with such ease, and for whatever reason, it just drove him to want to make her wrong....and maybe scare the shit out of her just a little. Maybe it was the Jinn in him, since their reputation for things that go bump in the night preceded them...or maybe it was just the way the little minx's voice dripped with sarcasm. No matter the reason, the words escaped him before he could stop himself.

"You're a writer. You lost your mother...she died. You've never known your father. And funny you should mention lawyers and loopholes, because whoever did that to your eye is the one who deserves that title, not me. Oh...and you're 33."

She gasped out loud and suddenly looked very uneasy and began looking around her in every direction.

"Did Derek put you up to this? Did he hire you follow me?" She turned to run, but he caught one of her arms and held it fast and she raised her other arm to protect her face out of habit.

He noticed how pale she looked and instantly realized that she was truly afraid as more pictures began to appear in his mind...people, places, and events that had happened.

He began to pull her closer to him, wanting to try to offer her some sort of condolence for some unknown reason, but she pushed him away.

He shook his head in frustration. "Well...damn. Look, I didn't mean to scare you...at least not that bad. And no, he didn't hire me and I'm not following you...at least not because of him."

She stared at him as tears welled in her eyes and he reached out to her again, wishing he could somehow offer her some comfort but knowing she wasn't going to let him anywhere near her. He felt uncomfortable for a moment marveling at the strange sensation coursing through his veins. He cared that he'd frightened this woman!

His next words baffled him even more, but they seemed to spill from his lips of their own accord.

"I promise you, you're safe with me. He's not coming anywhere near you."

She took a deep breath and started to walk away, but he held her hand and wouldn't let her go.

"What about our bet?"

"I don't' give a damn about you or your bet! How did you know that stuff about me? Did you steal my wallet...or are you lying and he hired you? There's just no way you could know those things unless someone told you."

She angrily wiped away a tear that trickled down her nose.

He sighed heavily. He'd really scared the shit out of her and although for a Jinn that was not necessarily a big surprise since that's what Jinn do...somehow it didn't feel right.

"Look. It was a lucky guess."

"That was *no* lucky guess."

He stared at her in silence for a moment knowing the risk he was about to take.

"Listen. You have secrets, right? Well, what if I tell you one of mine. Will you believe me then…that I'm not one of this Derek guy's hired guns?"

"What do you mean?"

"I mean exactly what I said. I'll tell you a secret about me."

She stared at him in silence and he wondered how much of it was anger…or curiosity.

He was about to find out.

"I can see things about people when I touch their skin."

"That's not possible."

He laughed out loud. "Yeah. It is…obviously or you wouldn't be pale as a ghost and pissed off as a wet cat."

She shook her head and started to walk away again, but he stopped her.

"Let me pass. We're done."

"You don't believe me?"

"Of course I don't believe you. You're just some lame-ass carnival magician…and for all I know Derek already got to you. Now get out of my way."

"Do you believe in psychics? They have t.v. shows with people who've helped the cops find criminals and murderers. It's documented. Do you think they're lying?"

She paused. "Well…no, I guess not. But that's different."

"Why? Why is it believable when you see it on t.v. but not in real life. Doesn't that seem kind of the opposite of what it should be?"

She sighed and stared at him for a long moment before her expression finally softened almost imperceptibly.

"So, you're trying to convince me you're like one of those idiots from 1-800 Psychic Whatever who scams people's money telling them a bunch of made up crap?"

He laughed. "Well, sort of. Except I'm hoping I'm not an idiot and obviously I didn't make up any of the 'crap' I just told you."

He paused and offered her his arm, knowing she wasn't going to take it. He then nodded toward one of the concessions.

"So, are you ready to go try one of the mystery-meat hot dogs?"

"Stop trying to change the subject. You're sitting here feeding me this psychic bullshit and expecting me to believe it, when he probably hired you to poison me or something."

"Look…I'm not expecting anything. I just told you what I saw. No one hired me. I won't let this guy come anywhere near you. You decide for yourself whether you believe me."

She didn't reply but she didn't walk away either.

Maybe it was a good sign.

CHAPTER THREE

A few moments later, they stood in front of the nearest concession.

Her stance had eased just a bit on the walk over, although he'd noted she'd looked back over her shoulder several times before they reached the line where they now stood waiting to order.

"So, how long were you married?"

"Why don't you tell me?" she said with a hint of sarcasm.

He smiled. "Look, just because I can see certain things doesn't mean I can read your mind or see everything. No one can do that. I'm just a little bit psychic I guess."

That was somewhat of an understatement, but she was after all, human. Magic….real magic….angels, demons, things that go bump in the night, were all thrilling on the movie screen, but in real life, these frail beings would jump and scream like frightened children. To most Ifrit, and even to him on occasions in his not so recent past, that was quality entertainment…but for some reason he didn't find it very humorous right now. He could tell she was reluctant to tell him too much, and probably also wondered how much he already knew.

She stared at him for a moment and then finally answered. "I'm still married to him. And it was about ten months…I spent most of that time just trying to get away. I was with him for a whole year before we got married."

"How long before it started?"

"It was after the wedding. One night he came home from work and I accidentally broke a glass and he just…went nuts. He threatened me and told me he would make me regret the day I was born if I tried to run. Things went downhill from there. And every time I've tried to leave, he has me tracked down and brought back. And, well…" she sighed heavily. "You can guess the rest." Her voice was barely above a whisper.

He nodded. He hadn't been able to pick up everything, but he'd seen enough to know this man she was married to was a piece of shit; a human coward who needed to dominate and hurt those weaker than himself in order to feel powerful. Sure…the Jinn liked to rattle the windows and make things go bump in the night to scare the bejeezus out of people and set their supernatural radar off. There was little harm in that other than fear of the unknown. But physically beating a helpless woman….or any undeserving innocent? That didn't sit right with any part of him. Even the Law forbade a Jinn from using their power to cause the death of another, even if they were owned and their master commanded it.

They stepped up to the concession with 'Cheese Steak Louie's' emblazoned across the side in bold red letters, along with a hula girl holding…a sandwich. A middle aged man with a New York accent and day-old razor stubble stood waiting to take their order.

"Heya, Z! How's it going." He smiled at Scheri and then nodded back to Z. "What'll ya have, buddy?"

"Hey, Louie! I'll have the usual…some of that grilled steak, hold the onions, no bread. And a plain salad. Olive oil and vinegar."

Z turned around to face Scheri. "Whatever you want…I'm buying."

She shrugged. "I guess I'll just have whatever you're having. It sounds healthier than all the greasy stuff."

He nodded and smiled as he turned back to Louie. "Make it two."

Louie nodded and laughed. "You got it…and you know I only keep that health food crap around for you, Z. You're my bud so you want olive oil and salad, you get olive oil and salad."

Z laughed as Louie disappeared behind the concession counter to prepare their food. It came up quickly and as Z reached into his pocket to pay, Louie stopped him. "Nah...fah-get it. Your dinner date's on me today."

He winked at Scheri and she forced a smile, wanting desperately to point out that this was *not* a date, but Z had already turned and started to walk away with their food, so she just let it go.

They walked to a nearby picnic table where he cautiously slid in next to her on the bench after she sat down. "Is it okay if I sit here? I'll move if it makes you uncomfortable."

She shook her head. "No. It's okay. You've been...really nice. And thanks for the food."

Her eyes traveled to the thick muscle of his bicep as he took a huge bite of the steak and washed it down with a gulp of water.

She followed suit and took a bite, surprised at how good it actually was.

"I guess the jokes about carnival food were just a front. You have to eat pretty healthy I imagine, to maintain that much muscle."

He nodded. "Yep."

It was the truth. He could manipulate the matter of his body in deciding how he'd wanted to appear, but once it was created and took solid form, it required maintenance of every atom from which it was composed. So...eating, like for all humans, was a necessary part of his existence, and he, like every other human had to work to maintain the well-muscled physique he'd created.

Scheri looked over at him as he ate, and noted the large, colorful dragon that sat curled on his shoulder and bicep and trailed down his arm.

"Nice tat. Does it have any particular meaning?"

"Not really. I just like it."

He sat there in silence and she finally said, "Well?"

"Well what?"

"So that's it. You just like it and there's nothing else behind it?!" She laughed a little in exasperation.

He swallowed a huge bite of his salad and said, "I knew it!"

"Knew what?"

"That I could get you to smile. I mean a real smile…not that fake sarcastic shit."

He winked at her before gulping down a large chug of water from his bottle.

She blushed and was suddenly embarrassed that she'd felt comfortable enough to let her guard down, even for a minute, but at the same time grateful that he'd made her feel that way. She didn't want to trust him or anyone else, but something about him made her feel at ease.

"Yeah. I guess you did. Thank you…I needed it. But you still haven't answered the question."

No one had asked him about it before, and he had no intention of making up some 'deep meaning' that the dragon stood for…because there was none. But, he'd learned in recent times, humans seemed to place great importance on the meanings of the marks that they put on their bodies.

He'd had it engraved on his human shoulder the 'old-fashioned' way, pain and all for no other reason than so he could know what the sensation felt like. It was that simple. He'd chosen the dragon right off the wall because he liked the colors…and loathe as he was to admit he supposed he liked the idea that the dragon represented the 'snake' in some cultures. The snake represented Satan himself….the original fallen Angel, and since he certainly had no love or loyalty for his father's race, he had no problem sporting their antithesis on his arm for all eternity. Perhaps it had some meaning after all.

He coughed lightly, ready to change the subject.

"So, you're a writer. What kind of stuff do you write, Scheharazade?" He sounded genuinely interested but she looked uncomfortable that he knew her real name, given how unusual it was.

"How the hell do you know my real name? And yeah…I'm a writer, but I haven't done any writing in a long time. He pretty much put a stop to that…and it's not very easy to be creative when you're getting the crap beaten out of you every week or two." She sighed heavily. "But when I was writing, I mean besides my regular copywriting job, I had done a book of short stories that I self-published. I was working on a full-length novel when all of this started."

"So why don't you go to the police and report him? Go back to your life and your writing. You don't have to be a victim and you don't need him to make yourself a career doing what you love."

She shook her head. "I can't! Not right now anyway…maybe never. He knows so many people in the judicial system and he has money, and I mean a lot of it. He already told me he would make it look like I was having an affair and my non-existent boyfriend was the one who hit me. And if I leave any paper trails or electronic transactions…or get on a computer and even check my websites or email, he might be able to track me down and find me. So, I just had to disappear. I'm not stupid…or weak. I'm not a coward either, but there's only so much physical abuse I could take. I want to go to the police…to someone. But he could probably have me killed and walk away free as a bird."

She took a bite of her steak and they sat there in silence for a long moment before she spoke again.

"I know for a fact he had another girlfriend before me and she just…disappeared. I have this sick feeling that the son-of-a-bitch killed her! But I don't know where to begin to look for evidence. He's just too thorough. I wish more than anything I could take him down but I know that's never going to happen, so I just tried to leave. I would have just walked

43

away and never said a word if he'd just let me go and stay the hell away from me. I tried to several times and he found me and well….you can see where it got me last time."

She pointed to her eye and dragged in a deep breath, as her expression turned to one of resolve. "I finally got away, and I am not taking *any* chances on him catching me again. I need to stay moving and just try to think and come up with something…some way."

"Will your family miss you? I know you lost your mother…but is there anyone else?"

"No. I'm alone and I've never felt it more than now, believe me. But it's probably better this way, because if I had anyone close to me that he could threaten to kill or hurt to get back at me or try to make me come back to him, he would."

He started to reach out and take her hand in his own, but then drew back, remembering how pissed off she'd been when he touched her before. She'd warmed up quite a bit, but he wasn't going to push his luck.

He shifted in his seat, debating whether he should say what he was about to say. The debate was soon over, because the words just came out before he could stop himself.

"Well..look. You're not alone right now, right? Here we are…you're looking for a job, and I happen to need an assistant."

Her brows knit together. "How did you know I came here looking for work? And the other stuff too. You've somehow managed to avoid the subject , but now I really want to know."

"I told you…magic."

She sighed. "Look...if you can't be honest with me, how am I supposed to take you seriously? Obviously you're *not* some psychic and you can't read people's minds when you touch their skin or hold their hand or whatever. So how did you know that stuff about me? I'm pissed that you invaded my privacy but I want to know. I'm serious."

"So am I."

"So…you're not going to tell me…are you."

"First rule of magic: never give away your secrets." His expression was firm.

She stared at him in silence. He was offering an opportunity that she desperately needed, but how could she trust this guy. Was he for real?

She sighed in frustration. "Look…I really need a job. Are you serious about that?"

He nodded.

She still looked skeptical. "You told me I was a terrible assistant…so what made you change your mind."

"I can teach you," he said without hesitation.

She sat there, weighing his words and debating what to do. What if he was some kind of psycho who'd somehow rifled through her purse when she wasn't looking to find out a few details about her life to rope her in and then do God knows what? He was an illusionist and guys like that were fast with their hands. She hadn't let her purse out of sight, but if he was really good…maybe it was possible. And then there was always the other possibility….what if Derek *had* actually hired him and this was all some kind of show so she would go with him willingly somewhere instead of making a public scene and then….? She shuddered at the thought.

"Damn, woman, you're as good at creating these uncomfortable moments of silence as you are at giving me shit." He laughed. "Sounds like an easy choice. But hey…it's up to you."

She inhaled deeply and stalled a moment trying to buy a little more time.

"Don't I have to meet someone who runs this place or anything like that? I mean do I have to fill out papers or interview or something?"

He shook his head. "Nope. They pay me under the table and I'll pay you the same way. They won't give a rat's ass who I have helping me out as long as it brings people through the door and they pay for tickets. No one keeps track of most of the carnies going in and out of here…at least from what I've seen."

Up until now, he'd never had any human helpers other than the guys who set up tents and lights and ran the sound. It would be a pain in the ass, actually, teaching her how to act on stage and what he needed done, and he had no idea what he was thinking right about now offering to invest this much time and effort into helping her.

Scheri bit her lip nervously trying to decide what to do. He'd bought her dinner, promised her that Derek wasn't going to come near her…at least not while she was with him, and he'd offered her a job. She wanted desperately to believe that this was for real.

Her gut feeling was that he was actually sincere…and when she pushed the other doubts aside and went on that alone, she reasoned that given his size and physical conditioning, she would be safe when she was with him….if he really was offering what he said he was.

There was no way Derek or even two or three of his hired goons all at once could take this guy down, at least not without guns or some kind of weapons; and maybe not even then. He was fast on his feet, who knows what kind of illusions he could create on the spot and she had a feeling he probably could kick some major ass in a fight.

She took a deep breath hoping she wasn't about to make a huge mistake…a potentially fatal one. "Okay…I'm in."

Her hands shook just a little and she inhaled nervously as her heart pounded in her chest. She would have to keep her guard up at all times in the next few hours to make absolutely sure he didn't try to offer her a ride somewhere or any other instances where he might be able to take her away and hand her over to Derek…or worse. If she had to fill out some kind of application at least there would be some paperwork proving she'd worked here and someone might ask why she'd disappeared if anything happened to her.

But then again, carnies came and went by the week…sometimes the day, so that wasn't much guarantee of anything. She was just going to have to trust her gut on this one.

Z smiled and raised a brow. He was both surprised…and relieved that she'd accepted his offer. If that piece of crap husband of hers was after her, at least he could keep her from being beaten up for however long she decided to stay. He didn't know why he felt this strange and unfamiliar sensation called 'protectiveness', but he did.

And although she'd had been acting as cold as a well-digger's ass in winter even a half hour ago, she'd definitely warmed up since they'd been sitting here. He had to admit, he secretly hoped that maybe with a little time, she might warm up even more, and who knows? He just might get to taste those lips of hers after all.

He found himself staring at them again and as a mildly X-rated picture began to blossom in his mind, he had to force himself back to reality and try to make conversation. He figured he may as well find out something useful.

"So where are you staying? Do you have a place to live?"

She sighed. "I told you, I can't really stay in any one place very long because if I do, he'll find me. Right now I'm at the Valhalla Inn around the corner. It's pretty run down…it's a dump actually, but they're small and they don't have records going into some large hotel computer system. They let me pay with cash too."

"You know, since you're going to be working with me, we can probably find someone here who wouldn't mind another roommate in their trailer. Or if you want to just stay where you are, I'll pitch in a few extra bucks to pay for your room while we're here in town."

"Really?"

He nodded. "Call it an advance."

47

"Why are you being so nice to me? I mean...you don't even know me."

"Well, being as you've been so warm and friendly to me, since the moment we met, it's the least I can do." He laughed just a little.

She shot him a warning glare and he knew he'd better shut up while he was ahead. He'd barely won her trust so now wasn't the time for ragging on her...even if it was just in good fun.

His expression turned more serious. "Look, I know enough about you to know that you need a friend right now. Let's just leave it at that."

"Well I don't know anything about you! I trusted someone once, and look where it got me. How do I know you're not just some homeless, vagrant pervert working as a carny?"

"Excuse me, but I think it's the pot calling the kettle black on that one. Well, not the pervert part, but the homeless part. Although...how do I know *you're* not the one who's a pervert? Not that I would mind or anything."

She blushed and looked a little angry.

He realized he needed to watch his step....again. Damn. This wasn't easy.

"I'm just kidding. I know you've had it rough, so I'm just trying to keep it light. But let's just be honest, here. You're the one who's homeless."

She nodded. "Yeah, you're right. But this isn't my choice, you know."

"Do you think it's any homeless person's choice to be that way?"

He marveled at his own words, since he typically believed that most humans earned pretty much everything that fell into their lap. And yet, here before him stood someone who'd apparently done nothing to deserve the cruelty she'd suffered at the hands of another.

"No. I guess not." She felt stupid for having said anything in the first place, and wanted to change the subject.

"Where do *you* live? Do you live in one of the trailers or do you stay in a motel or what?"

"I have my own trailer. I owned it before I even started here, so the company doesn't have to pay anything toward my upkeep. I just bring in the crowds and make 'em money. They're happy. I'm happy. It works."

"Do you live with anyone? I mean…well…I don't want to pry but do you have any family?"

She avoided saying 'wife' or 'girlfriend' because she didn't want him getting the idea she might be interested in his personal life.

He smiled. "I don't have a wife or girlfriend, if that's what you're wondering." He held up his left hand and pointed to his ring finger.

"No. I wasn't," she said matter-of-factly, reminding herself that she really didn't care who this guy lived with…or slept with or anything else. This situation was going to be temporary and as soon as she had enough money to move on, she'd be out of here by the time the carnival was ready to pack up and move to their next destination.

For now, all that really mattered was that he'd offered her some honest work and help with a place to stay if she needed it until they went their separate ways.

"When do you want to have me start learning what to do, and helping you with your shows? And I didn't even ask how much it pays or when I get paid. I just need to make some money as soon as possible."

The words were barely out of her mouth when the realization hit her that she was going to have to stand up there on a stage with him every night…in front of large crowds of people, under all those lights.

She could only hope that no one Derek knew would see her up there, though the chances were slim, being that this was a little town far away from her life back in the city. But she also couldn't help but cringe at the very thought that Z was probably going to turn her in mid-air again, or do one of those illusions where she'd be 'cut in half'...or maybe make her disappear. God only knows what!!

Scheri...what have you done? she thought to herself. It was too late to worry about that now! The only comfort she could take in the situation was knowing she would make some much needed cash, and who knows? Maybe she would learn a few secrets that might come out in one of her books someday...if that day ever came when she would be able to live a normal life again.

Z saw that she looked a little worried and wondered if she was having second thoughts. "We can start right now if you want. And if you're hurting for cash, I can pay you by the day. I have another show at 6 and one at 8. You wanna get up there with me and do it?"

She dragged in a deep breath. "You mean like in an hour?"

He nodded. "Yeah. All we have to do is get you through tonight's shows, and then I have some ideas for something new we can work on for tomorrow."

"Are you *crazy*? How am I going to learn anything in that short of a time?"

"You don't need to do much. Just push the platform out onto the stage, put it where I tell you...if I hand you a prop, take it off stage. Then when I call you over, come sit in the chair. Oh, and hold on tight."

He looked more than a little mischievous and his smile was seductive as he stood up, drank a large gulp from his bottle of water and motioned for her to follow him back to the tent.

Time to see if this elevation in power was just a fluke.

CHAPTER FOUR

One hour later, as the music began to pump through the PA system, Scheri stood behind the curtain waiting for her cue.

Z had brought her back here, and instructed her exactly what to do...and she was quite frankly, scared shitless!

The lights came up and as an array of multi-colored laser light beams rained down, the crowd began to applaud loudly and she pushed the large platform on rollers out to the middle of the stage. It held nothing on it except for the large gold-framed, free-standing mirror.

She rotated the platform so the audience could see it from every angle and then took a quick bow and walked off stage.

Even with such a small task, her nerves were frazzled and she didn't know how he could do this every day...standing up in front of so many people!

Her worries were quickly superseded as smoke began to pour out from the bottom of the mirror. And as the floor surrounding it became filled with the misty vapor, Z 'stepped out' of it to the crowd's thunderous approval.

She gasped with renewed amazement because she had no earthly idea how such an illusion was possible. There had been no additional curtains, or other mirrors or anything else there that could hide him from view...unless maybe he was waiting under some trap door beneath the platform. She hadn't seen one, but she supposed it might still be there.

But the mirror wasn't facing the crowd with the glass side forward....it was turned so that the glass was facing off-stage. So there was no place out of the crowd's view for him to be concealed! So, how the hell had he done it? And how had he known the things about herself that she hadn't told him...or the ladies in the audience he'd just called up on

51

stage? Maybe he had someone out front who was monitoring them with a camera and listening to their conversations as they walked in. But then again, there was no conversation for him to have monitored for him to know the things about herself that he'd somehow known. It was really unnerving and she was beginning to wonder if maybe psychics were real after all.

She made up her mind right then and there that she was going to have to find some way to get him to tell her his secrets, 'first rule of magic' or not.

She was called out to the stage a short time later to be 'levitated' again, and she gripped the chair, in white-knuckled anticipation as she felt her feet lift from the floor, because she knew what was coming. It was a strange sensation, actually. The moment she sat in the chair she felt slightly less heavy or something. Her breaths seemed to be more shallow and she felt a little strange and light-headed. Probably from nerves she presumed.

A few minutes later, after she'd descended to the floor and did her best to keep an even expression despite the fact that her heart was pounding in her ears, she walked off the stage with the chair, and he proceeded with several different illusions before he finished the rest of the show.

She made her final appearance, to wheel the platform with the mirror back off stage, after he'd stepped 'into' it.

After she got back stage the curtain dropped and the lights dimmed back down and as she stood there, looking at the mirror from all angles and even going so far as to step up onto the platform to re-examine the mirror.

She stood there for a long moment staring into the mirror and reached forward running her fingers across the smooth surface. It seemed to just be a regular, everyday mirror....a little on the fancy side, with its heavy gold leaf finish, but just a normal mirror nonetheless. So...how?

Z stood in the 'in-between' area that led from the human world to the parallel world of the Jinn on the other side of the mirror. From his point of view, he was looking out onto the whole backstage area, and it was like watching her through a surveillance window, as she approached and touched the glass, unaware of his presence there, just inches from her fingers on the other side.

He watched her in amusement as she stepped up onto the platform to examine the mirror from her side, and he couldn't help but notice the soft curve of her cleavage from beneath her top as she'd reached forward and touched the surface. The way her hair hung down across her shoulders and the intelligence in those green eyes of hers.

An unexpected and unfamiliar wave of protectiveness surged through him as she looked at her reflection for a moment and then reached up and touched the place around her eye, dabbing the area to make sure it was well-covered with make-up so the faded bruise wouldn't show.

He resisted the urge to reach forward and touch the curve of her cheek and trail a finger down to her lips through the mirror...and he could only imagine how soft and warm they would feel if he stepped through the glass and kissed her right here and now. And how she would scream and probably pass out in terror if he did! Not exactly what he had in mind.

As he admired the curve of her breasts against her shirt, an image of her lying naked in his bed...with her long hair fanned out around her like a black satin cape against the pillows blossomed in his mind. He wondered if given time, she would ever allow him or any man to touch her in that way again, after what she'd gone through.

It didn't really matter he supposed, because she, like every other human, could never know who he really was, or where he'd come from.

He sighed heavily and waited until she'd turned around and started walking away, and after making sure no one else was standing by, he quickly stepped out of the mirror.

She gasped a moment later as she felt him brush up against her from behind.

She quickly turned to face him and backed up a step or two. "You scared me. And how did you....?" She looked over toward the mirror.

"You don't have to be afraid when you're around me. Or of me." His voice was quiet and reassuring.

He took a chance and laid his hand on her shoulder and was surprised that she allowed it and even more surprised at how it made him feel. He wasn't touching her skin, so no pictures appeared in his mind, but he could feel the warmth of her body against his hand and there it was again...that strange energy that seemed to not just flow through him, but also resonate with his own.

The hum in his chest felt almost like some kind of harmonic. Interesting. He'd never felt any such thing before in all of his existence here in this realm.

She nodded surprised at her own willingness to allow him to touch her. A calm washed over her and she had to shake off the feeling in order to pay attention so she could ask him the questions she was dying to know the answers to.

"Okay, so I checked out the platform. There's no trap door. And I touched the mirror and there's just no apparent trick doors or anything else that I could find that would make what you do possible. So how?"

He laughed teasingly.

"You really wanna know?"

"Of course!"

"Well, in order to learn a magician's secrets you have to become an apprentice and work with him...or her, and build a strong bond of trust. It takes time and dedication."

"I already agreed to be your assistant," she said, matter-of-factly.

"That's not the same thing. An assistant can come and go, like all carnies. Come in, push a platform...take away a few stage props, make a few bucks and then take off before the next town. An apprentice is in there for the long haul, to get an education, and then someday move on to become a magician in their own right."

"So...you're not going to tell me anything, then?"

He shook his head. "Nope. Not unless you agreed to become an apprentice and prove you're worthy of it."

She sighed heavily. She could never commit to anything more than what she already had....not that she'd made agreements on how long she'd be here, but surely he had to know that she couldn't stay on for very long.

"Well, then...I guess your secrets are safe with me, because I'll never know them. How did I do, otherwise? Was I as terrible as you thought I would be?" She raised a brow.

"You did fine. I told you it wasn't that hard." He paused for a moment. "But I have a new idea for us to work on. You'll have more to do."

She looked a little worried. "I hope it's nothing too complicated. I won't be here that long and I don't want you to have to invest a lot of time for nothing."

He stared at her for a moment and then took a big chance in reaching forward to trail a finger down the side of her cheek and across the fullness of her bottom lip like he'd been longing to do a few moments ago from inside the mirror.

"Any time I can buy you where you're safe from him is certainly not an investment for nothing."

Where the hell had that come from? He didn't know...but he'd certainly said it.

She couldn't help noticing how handsome he looked there in the dim lighting...his skin like rich coffee with cream, and his hair black and shiny, hanging loose around his shoulders. He had beautiful straight white teeth and his smile...well it was like something out of a magazine. Those golden-flecked eyes of his were a little unnerving, but something about the way he looked at her brought her a sense of calm....and trust.

She resisted the urge to reach up and rest her hand on his as he traced the curve of her lip with his finger and didn't want to admit to herself that she welcomed the feel of his skin against her own. Or the fact that she could imagine those hands of his woven through the length of her hair...or tracing every curve of her body.

She quickly shook off the feeling, reminding herself that he was now her employer and aside from the fact that she barely knew this guy, she also had promised herself that she wasn't going to allow herself to feel such things for a long time to come...if ever. Not after what Derek had done.

Yeah, this 'Z' certainly had promised to keep her safe, and offered her a job. But aside from that she knew absolutely *nothing* about him and she needed to keep her distance.

He walked toward the exit and motioned for her to follow. "Come on...you can wait here for a few minutes while I go out and shake a few hands...unless you want to join me?"

She shook her head. "No. It's already risky for me to be up on stage in front of people. The last thing I need is to get too close to anyone. What if someone Derek knows is in the audience? I mean the chances are pretty low...but nothing is impossible."

He shook his head. "Yeah...I agree. So, you wait here and I'll be back in a few minutes."

She nodded and stood back stage peeking out from the curtain once to see him smiling and shaking the hands of some of his eager fans. He was charming...magnetic. There was no doubt about it.

He waved one last time and took a bow and then quickly headed back stage to where she stood.

"Alright...let's go take a break. One more show tonight and then we can go over what we'll be working on for tomorrow. I have an idea."

"What kind of idea?"

"Well....your name is Scheharazade and it got me thinking. We could work some kind of theme like that into the show. I'm thinking instead of levitating a chair, we're going on a magic carpet ride."

"Are you serious?!"

He smiled. "All you have to do is worry about rolling the carpet out onto the stage, and sitting where I tell you, when I tell you. You leave the rest to me. I'll get some props together and we'll change up the show a little too. Some new illusions."

He looked down at her clothes. "We've gotta get you into something a little more 'Arabian Nights', too...harem pants and veils."

She looked down at her jeans and t-shirt.

"You mean, like Princess Jasmine or something?" She cringed and shook her head in disapproval.

"Why not?"

"Because I'm supposed to be a magician's assistant, not a stripper!"

He laughed. "I did't say you had to do the Dance of the Seven Veils. Although...on second thought we could have you do something like that, and have the veils disappear as you remove them, and then have *you* disappear into some mist at the end. I'm liking that idea."

She looked a little worried and intrigued at the same time.

"I am *not* taking off my clothes! No way. And just where am I supposed to get the money for whatever get-up you want to dress me in even if I did agree to this Arabian Nights thing?"

57

"I've got you covered," he said, as the picture of her, with bare midriff, bejeweled and veiled, with those long legs draped in chiffon and gold materialized in his mind.

"From the sounds of it, you aren't going to have enough of me covered!"

He smiled. "Yep. That's the plan."

She stared at him in silence for a moment and he motioned for her to follow him back toward a curtained off area where he would spend the next 45 minutes recapping the order of the entire show in preparation for their next appearance.

The second show of the night went even better than the first and the lights came up as she stood backstage, waiting for Z to appear. She wondered where he had gone off to again, and peeked out from the side curtains to see if he was already out front shaking hands with some of his fans.

He was nowhere to be seen and as she turned around to head backstage, she hesitated for just a moment as a movement in the glassy surface of the mirror caught her eye. She did a double take, because she could have sworn she saw a reflection in there...but no one had walked by or was standing there. Not to mention a tiny trail of mist that seemed to be billowing from its base.

She walked over to the mirror to inspect it and see exactly where it was coming from. There must be some kind of vent near the base where it poured out.

She knelt down and checked from every angle. There was nothing.

Her brows crinkled together as she stood back up, and stared into the glass. For a split second she could have sworn she saw Z's reflection there...but it wasn't really him. It was like he was faded and ghost-like.

Her breath caught in her throat and she spun around to see if he was standing behind her, but there was no one there.

She turned back around and saw only her own reflection. Maybe she had imagined it? She shook her head, turned around and walked toward the backstage exit to see if she could find Z.

A moment later, a thin trail of mist billowed out from the glass and he stepped out of the mirror, to catch up with her.

CHAPTER FIVE

Derek Worley took a large gulp of the whiskey in his glass as he stared out the window of the high rise apartment that only two weeks ago had been both home and prison.

The little bitch had run off again...only this time she'd been a lot more careful. She hadn't taken her phone, or her credit cards. She'd left her car here and most of her belongings. She'd definitely taken much greater care in her planning this time....but it didn't' matter. He would find her one way or another.

He never really had any interest in marrying. That was too dangerous for a serial killer like himself.

The last girlfriend he'd had lasted less than a year before he'd taken care of her...permanently. And as far as anyone knew, she had simply 'disappeared'.

His explanation to those who'd asked was that she'd broken off their engagement and packed all her belongings and taken off without a word. No one questioned it...he had acted the part of the jilted lover, broken hearted and all alone.

Scheri Bloom had been working as a copywriter in one of the offices in his building. She was more than a little pretty, and smart too. He'd enjoyed wining and dining her, and taking pleasure in that delicious body of hers as well. And sometimes when she'd look up at him with those green eyes of hers with her hair splayed out across his pillow he'd almost felt something...an emotion that was foreign to his very being.

And he'd had to remind himself that she was no different than all the rest...just another useless female using him for position and power and they deserved exactly what they got.

He'd scrutinized her background before getting too 'involved' to make sure that she, like the others before her had no family to come forward looking for her after her disappearance.

And as his mind drifted back in time, his heart began to pound with excitement remembering the climactic end to his last relationship, before Scheri. The feel of his lover's throat beneath his fingers as her eyes had rolled back in her head and she'd drawn her last breath. The feel of her dead, cold flesh against his body, and her hardened lifeless lips beneath his own as he'd kissed them one last time before he buried her charred body two days later along the banks of the river at the edge of town.

The anticipation of another moment like that excited him to his very core, and he could feel the arousal between his legs as he reached down to fondle himself. Scheri had escaped for now, but she would soon be found....and she would end up just like her predecessors.

He'd already let things go too far in that he'd married her, but he'd figured that this time around at least a couple of his ethical associates that worked in the firm, had grown fond of her, and it would look better if he went ahead and made the commitment. He also had to admit that at least some part of him enjoyed the extra challenge of figuring out the legalities and logistics of killing one's wife as opposed to just a girlfriend who could 'disappear' from your life with less ado.

He'd made sure he altered phone records to look like she'd been having an affair, and he'd drained his accounts so it would look like she had been a gold-digging whore, who'd stolen his money, broken his heart and run off with a lover. He would play the heartbroken husband ...and of course what was left of her when he was finished would never be found. If it was, there would be nothing that led back to him. He'd cover his trail carefully and no one would ever question anything. He was after all a well-respected lawyer...a pillar of community.

It was a beautifully thought out plan, but one that may never come to fruition if he didn't find her. And now that he was so close, he couldn't leave her out there…a loose end, to talk about the things she'd seen or the reprimands she'd endured for defying him. She was going to pay with her life, but not before he had a little fun watching her scream.

He sat the glass down on the ledge of the bar sitting by the sliding glass door and walked over to a small alter sitting in the middle of the living room.

He drew a large circle on the floor with salt, and a pentacle within it. Candles of green, gold, white and red had been placed around the border of a gold framed mirror laid across the surface of his altar in the four places corresponding to the directions of the wind.

He wasn't very good at this occult shit…at least not yet, but he hoped with time and practice, he'd get better.

He read the page of the open book sitting on the altar and then grabbed a pouch sitting nearby and poured the contents into a metal cup sitting in the middle of the altar.

A moment later he sliced open his hand with a knife that he'd 'blessed', allowing the blood to drip into the cup. He bowed and then welcomed the four winds and what he hoped were some spirits or ghosts or whatever the hell you wanted to call them that were hanging around somewhere nearby that might guide him in his mission for power and wealth far beyond what he had now.

He'd held a similar ceremony after he'd knocked her into a state of near unconsciousness a few days before she'd left, forcing her to drink the blood and herb mixture…and after he'd dragged her body to the center of the circle, he and two of his partners who also had an interest in creating their own little haphazard 'coven' had raped her there on the floor.

She'd woken up dazed and couldn't remember any of it, not that he cared if she did. But she'd seemed particularly fearful in the days after and he wondered if perhaps some repressed memories were working their way to the surface from the deepest recesses of her mind.

Just before he'd assaulted her he had been trying to call on a few of the so-called 'dark entities' with names he could barely pronounce, who would then supposedly blanket their bodies as they raped her and by doing so, taste of her flesh and drain some of her spirit and transfer it to his. At least that's what the books said.

He was trying to call them forth again here and now figuring maybe he could ask them to guide him to her...*if* he had done the ritual correctly. He would know soon enough. And even if it didn't work, he would still track her down. Once he found her she would rue the day she'd dared to defy him or to try to outsmart him.

He took another large swig of the amber colored liquor in his glass as his cell phone rang and he was jolted back to the present.

He picked it up quickly. "What."

"It's me. I have a buyer for the shipment of blow you paid to have brought in last week," said a male voice from the other end of the line.

"Excellent. Any word on where she is yet?" His voice was quiet and even, despite the quiver of anticipation he felt at the thought she might be captured and brought back.

"I'm workin' on it."

"Well, work faster."

"These things take time."

"Bullshit." Derek's voice dripped with all the venom he felt. "Get a few more of those pieces of shit that you call your 'street crew' working on it."

"Look, I just need a few more days," The voice paused for a moment and then continued cautiously. "So...if we can get back to the other subject for a minute. I can arrange for us to move this shipment out by week's end then?"

"I want every dime by Friday at 3. Period.

"Fine. I gotta go."

"Not so fast." Derek said menacingly. "Find her. If you can't, someone else more useful will. As my father used to say, 'It's always a tragedy when someone has outlived their usefulness,' He paused for a moment for emphasis. "Wouldn't you agree?"

There was silence on the other end of the line for a long moment before the voice finally replied. "I'll get on it."

"I want some kind of lead by tomorrow. No excuses and no more of your bullshit."

He hung up, walked over to the bar and poured another shot of whiskey.

He had plans and this little bitch wasn't going to be a loose end that may stand in the way of him achieving he levels of money and power he'd sought his whole life.

Yeah, he was making…and laundering more money than he could keep track of through the firm, and through the large shipments of illegal street drugs he now had a market on in at least five states with no one to suspect or stop him since he worked so closely with the DA. But he wanted more, and he had his eye on politics and higher government.

There he could have anything he wanted.

He had gotten over any stirrings of his conscience long ago and at this point there was pretty much nothing he wouldn't do. Surely there was someone in a higher position than he who could use his talents.

He drained the glass, set it on the counter and headed upstairs to bed.

A few moments later in the dim light of the empty room, a thin trail of smoky mist rose from one corner of the glassy surface of the mirror where it laid on the altar as the candles burned down and their flames were no more than a dim flicker in the darkness. For a split second, a ghostlike impression of a man's face appeared briefly and then faded away.

Abdul al Leil smiled as he looked out from the other side of the mirror into the living room of the foolish human who'd unwittingly, through the right incantation, and the right mirror....which he'd picked up just last week at an antique store; opened up a portal through which he could now enter the human world. The world in which his most hated enemy, Azizi, resided.

Azizi had willingly defied Jinn law and somehow managed to come here of his own free will and not lose his powers. Abdul had tried for years upon years to figure out he'd done it, with no such luck. And he'd been patiently waiting for an opportunity such as this one. He could not be held liable for materializing into the human world, since he'd come forth through the portal along with the other entities the human had engaged. And if the legends were correct, since he'd been *called forth*, instead of violating The Law and materializing on his own, his powers would likely remain intact because he was supposed to be here granting wishes.

Smoke billowed out from the mirror and second later, Abdul stepped forth from it dragging in a deep breath as he adjusted to the feeling of the human body he now occupied and the feeling of the material world around him....every atom touching his skin and flowing in and through the energy of his mass.

He stood there for a moment stretching his fingers, and working the muscles of his arms, legs and neck to get used to the clunky feeling of their solidity. He'd never taken human form before and he had to admit he liked the interesting feeling of it. It was no wonder Soheila had enjoyed it so much and he could only imagine...and envy the physical pleasures she had known with that damned Angel of hers.

He composed himself and walked across the room, getting a feel for movement and motion. He also realized that for now, until he was more familiar with this place, he would have to stay close by the mirror so he'd have a place to escape to if needed.

Since he'd been called forth along with a few other entities lurking nearby, he was indeed bound to serve the human who'd called him...but perhaps the human was not aware of this fact, since he had not called him specifically by name nor had he acknowledged him in any way. In fact, he suspected the human did not even know he had come forth at all! It was likely that it had been an accident...he'd been near the right mirror at the right time. And it would serve him well to keep it hidden if this were true.

For now, all that mattered was that he was here and finally would have the opportunity to track down Azizi and make sure he paid for his disregard of The Law and for influencing Soheila to refuse his offers.

CHAPTER SIX

Z materialized from the other side of mirror. He'd dropped off the woman named Scheri at her room and come back to the in-between-area for some peace and solitude to try to figure out what the hell was going on.

First he'd had enough power to not only levitate the chair with her full weight in it, but also to turn it completely over on its side. He'd felt a strange surge of power when he'd touched her skin…and as the evening had progressed he'd felt that strange hum that seemed to flow through his human body and up into his chest. What the hell was it?

He materialized and stepped back out into the material world to test a few things out and was surprised to discover that his power had increased since he'd touched her.

He wasn't sure why he felt the way he did, but at this point he was sure that whatever had happened that caused his powers to increase had happened since she came around, and it didn't' seem to be a one-time thing. He couldn't help but wonder if they would continue to increase and if so, would he eventually reach his the full potential he'd known before coming to the world of humans? Perhaps that alone was reason enough to keep her around in case she had something to do with it. But something inside of him told him that wasn't his reason at all. All he had to do was recall the memory of the way she looked standing there on the other side of the mirror trying to figure out how it worked as he'd watched her through the glass and he knew exactly what his reason was….he was drawn to her, and not just for the physical pleasure he might know with her body. Hell that wasn't likely to ever happen anyway. This was something else. He shook off the feeling, remembering who he was….and who she was. A human.

Regaining his powers had been something he'd let go of a long time ago, and then along comes this woman, and suddenly the impossible seemed possible. That was going to have to be reason enough.

Sunlight peeked through the narrow crack of the drapes drawn across the window of Scheri's room at the inn as a loud knock at the door woke her from her dreamless sleep.

Z had accompanied her in a cab back here to her motel last night to make sure she'd made it safely, and had even come inside to inspect the room before heading back to his trailer at the carnival grounds. She'd been cautious about not going anywhere alone with him, but since it was in a cab and the driver was outside waiting, she felt it was safe enough.

She sat up abruptly in the bed and noted it was just past 7 am. She quickly got up and walked over to the window to see who was there. Although the chances were slim, it was never completely out of the realm of possibility that Derek might have found her and she felt a shiver travel up the length of her body at the thought of it. She took a deep breath and was relieved when she peered through the narrow crack in the drapes to see Z standing there. He was alone and there was no cab driver this time. He'd either walked or driven over....or maybe his cab already left.

She opened the door, cringing as a ray of the early morning sunlight hit her squarely in the eyes.

"What are you doing here so early?"

She ran her fingers through her tangled hair, hoping it didn't look too bad and reached up remembering that she had no make-up on to cover the still fading bruise around her eye, and then wanted to kick her own ass for caring what she looked like.

Who was she trying to impress? Him? Yes, he was certainly nice...and gentlemanly...and funny. Not to mention ridiculously good-looking, standing there with that long black hair of his loose around wide shoulders. He'd offered her a job and his friendship for whatever reason…but there was no room in her life or her heart for those kind of feelings of physical attraction again. She wasn't going to allow it no matter how much her body begged to disagree. She motioned for him to step inside.

He stepped over the threshold cautiously, remembering how hard it had been last night to fight the urge to move in and take those lips of hers with his own as they'd stood here in the doorway. Instead, he'd been a complete gentleman and left quickly after checking her room. He knew to do anything else would be to break her trust after working so hard to gain just a little of it, and probably get the shit slapped out of him in the process.

Now here she was….standing there in a little tight nightshirt and as she turned to walk away toward the sink, his eyes kissed every curve of her body.

He cleared his throat and tried to look away. He supposed he was just going to have to accept the fact that for some ungodly reason he wanted to bother with this one. This angry, beautiful female…that was driving him out of his mind right now!

"It's getting late and we have a lot of work to get done before tonight."

He smiled and struggled to regain his senses. No such luck as she bent over the sink to brush her teeth and a hint of her behind peeked out from beneath.

"Late?" she said. "It's barely past 7."

She spit out a mouthful of toothpaste and looked at him from the mirror, as he stood by the bed.

"And that gives us less than twelve hours to get ready for this new show."

She nodded as she turned back around drying her face. "Don't you think you're pushing things a little too fast? Can't we take a few days before doing the new thing…I mean I haven't even learned your old one."

"It's time to move on," he said matter-of-factly. "Life's all about moving on from one thing to the next."

She looked at him for a moment. "Moving on? What about loyalty? Staying true to the ones you love...your friends?" She sighed. "Never mind. You're a carny and you guys are all about staying on the move."

"What makes you think you know what I'm 'all about'?" He sounded almost humored.

She stared at him for a moment.

"You know what? I don't. Hell I'm certainly no judge of character. Look at me...my life. All because I thought I knew the man I married."

"Anyone could have made that mistake."

She ignored his comment.

"You know...I could have just gotten up and come to the carnival myself."

He sat in silence, ignoring her business-like tone while admiring her every move as she leaned over to grab some clothing from her suitcase and headed into the privacy of the separate toilet and bath.

"I'll be right out. Just let me take a quick shower."

A moment later through the crack of the door he could hear the water turn on and see billows of steamy air that drifted out from the small room that housed only a toilet and bathtub with a shower stall. He had to fight with every last iota of his being to not get up and peek through the crack in the door, hoping to catch a glimpse of that body of hers...now naked, wet and slippery with soap.

He could feel himself getting aroused at the thought of it, and forced himself to stand up and walk over to the door, and slip outside for a moment into the chill of the morning air to cool down.

For all intents and purposes, she was just another pretty face passing through, and their work relationship would be short-lived...but something drove him to want to gain and keep her respect and not do anything stupid that would further strengthen her hatred for the male of the species.

He knew he wouldn't be around to appreciate it, but maybe if he showed her respect and some level of reliability, she might regain some faith that not every male was like the one she'd run from and someday she might allow someone in. And that next guy, if he was a decent man, might have a chance.

He heard the shower turn off and as he walked back into the room, he saw her naked reflection in the steamy mirror for just a split second a picture bloomed in his mind of that 'next guy' being him.

He quickly shook off the feeling and felt a little angry at himself at the same time. This 'guardian angel' shit was getting out of hand and he needed to rein it in and remember who he was. He'd offered to help her and intended to follow through, plain and simple.

Trying to get her into bed definitely wasn't on the list of 'things that help'…although it certainly was something that would remove him from the 'good guy' roster, which he had no real desire to be on anyway.

He'd only just met her a day ago, and knew little of what kind of personality lay beneath her feisty demeanor other than the fact that she was intelligent, distrusting and that she'd gone through some rough times that had brought her to where she was now, emotionally and physically.

He'd never once in all of his existence had any interest in helping a human…but if he could keep her safe from that piece of crap husband of hers even for just long enough so she could get her back on her feet before she took off on her way, well…then he'd have done a good deed, which was never easy for a Jinn.

Maybe she would go on to better things. Either way it didn't really matter…but he was determined to figure out exactly why he'd had enough power to turn the chair over last night and why he could feel his power flowing more fully and freely since he'd touched her.

She emerged from the shower room fully dressed a few moments later while running a comb through her long, wet hair.

Not bothering to even look in the mirror or put on any make up, she grabbed her purse and a jacket from the hook by the door.

"Okay, I'm ready. I didn't see a cab outside, so I'm guessing we are either walking....or you drove over here, because you know I don't have a car."

"Yeah. I know. I took a cab. I didn't want to make him wait because I didn't know how long you'd be, so I sent him on his way. Actually, I was surprised you even invited me in."

She laughed, feeling slightly embarrassed.

"Well...to be honest? I figured that it's broad daylight and there are lots of people out on the street. If you tried something and I managed even one scream someone would have a pretty good chance of hearing me and would probably come check it out. So, I took the chance."

"Jesus. Why don't you tell me how you really feel about me?"

"Why don't *you* tell *me* how I really feel about you? You're the mind reader," she shot back sounding surprisingly playful.

"I already told you, I can't read minds. I see pictures."

"Same difference," she said matter-of-factly.

"No. It's not," he said with equal fervor.

She picked up the phone and quickly called to have another cab sent over which arrived almost immediately.

Their banter continued as they walked out the door and got into the cab.

CHAPTER SEVEN

They'd spent the morning going over a whole new routine out on the stage, which included among other things, him rolling out a huge woven rug that they would 'ride' on, like Aladdin's magic carpet ride come to life. He hadn't actually levitated the rug with them on it, yet…he said he had a few technical issues to work out first.

The 'issues' were really pretty much him trying to figure out how to explain to her how the rug was able to fly without any wires or lifts underneath, and he was kicking himself in the ass right about now wondering if offering her a job wasn't a mistake after all . This wasn't going to be easy.

Meanwhile, Scheri sat on the floor behind the stage in front of a large trunk that stood open…its lid thrown back on hinges that creaked with every movement.

Her arms were draped with several pieces of cloth including a long pale pink veil and another made of see through purple chiffon. There were many beautiful pieces of clothing inside as well, including beaded vests, harem pants and little halter-like tops intricately beaded with pearls, bugle beads and tiny strings of golden rope sewn into place.

She pulled out one of the tops and turned to make sure Z wasn't watching from his place where he stood over by the curtain before lifting the material to her nose and sniffing it. She couldn't help but wonder where it had come from…or if someone had already worn it. Carnies came and went, and god only knew what kind of clean or dirty body may have been in these things…beautiful or not. They smelled fresh but she still crinkled her nose cautiously.

"You look like you ate something bad," he said laughing lightly.

She blushed a little. "No actually I was seeing if I *smelled* anything bad. We're at a carnival, and I wasn't sure if maybe someone else wore these and didn't' wash them."

"They're clean. I went over to see Marlena. She is about your size and she has lots of extra clothes."

"Who's Marlena?"

"She does a low-wire act right after I go off the stage. Not as big and fancy as a circus…this tent sure as hell isn't high enough to do a real high wire, but it still keeps people coming. She's…a friend. And she's good at what she does." He smiled mischievously and winked.

Scheri nodded keeping an even expression.

She'd seen a poster as she'd walked into the tent with Marlena's picture on it. She was blonde with blue eyes and a body that pretty much any woman would kill for, from years of physical training.

She turned back to the chest of clothes, refusing to allow her thoughts to meander anywhere near the direction of wondering how good of friends Z and Marlena were. It was none of her business.

Z walked over to where she stood and leaned in. His fingers brushed hers as he pulled the purple chiffon from her hand, and reached in and grabbed a pair of harem pants and a gold brocade vest and bra. He handed them to her.

"Yes, these colors look good on you No, you won't look fat in them…and yup, I've slept with Marlena a couple of times."

Scheri's mouth dropped open and she shot him a look of annoyance.

"That's not what I was thinking and I don't care whether you've been with…" her voice dropped off in exasperation and she sighed. "Just never mind."

She knew it was useless to protest. He somehow had known exactly what she was thinking! Maybe he really was a psychic. It was…unnerving.

He looked at her for a moment as if surveying her and she suddenly felt…naked.

"Can you dance?" His voice was blunt.

"Yeah… I guess. What kind of dancing? I mean if you're looking for a pole dancer, forget it."

He laughed. "No…you need to practice with those veils. Wrap them around you and then learn how to unravel them from your body…seductively. You know. That 'Dance of the Seven Veils' thing we talked about."

Her brows knit together. "Um. I never actually agreed to that part and what the hell is this Dance of the Seven Veils thing you keep mentioning?"

"It's actually from the Bible. Salome danced so seductively for King Herod that he was willing to behead John the Baptist because she asked him to."

He sighed, yanked off his shirt, walked over and grabbed a couple of the veils, wrapping them around himself, and then mockingly began to move and unwind them from around his body.

She busted out laughing at this huge man wrapped in pink chiffon trying to show her how

75

to…belly dance? It was hilarious, though she had to admit he was graceful and she couldn't help but notice the play of his muscles in his arms, back and torso as he moved and lifted the veils overhead.

He broke out laughing with her and shrugged.

"C'mon. Just do it. I'm sure you'll look a lot better in these things than I do."

She wondered if anyone male or female, could possibly look better than he did right now standing there in front of her…tall, tan, thick with muscle and shirtless. But she pushed the thought out of her mind and kept an even expression.

He grabbed his shirt off the floor and slipped it over his head as he walked back over to the other side of the stage and began hauling out some large pieces of plywood. She got up from where she sat and followed him over, watching as he began measuring some two by fours.

"What are you building?"

He started to draw out a design on paper as a way of stalling for time. What was he going tell her? The truth?

Building the wooden support was the only way he could think of right now to explain how the carpet would be lifted. The platform would be staying on the ground, even though he knew that he could now lift it easily…but the breathtaking effect would only come if the 'illusion', which was really no illusion at all…was that the carpet was actually floating with no support. And the idea was that she just had to *think* the platform was under them when they flew, and seeing him build it and laying the carpet on it now would make it believable later on during the actual show, when there would be no support…only the carpet beneath them floating high in the air.

He decided that blindfolding her was the only way to pull it off. If he covered her vision before the 'illusion' then she wouldn't know how the carpet was being lifted other than knowing he'd built this platform and assuming that was how it would be lifted. Otherwise she might get too suspicious…and scared.

Sounded workable enough….at least he hoped it would be. If not, he was going to have some explaining to do, and he wasn't sure exactly how he would handle it, but any activities like this that bought him some time to think up something better were all he had right now.

She picked up one of the nails that had fallen onto the floor next to the sawhorse where he was standing.

"So…how does it work? If it's held up by wires, they'd better be thick enough to support our weight or I am *not* getting on that thing."

"Just leave that part to me," he said quietly, happy that she hadn't pressed for any more information.

"Can I use your dressing room? Well, if that's what you call it since it's not really a room. I need to see if these fit.' She held up the chiffon 'treasures' she'd pulled from the chest.

He nodded. "Yeah, of course. It's right through that flap."

She headed toward the small area that had been sectioned off with canvas drop cloths. He was hoping maybe she'd forget to close the flap, but no such luck. She came back a few minutes later looking satisfied and laid the clothes across a chair sitting nearby.

He stared at her for minute controlling the slight disappointment he felt that she hadn't come out to model her costume, but it quickly passed when he realized that it was just a matter of hours before he'd see her in it. For now he had to get back to his task and find something to keep her busy and away from here so she wouldn't ask too many questions while he worked on this damned useless platform that he had to go through the trouble of building just to satisfy some human's idiotic questions.

He stopped tapping a nail that he was driving into one of the two by fours and shook his head. This was a real pain in the ass.

He put down the hammer and started toward the exit of the tent motioning her to follow.

"Where are we going?"

"Not we…you. I need to finish the platform and get out the jigsaw and make a mini Taj Mahal."

She crinkled her brows. "What are you talking about?"

"Props. We need an Arabian themed set and I need to cut something out and get it painted. We don't have much time."

"I'll help you. Just tell me what you need me to do."

"Later. First I have to get the plywood cut and then you can help me paint" He paused for a moment before going ahead and ragging on her a little to lighten the mood. "You can stay in the lines right?"

"I passed Kindergarten art, thank you very much."

He smiled. "Well, we're all good then, Picasso. Now, I just need an hour maybe to get these cut and sanded, so I was thinking maybe we could take you over to hang out and help Louie for awhile. We're done showing you what you need to know for the show tonight, so for now, maybe make a few bucks in tips. I know you can use all the money you can get right now."

"You know I could I just go back to the inn so I'm out of your way."

"You could. But I thought maybe it might be a good opportunity for extra cash…and maybe you'll meet a couple of the concession workers."

He smiled mischievously. "Besides…it'll give you a break from my charm and wit for a couple of hours. I know how hard it will be for you, but they'll help you through the devastating loss, I promise."

She rolled her eyes. "You and your ego are unreal!"

He almost laughed out loud. *Unreal? If only she knew just how 'unreal' he really was!*

She sighed. "Seriously, though. I don't really feel comfortable being alone right now. Out there I mean…with a bunch of strangers."

"*You* not comfortable being alone? After yesterday's 'Do I have to call security to get rid of you' speech? "

"Well…I didn't know you then."

"And you don't know me now either." His tone was matter-of-fact.

"True. But so far…I like what I've seen." She couldn't believe she'd just allowed herself to say it, much less think it. But it was the truth.

"And what exactly do you think you know about me?" he said quietly.

"Well…" she took a deep breath. "When I'm with you, I feel safe for the first time since I ran away from Derek."

He moved in closer to her and she began stepping backwards until she ran up against the canvas tent wall. She couldn't back up from him any further, and he wasn't budging. There was no escape…no distance she could put between her body and his.

And in that moment she realized she might be safe from Derek, but she certainly didn't feel very safe from all the things she was feeling when Z looked at her the way he was looking at her right now.

She noted the golden flecks in his eyes as she stared up at him. They were so strange and uniquely beautiful. *Dammit! Why did he have to be so handsome!?* Her thoughts were running wildly out of control now, and she sincerely hoped he couldn't actually read minds so he wouldn't know what she was thinking. She shouldn't be thinking it at all, and yet….

He stared at her for a moment and reached forward and trailed his forefinger down the side of her cheek and then took her hand in his own without saying a word.

She looked down to where his fingers intertwined with hers, knowing that he might be reading everything that was going on in her head right now…but instead of pulling away, she held on tight and walked out of the tent with him. He kept an even expression for the whole walk. If he was reading her thoughts, he certainly wasn't letting it on.

A few minutes later she stood behind the counter at Louie's concession stand, watching Z as he walked away, back toward the Smoke & MirrorZ tent.

Louie handed her a knife and nodded toward a basket full of onions sitting there.

"Well..I ain't one to like to see a lady cry or nothin', but this time, better you than me."

He smiled a toothy grin and laughed good naturedly as he handed her a large stainless steel bin.

"Once they're all chopped, you can just brush 'em off right in here and then put 'em in the fridge."

He nodded to the small refrigerator standing against the back wall.

Scheri smiled. Louie seemed warm and friendly, despite his thick New York accent and his 'I'm a tough guy' demeanor at first glance.

She began chopping the first onion in the pile and figured this might be a good opportunity to find out more about Z and if he was for real, or just some player...although if he and Louie were really good friends, it wasn't likely Louie was going to disclose much damning information. Still, she had to try, because something was better than nothing.

"So...how long have you known him?"

Louie shrugged. "Oh, I dunno....five or six years maybe?"

She nodded. "Well he seems like a nice enough guy."

"Z's a good man. Sometimes he doesn't know it himself, but he is." Louie raised his spatula for emphasis after dumping a pile of meat, green and red peppers and onions onto the grill where they began sizzling almost instantaneously.

The smell of it began to fill the air, and she soon could hear her stomach growling. She looked down at her watch and realized it was nearly 1pm and she hadn't had breakfast or lunch.

A few minutes later, Louie plopped a large portion of the heavenly mixture on a bun and then onto a paper plate and handed it to her.

"Here…have some lunch."

He then prepared another sandwich for himself, and took a huge bite out of it, and proceeded to chew it while scraping down the flat surface of the grill and then wiping down the chopping board with a clean cloth.

Scheri took a large bite of her sandwich, noting how good it was.

"Do you know how Z does it?"

"Does what? I mean…he does a lot of things," Louie said humorously.

"Well, for one thing…that mirror. How does he make it look like he's stepping out of that thing? I know it's an illusion, but it's so real. It's scary."

Louie shrugged. "Beats the hell outta me. It's the damnedest thing though, ain't it?"

"And then, he knew all this stuff about me, supposedly after he touched my skin. Now we both know that is a complete crock of you-know-what, so how did he know? Does he have some kind of hidden ear wire with a microphone on it or something and someone hidden somewhere feeding him information? I saw some show where there was this illusionist doing that."

"I dunno on that one either. But you know that's what sells. The mystery I guess. If we knew how he did it, it would kinda ruin the whole thing."

"Yeah…I guess it would sort of. But it's driving me nuts!"

Louie nodded in agreement. "Hey, get in line. So, what's your story? Booze…drugs? Divorce? You seem way too nice for any of that, but you know…life's a bitch."

She wrinkled her brows in between bites of her sandwich. "What makes you think it's any of the above?"

"Well, I'm sure you can imagine how many people flock here because being a carny is their career choice."

He laughed out loud and walked over to the cooler and grabbed a couple of cold sodas. He handed her one and then popped the top on his own, before gulping down several large swigs.

"We get the down and outers, the bums looking for a quick buck. The illegals…the druggies and boozers. And they all got a story." He finished off the sandwich and dusted the crumbs off the front of his shirt. "So what's yours?"

She sighed. "I'm on the run."

"Damn I'da never guessed." He winked. "Felony?"

"No!" She laughed a little. "Jesus. I'm running away from my husband."

"How come?"

She paused. "He beats me up….pretty bad as a matter of fact."

Her eyes traveled to the floor as Louie moved closer to where she stood and reached out to lay a hand on her shoulder and his expression became more serious.

"Hey, I'm sorry. You okay?"

"Yeah. I'm fine. I got away…not without a few bruises, but at least I'm alive."

"Well, that piece of shit better never come around here. Any man who hits a woman ain't no man in my book. Have you reported him to the cops?"

She shook her head. "I can't. He's an attorney and he's got his whole 'good ol' boys club' thing going on and he'd just pay someone off to kill me, I'm sure."

Louie sighed. "Well, look. You stay close to Z...he'll take care of you, and I got your back too. You ain't never got to worry with us around and if you need anything, you just come over here. If I ain't on duty, come knock on my door; I'm in the big trailer that's got 'Lou's Limo' painted on the side with the hula girl on it....she's my mascot, in case you hadn't figured it out yet." He smiled and winked before adding, "It's in the lot across the street."

She smiled. Lou had a kindness in his eyes beneath the gruff exterior. He was a typical New Yorker...and once you are friends, they have your back. Anyone messes with you, they mess with them too.

"Thank you, Louie. I really appreciate it."

She paused for a moment. "So how did you end up here? What's your story...if you don't mind me asking, that is?"

Louie shrugged. "I was one of the down and outers. It was oh, maybe six years back. I had just gotten out of county lock up and my old lady left me while I was in. I learned my lesson in there and I wasn't goin' back. No way! But nobody wanted to hire me, so I came here. I got a job cleaning up garbage on the lot. It was shit pay, but I worked my way up to helping at one of the concessions after a few months. I was trying to save up enough money to get a place of my own again....maybe go to trade school, but then the guy that

84

owned the cart dropped dead. Heart attack. He just went down like a lead balloon one night after work. Boom!" Louie clapped his hands together for emphasis and pointed to the floor.

"I thought about it and figured maybe this was an opportunity that would be easier than tryin' to put myself through school and then find a job out there when the market is already flooded. So, I worked a deal with the carnival owner to buy the concession and pay it off slow. I had this idea to bring in some real cheese steaks and hotdogs to the carnival. Not that fake crap they sell in the malls….I mean the real deal the street vendors sell in Philly and New York City. And well….I been here ever since."

"Wow…well, I'm really happy for you that you got your life together and made something of yourself."

Louie laughed. "Well..it ain't much. I mean this place ain't sure as hell ain't The Four Seaons but you know, for a guy who came outta jail and made something for himself instead of going back inside, it ain't bad."

She smiled back at him. "All that matters is you found a way and you did it."

The words seemed bittersweet, reminding her that somehow she still held on to some small hope that she could find her own way and get a divorce from Derek, go back to her writing and be able to live a normal life again.

She paused for a moment and then added, "You know…I'm good with ad wording and graphic design too if you'd like me to write something for you, just let me know. If you have a computer I can use, that is. I can write you an ad and put your hula girl on it."

Louie nodded. "Yeah, I'll keep that in mind. I ain't got a computer but Z does."

She smiled. It was the first time since leaving Derek that she'd even remotely thought of some way to try to have some normalcy in her life…to work doing what she loved.

Here she was at this run down little carnival, with this ex-con concession worker, and of all the people in the world, he'd given her hope. A place like this…a job like this was the farthest thing in the world from something she'd ever ask for or want in her life, and yet, she marveled how sometimes the things we don't ask for are the things we need the most. *Damn!* Hadn't Z said that to her just yesterday? It was downright eerie.

A few minutes later a line began to form outside the stand and Louie pointed his spatula toward the crowd and said, "That's our cue. Time to serve them our seven course meal."

Scheri laughed. "Okay, 'Chef Louie'…you tell me what you need me to do."

And the next couple hours was an ebb and flow of making sandwiches as Louie finished grilling batch after batch of fresh steak and onions, running the register and handing out drinks.

A short time later, she looked up to see Z walking across the lot toward the concession.

His hair was loose around his shoulders and he had on a grey t-shirt that fit pretty snug and it was damp from sweat, where he'd been working in the tent. His coffee with cream skin looked so smooth and beautiful as he walked and the sun glinted off the blue black highlights in his hair. Damn. That was a beautiful man.

And damn did she ever need to pull herself together! She barely knew this guy.

She closed her eyes for a second trying to push the image out of her mind before he got here, because she needed to try to keep her head on her shoulders and not let any stupid physical attractions or idiotic school-girl crushes distract her from why she was here; which was to work and make money so she could pack up and move on to the next destination. But the only thing that came to mind was the way he'd looked at her when they were back in the tent before he'd walked her over here.

A second later he walked up to the counter.

"Hey...what do I have to do to get service around here?" he said playfully.

"We don't serve low-lifes like you...now get the hell outta here." Louie shot back before laughing. "Hey, Z. Whatcha need, buddy?"

"The usual is fine." He pulled out a twenty dollar bill and threw it in Lou's tip jar. "That's for the lady, by the way."

Lou nodded. "Hey, she earned it. She's a good worker! I might just haveta borrow her from ya once in awhile."

Z looked over at Scheri and then back at Louie. "So I have competition already, then? Damn."

Scheri took off her apron and stepped out through the door on the side of the concession.

"Hey!" She smiled and stood at a polite distance trying not to remember the way his fingers had felt entwined with hers. "Did you finish up sawing and pounding those nails so we can paint?"

He nodded. "Well...not exactly. But it's done."

He'd finished up what he needed to do, but not by pounding nails and cutting plywood. He'd decided to try seeing on a whim if he was able to conjure up the large pieces he needed for his props. Usually he was only able to conjure up small stuff…and usually on the other side of his mirror, and then he'd bring them through with him.

But this time, he decided to see what would happen if he tried to materialize them here instead. He didn't expect it to work, but he'd focused the energy flowing through him and to his surprise a moment later, the images of what was in his mind materialized, in three dimensions, only they weren't just props…they looked and felt like the real thing!

The mini Taj Mahal he'd wanted to cut and built as a cheap looking piece of plywood painted by hand, was instead a nearly exact replica of the real one because when he'd envisioned it that was what he saw, complete with bronze finial on the top. It wasn't made of stone and mortar…but it was made of a more lightweight sandstone type of material but the tiles were pretty damned authentic. He had no idea why it was the way it was, other than maybe that was how he would envision his stage if he could have it the way he wanted it. It was role reversal. The genie making a wish…sort of.

He wasn't sure how the he was going to explain it to her, other than to feed her some story that he'd slipped out to visit some guy he knows who does set design for tv and movies who just happens to live here in this one-horse town….and who just happened to have a few pieces laying around that he picked up for a reasonable price.

It probably sounded like a complete crock of shit, but he really didn't have anything better. She was just going to have to buy it, and if she asked too many questions, he would give her his stock answer…magic. After all it was the truth; this time more than ever.

She eyed him for a moment. "Okay, so it's done but you didn't build it? How's that?"

"Just come on and I'll show you." He nodded toward the Smoke & MirrorZ tent as he waved to Louie.

Her breath caught in her throat when she walked in and saw the stage.

There was a Taj Mahal sitting in the middle that looked…well, exactly like the real thing. It was large enough to walk through the door and stand inside. It was flanked by the miniature towers that stood by its side and ran in two rows from the front of the stage to the doorway. In between the rows of towers was a narrow trough of water lit by candles on either side. Chiffon drapes of gold, pale purple and maroon hung down from the ceiling…some tied back by ropes of gold. The lights overhead had been adjusted so they lit through the chiffon like lasers and a net of lights had been suspended behind that mimicked starlight against an indigo backdrop.

Her mouth dropped open. "How did you do this in what? Three hours? You must've had a couple dozen people in here working with you!"

He shrugged and smiled. "Well not exactly that many."

"I would have helped you, you know! You should have let me stay."

His mind clicked immediately and he blurted out, "I wanted to surprise you."

Hey, it sounded good.

She bounded up the steps of the stage and stood beside the Taj Mahal, running her hand along the smooth wall.

"Where did you get this? It's amazing!"

He proceeded to tell her the 'I know I guy who builds movie sets' story and then waiting for her to give him the 'Herb' look. He was surprised when it didn't happen.

Instead she was walking around surveying everything like an excited kindergartener.

"Can I meet they guy who sold you these? I'd love to see what else he has. Just out of curiosity. I mean that's just such a cool job having beautiful pieces like this."

Z nodded and shrugged. "Yeah...someday. He travels a lot for his job. You know...movies." He stumbled over the words and was grateful she didn't even notice .

It was a 'someday' that would never happen but as long as she was satisfied, he wasn't going to argue. They had their set design and now it was time to go relax for a little while before trying it all out tonight, though he had to admit picturing her in the purple harem pants just sent any idea of relaxation out the window.

He watched her as she walked around looking at the stage and glowing like a little girl in a doll shop. She looked...beautiful and alive. Much different than the angry, abused woman he'd seen just yesterday who'd come here looking for a job and a safe haven for a few days.

He walked to the center of the stage and stood in front of the set, as the strains of Etta James 'At Last' began to pump through the speakers. Someone was testing out the sound system no doubt.

He walked over to where she stood and without warning she asked him, "Can you dance...I mean besides in pink chiffon like the show you put on earlier. I love this song."

He laughed. "I dunno. Let's find out."

He pulled her body in next to him and they began swaying to the music, eyes closed in silence as the strings swelled and for a moment in time there was no stage, there was no set or lights or anything but the two of them there. Two lost souls searching for salvation from the hand the world had dealt. When it was over he'd had to force his arms to move and his hands to let go after feeling the smooth skin of her back against fingers and the smell of her hair as he'd rested his chin on the top of her head.

The music had stopped and he slowly let her go and a moment later she walked toward the place where she'd thrown her costume over the back of a chair; and as he stood there entranced by the way the black cascade of her hair fell down to the curve of her back and the graceful way she moved, he smiled.

It was...magic.

CHAPTER EIGHT

Three hours later, the stage was dimly lit and ready as an attentive audience marveled at the beautiful scenery which seemed way too nice for a carnival.

Scheri wheeled the platform with Z's mirror out to center stage. She stood there draped in purple chiffon and gold brocade, the lower part of her face veiled and her eyes rimmed with khol. Large gold hoops hung from her ears and stood out in gleaming contrast against the black curls that framed her face and cascaded down around her shoulders.

Z could see her from inside the mirror as she stood there and for a moment he almost forgot to materialize and step through the mirror on cue.

When he finally did, and the mist cleared he could barely take his eyes off a vision of the real Scheharazade from 1,001 Nights come to life standing there beside him.

"You look...beautiful," he whispered.

She stared at him for a moment and she was glad he couldn't see her smiling through the veil she wore across her face, because she had no business caring whether he thought she looked nice or anything else.

She left the stage on cue, and the show went off without a hitch. She marveled watching some of the illusions Z performed. How the hell did he levitate a glass of water off the table? He'd shown everyone that it was an ordinary glass, and then filled it with water from a pitcher right there and drank some of it. And how did he know the lady's name and all the things he told her about herself when he called her up on stage? Was she a part of the show...someone he'd already picked hours earlier...or a carny that worked here who was just pretending to be part of the audience? There were several other things he did, some of which were explainable, but plenty that wasn't.

He had grudgingly agreed to give her a few days to work with the veils before trying it out on stage, and as she watched him perform….his confidence, and the way the audience warmed to his ability to entertain, as well as the humor he threw into his show, somehow gave her the courage to feel like maybe she could try it after all. Maybe even tomorrow. His energy seemed contagious….especially to the female fans in the audience who she couldn't help but notice were screaming and whooping over practically every move he made.

He ate it up. It was no wonder he was so damned cocky…he could pretty much have any of them he wanted she was sure. Not that she cared, of course, but it was interesting to note how many women threw themselves at this guy.

When it came time for the grand finale, which was a magic carpet ride off the stage, he stepped forward to put a blindfold on her, while cracking a joke to the audience, "My assistant here is afraid of heights."

Scheri wanted to elbow him for telling everyone she was afraid, but instead sat quietly on the carpet as he blindfolded her. She was tempted to just pull off the stupid bandana.

He slid behind her and as he moved in closer and whispered against her neck, the smell of her hair reminded him of jasmine on a warm summer night.

"Time for lift-off," he said quietly

"I still don't see why you have to blindfold me. What's the big deal? You've already turned me upside down in the chair how many times?" she whispered back. "It's not like I'm going to be scared being fifteen or twenty feet up on a large platform like this. People are going to think I'm some kind of incompetent fraidy-cat."

"Shhh." She could feel his lips against the back of her neck as he nuzzled her hair.

She felt his arm go around her waist and he pulled her back against him between his legs.

She tensed up and he whispered, "Relax."

Yeah. Right! The feel of his arm around her waist and the way his fingers brushed the bare skin of her midriff sent chills up and down her. She wanted to stand up and run to try to escape the way he was making her feel just being this close to him, but where would she go? They were on a freaking 'magic carpet' ride in front a hundred people!

She leaned back into him and he soaked up the warmth of her bare back against his chest as they rode the short distance up into the air and around the perimeter of the stage. It was over all too soon as they landed and the time had come to let her go. It had to be short and plausible...so he'd only gone upwards into the air in a straight line and circled the stage so it would seem realistic as an 'illusion' with wires or some other mechanism keeping them afloat, even though he'd rigged a large hoop for the carpet to float through showing there were none. It was just enough to keep them guessing.

What he didn't let on was that he was on edge wondering if he was going to have enough power to keep the capet afloat with their combined weight and have everything hold together. It had...to his relief.

They bowed and as the end-of-show music began booming through the PA, he walked over to his mirror, which had already begun to billow out large clouds of mist, and stepped into it, just as he had every night for decades.

The lights went down and he could hear the applause lingering even from his place on the other side of the mirror as she wheeled him backstage. And the feeling of her warmth and her scent against his human skin lingered even longer in his mind's eye.

She stood in front of the mirror for a long time, eyeing it suspiciously and trying once again to figure out how he stepped in and out of it.

If she stuck around here too long, his opportunity to go out and meet his crowd would pass by, so he needed a distraction. No better time than the present to channel his true inner Jinn and rattle a few chains or create some creaks and groans from afar to get her attention. Since his power had increased, he had regained the ability to do it even from this side of the mirror out to the other side.

A gust of wind suddenly blew up on the far side of the stage and a chair tipped over. She jumped with a start and went running over to see what had happened, and without missing a beat, he stepped out of the mirror and walked over to the stage exit so when she came back she would think that maybe he'd just come in. She came back over and spied him standing there.

"When did you get back here?"

He shrugged. "Just a few moments ago. I heard the chair topple but I didn't bother because I saw you already heading over there to check it out. Someone must've left the other side flap open."

"No actually…it was tied shut. I have no idea where that gust of wind came from!"

"It doesn't really matter. Chair is right side up, and all is right side up with the world. You wanna come out there with me tonight?" He nodded toward the curtain.

"It's no safer today than it was yesterday."

"Yeah….but tonight you have a veil. You can just cover up your face."

She sighed. "True. But I don't feel comfortable with it. You go ahead."

"I'll be back in a few."

He walked across the stage and parted the curtains and stepped out where the usual throng of people was standing in line waiting to exit the tent and began his usual routine of shaking hands and making a few girls hearts beat faster.

He began looking out at the sea of faces…particularly the eager group of girls standing to his right. There was a little blonde standing there, in a short black dress, heels and looking like an early Christmas present waiting to be unwrapped.

She smiled up at him and held onto his hand just a little too long when he reached out to her. Pictures flooded his mind of a bar, her kissing the tall, red-haired girl that was built like a 1940's pin-up queen standing next to her and a procession of men that she'd slept with over recent months. This one was a party girl…just his type. Five foot two…eyes of blue….damn, what's man to do?

"So you enjoyed the show?" He said, knowing damned well she enjoyed it and wanted to enjoy a whole lot more if he was game.

"Yeah! Oh, my god, you were awesome! Me and my friend are heading over to The Mix. You wanna come have a drink with us?"

Well, one thing he'd learned since he came here; when opportunity knocks you certainly don't turn it away. For him, it knocked pretty much constantly and here was one… or rather two more knocks because her red-haired friend was smiling seductively and he could tell that this was gonna be a two-for-one happy hour.

"Yeah. I would actually…hang tight and let me…."

His voice trailed off as the fantasy playing out in his mind screeched to a loud and yet, deafening halt.

His new 'student' was waiting back stage and he had to make sure she got back to her room at the inn safely before going anywhere. This 'savior' shit was definitely putting a damper on his lifestyle, which was pretty much 'party or sleep with whoever you want when you want'.

He sighed.

"Listen…I have to shut down here, and then I'll meet you over there in about a half an hour," he said, determined to bring back the decadent picture that had just escaped him.

He wasn't going to let his new 'charge' stop him from any of his usual activities...just because he was doing one good deed didn't mean he had to give up being who he was.

Scheri walked back over to the side of the stage where the mirror stood and began surveying it again, oblivious to the scene that was happening out front.

How the hell had he done it? There was just *no way* that anyone could step out of a mirror like that without some kind of trick door or something. It wasn't just baffling....it was creepy. She wondered if maybe he wasn't really doing it after all and had to remind herself that there was just no such thing as any human who could walk out of a mirror or make things float in midair like he did. But what if he was some kind of superhuman or something? Some person endowed with telekenisis or something. Did that even exist? There were plenty of tv shows about it.

She shook her head. This was nuts!! There had to be some plausible explanation and dammit, she was going to find it one way or another.

A commotion over by the back flap of the tent snapped her out of her train of thought and she walked over to investigate. She parted the canvas and stepped out to discover a couple of drunk guys standing there arguing. She walked over to try to calm them down before they got into a fist fight. She quickly discovered they didn't seem to give a damn about their fight anymore and didn't like the way the taller blonde man was looking at her. He started to come closer and she backed up quickly to try to get back through the flap of the tent but she'd walked further away from it than she'd anticipated.

"Hey girl....what are you doin' out here alone lookin' all hot like that. You sellin'?"

She looked at him with disdain. "Selling what?"

He reached out and grabbed a lock of her hair and started to pull her close to his body. She could smell that he had body odor and his breath about knocked her out. It was a combination of liquor, smoke and bad teeth. He got a grip on her arm and pulled her in towards him and started to put her hand on his crotch when she screamed, "Let me go!!"

The other man came up from behind and grabbed both of her arms and started to haul her behind a dumpster hidden between two tents. It was a dark little corner hidden away in the shadows where no one passing by could see what was going on.

His grip was like a vice and no matter how hard she struggled she couldn't get free.

"Don't matter whether you're sellin' or not. Cause we gettin' a freebie tonight," laughed the taller man.

"Get your hands off me!" She hissed the words through gritted teeth, as she continued to struggle

"Oh, I'm gonna put a lot more than my hands on you, baby," said the man behind her as he licked the back of her neck along her shoulder line.

She cringed and started to scream but the tall man had already come forward and put his large hand firmly over her mouth as he tore the bodice of the gold brocade bra she wore completely free exposing both of her breasts. Her heart was pounding in her head and flashbacks of the memory of Derek...and someone else raping her on the floor the night he'd knocked her unconscious, began to bubble to the surface. It was vague...and flashed in and out of her mind like scenes from a movie. She closed her eyes trying to just float away in her mind so she wouldn't have to confront what was about to happen as her attacker licked his lips and lowered his head to take a taste of her left nipple.

Suddenly and without warning, the other man who was holding her arms from behind loosened his grip and fell backwards against the ground dragging her down with him. She almost fell, but a pair of strong arms caught her before she landed on his body.

Z had appeared out of nowhere, and as he caught her, he pushed her behind him. She struggled to pull her torn top together to cover her naked breasts as she stood there catching her breath, shaken to the core.

Pissed off didn't even begin to describe his expression in that moment. He looked over at the blonde scumbag who was debating now whether to ditch his friend and try to take off running, or stand there and fight.

"Don't even bother, cause you're going down next to your shit-bag friend," Z said matter-of-factly.

The guy shrugged. "Ain't none of your business, pretty boy. She wanted it so get the fuck out of here and go play your magic show or whatever. I got some magic to make out here…with her."

Z dragged in a deep breath. Now that his powers were stronger, he wanted to direct a flow of energy at this asshole and send his body shooting across the lot to fall where it may. But there was no way he could allow her to see any kind of supernatural forces or she'd be so scared she'd probably never speak to him.

Nope. He was gonna have to handle this the old fashioned way. He walked over and without one more word, he hit the guy so hard he fell backwards ass over end and slammed into the dumpster, knocking him out cold. He then picked up each one of them by the collar and dragged them face down through the dirt and tossed them in the middle of the lot as people walked by staring in wonder. He pulled his cell out of his pocket and dialed security.

While they waited, he turned around to face Scheri.

"You okay?"

She nodded, hugging her arms around her body.

He stood there for a moment staring at her at loss for what to do. He couldn't just walk her back to the inn and leave her after what had just happened.

So much for a night at the Mix with Blondie and Jessica Rabbit, he thought to himself. *Damn.*

He dragged in a deep breath struggling with his own unfamiliar emotions of the moment, and then opened his arms. "Look, I know that you hate men right now and you probably don't want me or anyone else touching you, but if you need someone to hold on to, I'm here."

She hesitated for a moment and then nodded and a second later fell into his arms, burying her face against the strength of his chest as she struggled not to cry.

He wrapped his arms around her rubbing his hands down the length of her back and without thinking he kissed the top of her hair, smoothing it with his fingers. To his own surprise he felt no lust or anything else as he felt the curves of her body pressed against him...only compassion. It was strange indeed.

She stayed there wrapped in the warmth of his embrace for several minutes before finally pulling back from him.

"Thank you isn't remotely enough....but I don't know what else to say right now. If you hadn't come out here when you did, I don't know what would have happened. Well...actually, I do."

"I think from now on you'd better not go anywhere by yourself around here at night," he said matter-of-factly.

A few moments later a couple of security guys showed up with a police officer. They asked for her information and she immediately balked and said she decided she didn't want to press charges.

Z called her aside.

"What do you mean you don't want to file a report? You want to let them just walk away after what they did to you?"

"I can't....if I do, then there will be a record somewhere and Derek might find me."

"If he shows up here he'll regret the day he was ever born. You're filing that report."

She stood there staring at him with a pleading look as he rubbed the sides of her arms with his hands, sending a fresh wave of pictures flowing through his mind like a shockwave. There was no way he was letting her attackers get away with it. And he'd deal with Derek if he dared to show his face. If she refused to file the report then he was going to take care of them in his own way. But what was important was her letting go of her fear enough to do the right thing.

"File the report. Please." His tone was firm.

She took a deep breath and finally nodded. He wasn't going to let this go, and he was right...if she didn't these guys might try to do this to someone else, or even come back here for her.

She gave the police the information they asked for and watched as they then hauled the two men off the lot.

After they were out of sight, Scheri turned to Z.

"Will you take me back to the inn? I'm going to have to pack now and get out of here."

"You're not going anywhere."

"I have to! Don't you get it?"

"I get it just fine. You can't run for the rest of your life."

"How can I possibly stay? What am I supposed to do now, just wait for him to show up and do god only knows what?"

"He's not doing anything to you. I promised you that you're safe and I meant it."

"And just how do you plan to keep him away from me?"

He paused for a moment. "Listen...and don't take this the wrong way, but why don't you come stay at my place? I'll sleep on the couch; you can have my bed. Or if you don't want me there at all, I'll go stay with Louie. He's right next door. If you want I can get Marlena to come sleep over with you, but I don't think you should be alone tonight."

She shook her head. "That's your solution? You think having me sleep at your place is going to keep him from hauling me away when no one's looking or having me killed? You don't know what you're dealing with."

"Neither does he," said Z quietly.

She hesitated for a moment. "I don't have any of my things…a toothbrush or any clothes."

"We'll go get them. Or Walgreens is two blocks up. We can get whatever you need."

She thought about it for a moment longer and then finally nodded in agreement.

He took off his shirt and helped slip it over her shoulders while she held her broken top together and then without asking permission wrapped an arm around her shoulder and led her back inside the tent.

She noted again how thick the muscles in his shoulders were as he walked away from her and remembered how easily he'd knocked her attacker on his ass. He was a big man…and there was no denying that she felt safe with him beside her.

"Hang tight for a minute." He walked over and draped a large piece of cloth over the freestanding mirror and then removed it from the platform, carrying it under one arm. He walked over and flipped the switch on the light box before they walked out of the tent.

Z turned back around took her by the hand, leading her back outside. Her skin made contact with his and he cringed inwardly as the pictures of her two attackers began to flood his mind. He wanted to knock the shit out of them all over again, just for the hell of it and probably would have if they weren't already on their way to the downtown jailhouse.

He turned and looked at her for just a moment because he was also going have to admit there was something else he was picking up. He'd felt it at least three times now. When he'd held her hand walking her over to Lou's this afternoon, and again when they were on stage.

102

She was attracted to him, whether she wanted to admit it to herself or not.

He quickly pushed the images out of his mind and focused on clearing his thoughts and focusing on the present moment, which was helping her for a few days or a week or whatever and getting her the hell out of here and on her way so he could get back to his life and she could maybe move on to something better.

"Come on…my place is in the lot across the street, by Lou's. If nothing else, I'm sure the scenery over there will cheer you up."

Scheri looked at him like he was a little bit nuts but after they walked out of the exit and crossed the street, she began to see exactly what he meant.

There as a large trailer there, sitting right near the road, just as Louie had described earlier today. It had 'Lou's Limo' painted across the side in large tropical colored letters, and yep…it had a hula girl painted on the side, just like the one on his concession stand. The entire perimeter of the roof was lit up with multicolored lights and right outside his door, there were also several fake palm trees lit up with Christmas lights of different colors, a small thatch roof overhang and a blow up swimming pool with a mini tiki bar. A life-size statue of Betty Boop in a Hawaiian skirt stood nearby with a tray for holding drinks and a sign that said, 'Lou's Lounge' sitting right by the bar, with two folding beach chairs for seats.

She couldn't help but smile at the makeshift 'Trailer Park Tavern' that Louie had created right outside his door…it was not only humorous, but actually inviting!

They approached and as they walked by, Louie happened to step outside his door. He waved them over and as they approached he quickly walked down his steps.

"Hey…you wanna come in? I got a coupla cold ones in the fridge."

Z shook his head and set the mirror down on the ground leaning it up against his arm.

"Not tonight Lou…a couple of scumbags tried to rape her after the show tonight."

Louie's expression grew serious and he looked over at Scheri. "What? Are you alright? They didn't…" His voice dropped off.

Scheri shook her head.

"No. But if he hadn't stepped outside when he did they would have."

She felt like crying all over again, remembering the moment. "I'd rather not talk about it…at least not tonight."

Louie nodded and patted her shoulder. "Well, look, if you need anything, just knock on the door. And I don't mean nothin' rude by that…I mean if you need help."

Z smiled. "Actually, I might be the one who needs something. I offered to let her stay in my place tonight and if she doesn't want me on the couch, either you or Eddie the sound guy is stuck with my sorry ass."

He really didn't need to bother either one of them because he could just dematerialize and go to the other side of the mirror if he wanted to. But with her in such close quarters he was going to have to make things look legit.

Louie started back up the steps to the trailer. "You know you're always welcome. She is too. Just go get her tucked in. I'll leave the key under the mat. Oh…and if I forget, unplug the lights."

He waved and went inside, closing the door behind him.

"Louie's a really nice guy. I mean…despite the life he's lived, he seems like he has a good heart underneath it all."

"Yeah, he does. Sometimes you find good human beings in places you'd least expect.

He marveled that those words had just come out of his mouth. Good human beings? Where the hell had *that*

104

come from? He supposed he had to admit that over the past few years he'd grown fond of Lou, and a few others. And now there was this one, messing with his mind and possibly his magic. At least the magic part was in a good way.

He picked up his mirror and motioned for them to go to the next trailer over and as they walked he looked over at her…annoyed and intrigued at the same time that so far, in less than 48 hours, this human female had caused him to feel things he didn't want to feel or didn't know he was capable of feeling.

There were no lights on inside or out, and they could barely see to get up the steps as they walked up, and he quickly unlocked the door and flipped on the light switch.

"Home sweet home," he said as they walked in.

She took a deep breath, expecting to walk in and find a typical single guy 'man cave' type of place, but was instead surprised to see the place was decorated…elegantly. There was really no other way to put it. There were beautiful leather couches, velvet drapes, and a Moroccan style flavor to the entire scheme. Was this for real?

She looked over at him in mild shock.

"Wow. This is…impressive." She walked over to a book shelf studying some of the classic titles, some of which looked to be antiques, and various knick knacks that were neatly arranged across the top.

A red flag automatically went up in her head. Maybe this guy wasn't the knight in shining armor he was pretending to be. No one working as a carny could afford this kind of stuff. She'd learned the hard way that people are not always what they seemed.

She instinctively backed up toward the door.

He could sense her uneasiness and noted that she'd moved away from him.

"Louie's not the only one with a past," he said, quietly.

She seemed to be okay with the fact that Lou was an ex-con and had become a better man. So maybe if he played that same card, she would buy it and believe that he too, was some poor loser with a story who had turned his life around.

"What kind of past? she asked cautiously.

"Drugs."

It was a plausible explanation for the kind of money it would take to fill up a place like this with antiques and lavish décor. The truth was that he'd been collecting for a very long time…and had won plenty of money cheating at cards, spiriting into a few places he shouldn't have been and helping himself to whatever he wanted more than a few times as well. And with time passing by, some of those things became antiques worth a lot of money. He'd sold some of them off and bought whatever he wanted.

Pathetic, to have to do such a thing, since he was a Jinn and accustomed in his own realm to a lavish lifestyle…but here with powers that had waned over time, he had little choice in the matter. He had to work, beg, borrow or steal…or sell off things to survive. He'd pretty much done all of the above at one time or another but since the whole truth and nothing but the truth wasn't an option, this was gonna have to do!

Being a drug dealer seemed plausible enough since many dealers lived in shithole trailers and apartments tucked away in the kind of neighborhoods where their customers were readily available. Hell some of them had lavishly decorated dumps too.

"You were a dealer?"

"Yep."

"And you were a user too, I presume?"

"I've done my share but not like some." That wasn't a lie.

"How long have you been out of it?"

"Probably five or six years now."

She looked a little skeptical.

"Most people who've gone through rehab know to the day how long they've been without a hit or a drink. I guess you must've gotten cleaned up right around the time you started here....when you met Louie? He said he's known you for about that long."

"Well, yah....sort of. I was working this carnival before Lou came on."

He heaved a sigh of relief that he'd somehow managed to give a time frame that correlated to whatever Louie had told her. He hadn't thought about the fact that she'd spent a few hours with him this afternoon and God only knows what he may have said to her.

"So, then...you were still dealing when you started working the carnival?"

"Pretty much."

"But you're clean now....right?"

"Yep."

She nodded, trying to decide whether to open the door and walk out now. Was he telling the truth? What if he was still dealing or if he tried to hurt her now that he had her here alone? Then again, he'd saved her from a brutal rape just an hour ago...he'd offered her a job, protection and so far had done nothing but act like a gentleman, so it didn't seem to add up.

Her feet decided to stay where they were.

"Sometimes the worst of us become the best of us because someone gave them a second chance," she said, not sure whether she was validating him for his turnaround, or trying to convince herself that he had actually turned his life around. She remembered reading the words in the dedication of a book some months before. Either way, somehow, it seemed fitting here and now.

He smiled. "The worst of us? I'd say that's a little harsh."

He would have to admit he'd been rather selfish for most of his existence....and maybe callous, especially when it

107

came to humans. But that was expected...he was a Jinn! The whole drug dealer thing was a lie of course, and he'd never murdered anyone...so to lump him in with the worst of humanity? Well, that wasn't exactly a fair statement; especially since he wasn't even human. Still he had to play this one out.

"I got tired of being on the run and decided to start a new life."

That was actually the truth...he wasn't running from angry drug lords wanting money...or cops. He was running from more than a few pissed off Jinn and a handful of out-of-sorts Angels, which were in essence a 'police force' all their own he supposed. And it had been five or six centuries ago instead of five or six years ago. Years...centuries...who's counting? When you're on the run, you sort of lose track of time.

He stared at her for a moment.

"What about you? Don't you think you deserve a second chance? You're on the run too. Your life has been turned upside down pretty much and you don't really seem to have any plan in place for what you're going to do, except make a few bucks and run some more."

She sighed. "Yeah, I know. I'm going to figure something out."

He got up and walked over to the fridge and grabbed two bottles of water and offered her one.

"Why don't you relax and have a seat. You are staying right?" He smiled. "I know you were thinking about bolting a minute ago."

She blushed. "Well...what do you expect when you bring me here to this Breaking Bad mobile and tell me you used to deal?!"

"I'd say this place is a lot nicer than that. But I don't blame you...I was just asking."

She put down her purse and walked over to the couch and plunked down, fluffing up the pillow and putting her feet up to show him that she wasn't afraid of him, even though she still had her guard up.

"So earlier today you told me you've been here in this town for a month or so. When are you moving again?"

He shrugged. "Probably any time now. We usually don't stay in any one place too long. We'll hit one town for a month or six weeks, and then move out and go at least twenty miles away to another town or into the next county. We stay regional through the fall and then go south during the winter."

"I know I asked you this earlier today too....but when we were busy you never really answered the question. Do you ever get lonely being on the road so much? I mean it must be hard to make friends or have any kind of normal life."

She took a large gulp of water from the bottle he'd handed her and pulled a brown knit blanket that was draped across the back of the couch over her as she adjusted the pillow behind her head.

He smiled. At least she was loosening up a little.

"The carnies that stay on for a long time get to know each other. Everyone's got a story, but we've got each other's back. We're sort of like a little dysfunctional family."

"Yeah, Louie said something along those lines. Where are you from originally? Do you have any family?"

He almost laughed out loud. Well, now there was that question he always hated trying to answer when some clingy female would try to pry into his life after he'd slept with her.

Hell, he hadn't even slept with this one and she was already at it! But then again, he'd invited her in, offered his protection for God knows what reason, and getting to know him seemed to be her lifeline right now. What was he going to tell her? Yeah...I have family. Mom's a genie and dad's a no-show flaming avenger from Heaven above!

He felt a sense of guilt that she was here, opening up to him and offering up fragile trust that could be easily shattered and he had nothing to offer her in return except for his protection...and lies.

109

"Listen...I need to take a shower and get whatever I need out of the bedroom for the night so you can have the 'presidential suite' all to yourself." He picked up the tv remote and tossed it to her. "Make yourself at home....but can't promise you what's growing in the fridge. Whatever's in there, check because it might eat you first."

She cringed and he laughed out loud.

"I'm just kidding. There's fresh fruit in there...and some stuff to make a sandwich."

He walked down the narrow hallway toward one of two bedrooms ...the other served as an 'office' of sorts where he had a nice computer desk and hutch set up, a small leather loveseat, a guitar that stood in the corner and various music and media posters hanging on the walls.

He stepped into the shower and the hot water sluiced down his body, washing away the cares of the day, his mind traveled back in time to his past...when he was still living back in the Jinn realm not far from his mother Soheila.

She'd just found out that he'd been taking human form to come to the human realm and it was almost as if it were yesterday that he could see her standing there, with her long black hair drifting around her looking beautiful and timeless despite her stern expression.

"Azizi...I don't understand you. Why would you do this when you know the risk? You know I lost my powers to go there...and what of the trouble you have caused? The Jinn elders are now looking for you...and I cannot keep your whereabouts hidden forever. The Angels are angry as well, from what I have heard and they have more power to find you even than the Jinn. What do you expect me to do?"

He'd shrugged off her commentary.

"Nothing, mother. I've grown into my full power and I am quite capable of taking care of myself."

"Are you? Look at you! You go to the other side and you drink...you gamble. You sleep with them. You make trouble. And there is always the danger that one of them may

know enough magic to trap you. If that happens, you know I cannot help you."

"That is no more than legend, mother. No one is really even sure it can be done or if it was ever really done. These humans...they are inept. My God, they can scarcely find their own pathetic way out of the traps the material world creates for them, much less figuring out how to trap one of us!"

Soheila wasn't letting it go. "Who is she?"

"Who is who?"

"Why else would you go there except for some human woman?"

He laughed out loud. "A woman? One woman? Not a chance. Two or three at a time is more like it."

He sighed. "Mother, I did it because I can....because I wanted to know what it felt like. And somehow I had this feeling I wasn't going to lose my power. I don't know why, but I just knew."

Soheila took his face in her hands. "What if I had lost you? You are all I have left of him, Azizi."

"You weren't going to lose me," he said quietly.

He often marveled at how beautiful and loving she still was despite the hand she'd been dealt. His mother was a remarkably resilient woman...and one whose heart was more giving than he could comprehend. Perhaps that was why life had dealt her that very hand...and he was determined the same thing wasn't ever happening to him. He would leave the love and compassion to her. His life was going to be all about self-fulfillment. Nothing more.

" I'm sure dear old dad wouldn't be very happy to know that I was there, getting my human ass into every kind of trouble there is...and enjoying every minute of it, instead of forgiving some pathetic wretch of their sins so they can turn around and do it all over again the next day. If it would piss him off, that's reason enough for me."

111

Soheila stared at her son wondering how and why he had such bitterness in his heart for the man he knew little of.

"You know nothing about him, Azizi."

"I know all I need to know...so, let's just leave it alone." He paused, "So, why did you do it"

"Why did I do what?"

"Go there. How come it's alright for you but not for me?"

"It wasn't alright for me...I lost my powers. You know that. The only reason I'm even here...why you're here is because of your father."

"You didn't answer the question."

Soheila paused for a moment.

"There was a human...one who I as connected to. I influenced him from here on this side for a long time, but soon I wasn't able to resist the impulse to go to him. I felt as if we were twin souls. I had been taught this principle but never believed in it. But after I had started influencing his ideas, it felt as if we were one, in a way. I fell in love. I went there to meet him and soon afterward I found I had no power."

Azizi stared at her in disbelief. "You? Fell in love with...a human?"

Soheila nodded.

"I was lost in a world which in which I didn't know how to survive. And the one who I had felt the connection to...well...like most humans he made mistakes and was unable to control his impulses either, I suppose. Who was I to blame him after I had broken The Law to come here to take a chance on him? And yet...his feelings were fleeting, mine were not. I too, had made a mistake....given up everything to go to him. He was no twin soul at all...and I was no more than another passing fancy of his human desires. He deserted me for the next pretty face that came along."

"I was heartbroken, but I had accepted my fate. And then the worst happened...not only had I lost his heart, and

112

no longer had my powers...but one day I got word that he had been killed. Even though he no longer wanted me, I still loved him, and when he died, I felt as if a part of me died as well. Your father was there at his passing to escort him to the other side, and afterward he came back and made his presence known to me. Since I had no powers I could not see him as I normally would have but he came to me at first in a dream and then later materialized so I could see him."

"He felt sorry for me, at first, I suppose. And he began visiting me regularly Within a very short time, we realized that perhaps there was something much more between us. He stayed at my side despite his orders from above to abandon me...and he was cast out of The Order for his disobedience, stripped of his own powers. But his love never faltered...his compassion and his guidance got me through that terrible time when I didn't think I could go on. He was now a human and so was I....and we reveled in the time we had...the love we felt for one another. You are the product of that love, Azizi."

"Love? Oh, I see...that's why he's still here for you and why he was here for me all this time. Spare me the details," he said with contempt.

"He was accepted back into the Order because of his compassion for me....for us! His powers were restored. And he was granted a second chance to do greater things that perhaps we cannot understand right now. How could we turn away that opportunity for him to help others as he'd helped us? You are a part of him, Azizi."

"Mother, I love you, but I am Azizi ab'd al Jadu. My name means 'Servant of Magic' and that is exactly what and who I am. I'm no Angel. Not now. Not ever. I do not want nor did I ask to be a part of him or any of his agenda."

Soheila smiled with a far off look in her eyes as she laid a hand to his face.

"Someday you'll understand. Sometimes the things we don't ask for are the things we need the most."

113

She'd kissed his forehead and left the room and as she'd walked away he knew it was the last time he was going to see her...for a while anyway.

Later that evening he'd decided to come through the portal and stay here far out of reach of the Jinn who's wrath he'd stirred up, and out of sight and mind of his father's kind as well. It was all past history now anyway, and his life was here and now.

Except now included the woman named Scherarazade Bloom, and with her arrival had come a return of power that he could only hope would grow over time. But time was something they didn't have much of if she left as soon as she could scrape up the money she needed to move on.

He turned off the water and dried off, and slipped on a pair of clean pants and a shirt over his head, towel drying his hair and then brushing his teeth. He checked under his cabinet to see if he had an extra toothbrush and wasn't surprised to see that he didn't. He was either going to have to go to the drugstore, or go get his mirror, bring it to the bedroom and then conjure one up on the other side and bring it through. And go through trying to explain why he was carrying the mirror into the bedroom and then back out again when she took over the room. He wasn't comfortable leaving it out of his sight especially if he needed to go through it after she went to bed.

He decided conjuring one was his first choice and decided to give it a shot here on this side...after all he'd created a mini a Taj Mahal for the stage, and it seemed to be solid... and at least all day yesterday and through last night's show it had held together and not disintegrated or dematerialized..

He closed his eyes and visualized a purple tooth brush in his mind and a few seconds later felt it materialize in his hand. It was a strange sensation...different than on the other side where things were made differently.

Here they were put together atom by atom with polarity holding it all together. Over there, things were not as solid, because they were not made of the same type of matter….and once they were here on this side those things were not as reliable at holding together, either.

He turned the toothbrush over and over in his hand, marveling at its solidity and the fact that it seemed pretty damned normal. The possibilities were starting to grow. He would be watching over the course of the next few days to see whether his stage props stayed solid and didn't start to disintegrate and if so…then life was about to take a turn for the better.

He smiled, grabbing a pillow and blanket from the closet on his way down the hall and headed back to the living room wondering whether she'd even still be there, given the fact she'd been thinking of walking out the door only a short while ago. He was surprised to find her sound asleep on his couch.

She looked so peaceful…and beautiful lying there with her thick lashes spread out like little fans on her cheeks and the black cascade of shiny, long curls spread out on the throw pillow under her head.

He knelt down beside her and brushed his fingers along the side of her face. She moved slightly but didn't wake up. Her lips looked full and delicious and he could barely control the urge to lean in and taste their softness.

He stared at her for a moment wondering whether to leave her there on the couch or wake her up. He decided on neither and instead picked her up in his arms to carry her to his bedroom.

As he leaned in and picked her up, the top of his shirt that she was still wearing from earlier, fell open exposing a hint of cleavage and he pushed the image out of his mind of tracing the curve of her collarbone with his lips and trailing a wet path with his tongue down to where the tops of her breasts were peeking out.

He'd been wondering what kind of body she was rocking under the baggy clothes she'd showed up in yesterday, and he'd gotten more than an eyeful of it in her room at the inn this morning and again tonight in the harem girl outfit he'd been fantasizing about all day. Not to mention he'd pretty much seen both of her naked breasts when the shitbag who'd tried to attack her had torn her top completely open.

She woke up with a start half way down the hall.

"What are you doing?"

"Taking you to bed."

Her expression turned to immediate alarm.

"Put me down! Now."

"Shhh. I don't mean that. I'm just carrying you to the bedroom. I was going to lay you down and let you sleep but you woke up."

Her face was only inches from his and he had to force his gaze away from hers because he was being driven insane now looking at how soft and sweet those lips of hers looked up close and the desire to taste them was growing by the second.

He kicked the door open a little wider than it was and then set her down on the corner of the bed, and then made himself step back when he noted how nervous she looked.

What he'd much rather do was lay her back, lift his shirt up over her head and explore and taste every curve of her body until they were both damp with sweat and lying in the afterglow of the many explosive sensations the human body could enjoy. But something made him keep a polite distance.

She turned away and was oblivious to the way his eyes were kissing her body as she ran her hands along the thick brown and gold damask bedspread as she looked around his room, marveling at how beautifully decorated it was…almost palatial, despite its modest size.

The windows were hung with brocade draperies tied back with gold ropes, there was a potted palm tree in one corner, a large chaise chair on the other side and carved headboard, end tables and dresser. Carved wooden and leather animals were perched at various locations around the room and a fisherman's net hung overhead strung sparingly with dried starfish, sand dollars, gold coins and pieces of hand blown glass.

She got up and walked over to peek inside the master bathroom. It looked as beautifully kept as his bedroom.

She turned to face him. "I guess I shouldn't be surprised since the rest of your house looks this good."

He shrugged as she walked back over and plunked down on the bed.

"So…you're a story teller, Scheharazade. Why don't you tell me a story?"

"What kind of story? You mean like a fairytale?" To his surprise, she sounded intrigued.

"A bedtime story." He laughed.

She blushed and looked slightly annoyed.

"Sorry. I think you want one of those 1-800 late night numbers?"

"I didn't say it had to be pornographic. Just a story. Kind of like 1,001 Nights. Pretend I'm your king and your life depends on how well your tale entertains me. What kind of story would you tell?"

She laughed. "You? My king? Okay, that is a fairy tale right there! I thought you were just a little off your rocker, now I know you're completely out of your mind. And you're an egomaniac to boot. Nice combo."

"Guilty on both charges. But I'm serious. You should start thinking up stories every day. It'll keep them fresh in your mind for when you start writing again. Can't hurt, right?"

She smiled. "You know, when I was a little girl, I used to love to tell my mother stories. Sometimes I would go in her closet and take her clothes and put them on so I could be in character. And no matter how good or bad it was, she would always sit and listen as though it was the best story in the world." Her eyes clouded up. "I miss her so much some days."

"You know, by telling me about her…and by remembering her, she's with you even now. And anytime you want to share a story, I'll listen."

He paused for a moment trying to come up with anything that might cheer her up. "Now… if you want to dress up, I won't argue either, but I can't guarantee you'll find any princess gowns in my closet. But hey, you know I can rock the pink chiffon."

She smiled through her tears at his attempt to lighten her mood, but her emotions were still raw.

"I just feel like she wouldn't be very proud of me. For everything that's happened. The mistakes I've made."

"What mistakes?"

"Well, look…I married Derek. I invited this psychotic sadist into my life, and look what I've become."

"Don't you dare blame yourself, Scheri."

She shook her head and began to cry.

"But this never would have happened if I had just not gotten involved with him."

"There was no possible way you could have known what he was like. People like him keep it hidden …they beat their victims down until they are convinced that they somehow asked for it."

She looked up at him and wiped the tears off her face.

"You're right, I know. Sometimes I just feel like I let her down. She had such high hopes. I loved her so much and I just wanted to make her proud."

"She is proud. She's proud of you even right now, if for nothing else than for having the strength to escape from that situation."

She nodded. "I just wish sometimes that she was still here with me. I would give anything if I could have called her tonight...or gone to her house and sat with her after what happened. I just needed my mother. But you know if she was here Derek would just threaten to hurt her...so I guess it's for the best."

"She'll always be with you. Just listen with your heart and you'll hear her there whispering to you."

She stared at him for a moment.

Who was this man? Everything that came out of his mouth seemed to defy the cocky, bad-boy image he seemed to have when she met him standing in the lot of the carnival. Instead he seemed to be insightful and compassionate...and down to earth. Although right about now, he seemed more like an angel from above than any earthbound male human.

She dragged in a deep breath as though to center herself. "Well...I guess I need to pull myself together here and try to move on with the rest of the night.

She walked over to his closet and opened it. "Do you have a long shirt, or a pair of pajamas I can borrow, since we didn't go back to the inn to get any of my stuff?"

"Yeah."

He opened one of the dresser drawers and grabbed a pair of pajama bottoms and a long sleeved t-shirt and tossed them over to her.

He nodded toward the bathroom.

"There's towels in the stand-up cabinet in there and there's soap and shampoo in the shower. You can use my razor if you need it. It's on the sink."

She started toward the bathroom and then turned around.

"You know, you never answered my question earlier. Where are you from originally...and do you have family?"

He sighed. What was he going to tell her? He'd avoided the question earlier and he realized that anything he said from this point on, he was going to have to make sure it

119

correlated with what Lou knew about him since he may have already told her whatever he knew…or thought he did.

"I came from…out west. And yes, I have family. My mother is alive and my father is too…somewhere. But I haven't seen either of them in a long time. It feels like centuries."

She walked over to where he stood and stared up at him. "It doesn't really matter where you came from or where you've been. Or who you've been. All that matters is who you are now. You saved me tonight. I…" her voice dropped off and she looked at the floor. "Thank you."

He stepped forward and wrapped his arms around her again, resting his chin on the top of her head and closing his eyes while reveling in the warmth he felt with her body pressed in close to his. He kissed the top of her hair and held her there for a long moment.

In barely two days this woman had come into his life, wrangled her way into his work….caused him to feel things he didn't know he was capable of feeling, like compassion, guilt, and God knows what else. And somehow he just knew that she had something to do with his increase in powers.

He didn't want it. He didn't ask for it…and he was beginning to wonder if maybe his mother was right.

Sometimes the things we don't ask for are the things we need the most.

CHAPTER NINE

Derek tapped his fingers on the desk in his office. He was pissed.

So far there was just nothing...the little bitch had completely dropped off the face of the earth for all intents and purposes, and no amount of money or man power had been able to locate her. Where the hell was she and how was she staying off the grid? His phone rang a moment later.

He composed himself, but had already told his secretary that had a headache and to hold his calls. It wasn't a lie actually...his temples were throbbing as a reminder that he needed to find some way to keep his personal life out of his business. There would be time for dealing with the issue of finding his estranged wife soon enough.

He picked up the phone. "Alicia, I told you I don't want to take any calls this morning for at least a couple hours."

"I know, Mr. Worley, but there's a Mr. M on line 2 and he says he has something important to tell you. I tried to explain to him, and take a message, but he's called back three times. I'm sorry but the only name he would give was Mr. M."

Derek felt a tingle of excitement flow through his veins as he told her to put him through despite his anger that the idiot had called him on his work line instead of his private cell.

"What do you have?"

"This isn't written in stone...yet anyway. But one of my friends works in dispatch for Morgan County Police Dept. and there was a call-in the other night .A woman fitting her description was attacked outside a carnival. She didn't want to file a report...something about not wanting her name attached to any police records, but whoever she was with

121

made her do it, cause otherwise they wouldn't have been able to haul in the two guys that tried to rape her."

"Morgan County? Where the hell is that…and she was raped?" Derek sounded almost enthused at the picture…almost as much as when his co-horts had violated her on his living room floor.

The voice on the other end of the line continued.

"My buddy wasn't sure, but said she had a strange name like Sharizanne or something, so it's gotta be her"

He hung up the phone and his expression remained a mask of calm despite the waves of excitement that flowed through him like waves crashing to the shore.

He stood up and walked out to Alicia's desk.

"I'm going home for the day….this headache is bad enough that I can't think straight. I'll call in for messages in a couple hours."

Alicia nodded. "Feel better."

He walked to the elevator and got in. He was feeling better alright…just imagining the look of bloodshot eyes staring up at him, when he finally had her in his custody again, pleading in those final moments as the last breath exited her lungs was all the medicine he needed.

The morning sun peeked through a crack in the blinds of the window of Z's bedroom as Scheri opened her eyes, disoriented and confused for a moment until her vision cleared and she remembered where she was.

She sat up and stretched the kinks out of her back before padding to the bathroom to clean up and then go see if there was coffee in his kitchen.

She walked out to the living room expecting to see him sprawled out on his couch since it was so early, but he didn't seem to be anywhere in sight, including the hall bathroom, which she checked next.

Maybe he'd gone out to the store?

She shrugged and decided to head back to the kitchen to make some coffee, if he had some. She quickly located it in the cabinet next to the stove and soon had a nice pot brewing.

The gold mirror stood in the living room next to the couch and she couldn't resist the urge to walk over and inspect it…again…for the hundredth time.

She stood there for a moment and then suddenly smiled. How could she have been so stupid? He was obviously somehow projecting a picture of himself from some remote location and as the mist poured out from under the platform…a smoke machine like the kind they used for rock n roll stages would work, he was probably hiding under the platform and then standing up and it was so misty you couldn't tell. That had to be it. It was the only explanation.

Ha! So much for his 'first rule of magic.'

She stared at the mirror for a moment nonetheless and reached out cautiously to touch the glass, wondering if it would feel strange or swallow her up or something. Just standing here next to it made her feel weird, like she was being watched. It was….creepy.

She wrote stories…she had an open mind and wild possibilities of fantasy were always a part of her imagination. And maybe, though she was embarrassed to admit it to the average person, she wanted to believe that magical realms and otherworldly things could exist. And yet, there seemed to be something almost otherworldly about this mirror.

Finally after walking around it a few more times, she headed to the bedroom to see if she could find something in his closet to wear long enough to go back to the inn to get some of her own clothes.

Z woke with a start. He had been sleeping in the comfort of his large bed on the other side of the mirror, where he'd come after she'd gone to sleep, to rest and think in the privacy and quiet of his own space. It was peaceful and the bed was much more comfortable than his couch in his trailer.

He watched as she circled the mirror.

She looked more determined than ever to discover its secrets but he also knew there was no chance of that because she couldn't see into it...anything inside wasn't visible to human perception. She'd smiled, as though satisfied with herself, and she probably thought she'd figured it all out.

For just a moment he allowed himself to envision what it would be like to be able to share his secret with her...what her reaction would be and whether she would run in fear or stay connected to him, but quickly pushed the thought away. No human could ever know the truth. His destiny was one of magic, mystery....and loneliness.

Lonely? Him? He almost laughed. Where the hell had that come from? He always had good company...Louie, his friends here at the carnival...and whatever women he brought home on any particular night for some fun and games. He was never lonely. And yet watching her here and now standing before him unaware of his presence, he'd never felt more lonely in his entire existence. He was surrounded with people all the time, and yet none of them were ever really with him. The real him.

He watched her as she walked down the hall toward his bedroom, admiring the gentle sway of her hips and the tousled curls falling down her back as she moved and the realization hit him that he liked seeing here here...in his place...wearing his pajamas.

As soon as she closed the bedroom door to get dressed he quickly stepped through the mirror, and then opened and closed the trailer door to make it sound like he'd just come in and then went to the hall bathroom to clean up and wash his face.

She emerged a few moments later from the bedroom and ran into him in the hall.

"Where were you? It's barely even daylight."

"I stepped out for a minute...I thought I heard something over by Louie's. It woke me up."

She nodded, walked to the kitchen and pulled a mug out of one of the cabinets. "Want some coffee?"

"It sounds funny, you offering me a cup here in my own house."

She blushed. "Yeah, I guess it does. I'm sorry. I hope I'm not being too forward, making myself at home?"

"No, you're not. I...like it, actually."

She poured him a mug of coffee and handed him the sugar and some powdered creamer she found in his cabinet.

"So what's the agenda for today?"

"Same as every other....smile and the show must go on."

She sighed. "I'm scared."

"Of what?"

"What do you think! Last night...I filed that report and I just know that he'll find me."

"He won't find you, even if he comes here."

"How are you going to stop him?"

He shrugged. "Look, you're in a new place...a new state. He doesn't have that kind of pull here like he does at home. Even if he sends someone here, you know I'm not telling anyone anything...and Louie's not saying shit to anyone either. He's from New York...he's got your back."

"What about anyone else who's seen me here?"

"We'll deal with that if it happens...I'd bet there's few if any of the carnies that have even noticed you walking around. It's only been a couple days."

"You're just way too confident. You don't know Derek like I do."

"I know enough," he said matter-of-factly, remembering the pictures that had flooded his mind every time he touched her.

"I just wish..." her voice trailed off.

"What?"

"I wish I didn't have to run anymore. I just want my life back."

He reached forward and took her hand in his own, turning it over and kissing her palm. It sent shock waves of energy through his body and mind and he was drowning in the desire to drag her body in against him and taste her lips and trace the curve of her hip with his fingers, with a familiarity that was both unnatural and unnerving. She was attracted to him he knew, but at the same time, she was afraid...of him and of men in general right now. And he knew if he gave in to the desire he would break any trust he'd built with her so far.

And yet, as the picture blossomed in his mind, he could almost taste the essence of her skin on his tongue as he imagined trailing a wet path down her collarbone, past the crease of her cleavage, and down the silky skin of her midriff toward her navel...and beyond.

"Your wish is my command," he said quietly as he reined in the torrent raging through his mind and body.

"What do you mean?"

"Exactly that. I'm going to help you get your life back. It may not be exactly the life you had before, but at least it'll be a life where you can walk around without looking over your shoulder every day."

She sighed. "Honestly? I wish you were some genie who could just go poof and give me my life back. But it's not that simple."

He smiled....oh, the irony of it all.

"Maybe I am...and maybe it is."

Funny, but for some reason it felt good to acknowledge that he was a Jinn...even in the half-assed pathetic state he was now in.

And for once in his life, he wasn't thinking about using power for his own selfish reasons. But here and now he had to wonder. Maybe magic wasn't always the answer to everything anyway. Real solutions here in the material world...ones that included thought, creative ideas, coupled with compassion and survival were pretty damned powerful forces themselves. So far being clever had served him well more than a few times. Maybe the time had come to try some of the others.

"Right now you're hiding, but what you need to do is the exact opposite. You can't run forever. Maybe you need to stop worrying about who knows you're here and just stand your ground. Be truthful with people."

"You mean just set up house and home here and get back on the grid? I don't think I'm comfortable with that. What if he shows up here? Or has someone else do it."

"So what if he did? He wouldn't dare lay a hand on you or hire anyone to make you disappear if everyone is watching and there's any question about his character."

"I don't know. He's such a conniving bastard, I just have this feeling he'd find some way to get to me. He told me if I ran away before that he'd make it look like I was some gold digger who married him for his money and had my lover beat me up so it would look like he did it and I could take him for everything he was worth, and then share the money with my lover after the divorce. And what if he or someone he hires tries to break into your place?"

"Whoever it is, they will regret the day they try breaking in to my place day or night. And hey...I can just make you disappear if I have to. Not sure how I'll work that yet, but remember, I'm an illusionist." He smiled.

She laughed. "Yeah, right! What are you going to do...take my hand and have me step into your mirror with you?" She raised a brow in mild sarcasm.

"If that's what it takes."

She smiled at his joke, but something about the way he said it felt too serious...strange...almost eerie. The same way she'd felt when she was standing in front of the mirror earlier feeling like she was being watched.

She took another sip of her coffee weighing her options. Should she stay here and trust in the safety Z was offering or should she leave now while there was still a chance she could get away before Derek found out about the police report.

She stared over at him.

He looked so handsome sitting there in the morning light with his black hair tousled around his tanned shoulders. She struggled with the undeniable physical attraction she felt for him, and yet, at the same time, she felt so comfortable with him. A sense of being at ease that simply didn't make sense…she'd only just met him, this man with the ability to make magic appear to be all too real.

Perhaps the greatest magic of all was that for whatever reason, he'd given her hope; something she thought she would never have again…and a belief that he would do everything in his power to help her get her life back

Was it all just another illusion? And if she dared to stay, would it be enough?

CHAPTER TEN

Derek sat on his couch talking to his informant who confirmed that she had been located.

"So you're telling me she's staying up there in Morgan County Where-Ever-It-Is in Bum-Fuck Egypt, and she's been seen more than once at some carnival? Who is she staying with?"

"I dunno but something about a magic show came up....when she filed the report she was with some magician. Some guy who goes by the name of 'Z'. No website, but I emailed you the picture. You want me to head up there?"

Derek paused for a moment. "No."

"What? After all the shit you've been giving me about finding her right away?"

"Exactly. We need to watch and wait. I don't want any red flags going up with her that might cause her to run. We need to let enough time go by so she thinks she's safe...that no one traced her from the police report. Then we make a move in a few weeks. Just have someone keep an eye on her for now."

He hung up the phone, his thoughts racing with all the possibilities. He couldn't help but wonder who this 'Z' was and felt a slight twinge of jealousy. Had he been sleeping with her?

Although he wanted the little bitch dead, something about her had always intrigued and attracted him to her physically. And although he'd gotten aroused watching his friends assault her on the floor the night they'd done their little 'ritual', it still hadn't quite sit right with him that they were savoring her body....the body that should only be his to enjoy.

His mind traveled back in time to the first time he'd ever heard those words.

He was just six years old, and he'd been playing out by the stream behind his house. His mother had gone out to the store and his stepfather Jonas was there in the house, drinking again as usual.

He could hear him calling his name and he knew what kind of danger he was in at that moment....and he wasn't going in that house not now, not ever if he could help it. Not after what Jonas had made him do last time his mother was away.

He heard Jonas's voice calling out to him again.

"Derek! You better get your little ass in this house now. If you make me come find you...you'll regret the day you were born you little piece of shit."

He still didn't answer and a moment later he saw Jonas come out of the back door of the house as he hunkered down in the tall grass hoping he wouldn't be detected.

Jonas looked around surveying the property and a moment later he could tell that he'd been spotted.

He took off running as fast as his small legs could carry him, but he was hardly a match for Jonas's size and strength, and as he swept him up under one arm he knew the beating that was about to ensue....before he was forced to do 'the deed.' That horrible thing that Jonas made him do when he would take down his pants.

It nearly choked him every time, but Jonas never cared and when he was through he would spit the evidence from his mouth and scrub his teeth over and over as Jonas looked on laughing, telling him that if he dared to breathe a word to his mother he would take his hunting knife and slit him from belly to throat.

He remembered the first time Jonas had forced him to do it and he'd struggled and cried as he had slapped his face and told him, "I don't want to hear your whining. I married that whore of a mother of yours...and took you in with her. You think anyone else wants you? Now I own her

130

and I own you too. Her body is mine to enjoy as I see fit....and yours too, boy."

The abuse had gone on and on for years, even after his mother found out....the bitch had either been too afraid or too stupid to leave or she just didn't care, and she, solely and with full knowledge had allowed that bastard to rape and abuse him, never once standing up to protect her own child.

One night when he was about thirteen years old, he'd run away from home and been hunted down and brought back, and no one would believe him when he tried to tell them what was going on. After all, Jonas was a pillar of the community. A rich lawyer...respected among his peers.

He'd stood in the middle of the dining room wiping the blood from his lip after Jonas had hit him so hard that his teeth rattled in his skull.

"Why? Why do you do this, Jonas?"

And he remembered the cold look in Jonas's eyes when he said, 'Because I can.' They were words that stuck with him for years. Not so much because of the cold blooded callousness with which they were said, but because of the utter and complete power and dominance for which they stood. In that moment when Jonas had said them, he'd realized that Jonas was a man of complete and total power. Not just from his position in life, but because of the freedom with which he lived. He feared nothing...and that kind of freedom came from only one thing: no conscience.

He'd made up his mind then and there, that he wanted that kind of freedom. Because with it came a letting go of all pain and fear...all the memories...everything. Once you didn't care anymore, you were truly free.

A couple years later, when he had planned out and orchestrated the murder of both his bitch mother, and that piece of shit...he made absolutely sure they'd suffered enough to make up for all the abuse they'd dished out to him over the years. Children are like sponges and it was time for him to show them exactly what he'd learned from example.

131

The look on his mother's face as he'd doused her with gasoline, while tied to that chair in the warehouse, her head held back, trying to balance that lit candle on her forehead was priceless. She'd somehow managed to do it for a very long time and when the candle finally fell to the side, it caught fire to a spot of gas on the floor, which he'd let burn until it was a few feet away from her before putting it out, to the sound of her screams through the duct tape on her mouth. The look of terror in her eyes was priceless. Maybe quite as intense as that which had burned in his own eyes the first time Jonas had raped him, but it was still pretty damn good.

And the battery he'd hooked up to Jonas's balls that would send shockwaves of pain every time he made a sound, was not only brilliant but also enjoyable.

And then there was every time he would cut a piece of flesh from Jonas's body and peel the meat back...waiting...waiting for the scream of agony that would come when he poured salt water on the wound.

He'd made sure both of their tortures went on and on....enough to cause agony and suffering but not death. He saved that part for later, when he'd taken them to the cliffs by the river where they would have an untimely 'accident' after being apparently kidnapped and their car careened off the road.

He'd driven them to the site and pushed his unconscious mother down deeper into the trunk of the car and had pulled the tape from Jonas's mouth.

He cocked his head as Jonas gasped for breath.

"Aren't you gonna ask me why I'm doing this, Jonas?"

Jonas stared at him in silence.

"Oh, wait. I'm sure you don't need a refresher but let me give you one anyway. My body is yours to enjoy, isn't that right?" He took off his shirt and stood there flexing his well-muscled form. "Enjoying it now?"

132

He put his shirt on and walked back over to where Jonas was propped up against the trunk of the car and punched him hard in the mouth.

"Go ahead, motherfucker. Ask me why."

Jonas slumped and said nothing.

"Ask me! Now."

Jonas finally dragged in a breath and said, "Fuck you. I'm not asking you anything, you little piece of shit. That's all you were then and that's all you ever will be."

Derek's mouth hardened into a thin line and he walked over and grabbed Jonas by his balls, swollen and sore from the many jolts of electricity that he'd shot through them, and began to squeeze until Jonas screamed in agony

"Ask. Me. Why."

Jonas gasped, ready to pass out as he whispered, "For the love of God...why?"

Derek smiled and said, "Because I can, you son of a bitch."

Tears of anger and frustration poured down his face. He punched Jonas one last time and then pushed him into the trunk, but not before making sure he managed to bring his mother around to at least partial consciousness so she could be aware of what was happening in those final moments.

He smiled, put on a pair of gloves and carefully wiped everything down to remove all traces of his fingerprints, then started the engine. He pushed the gas hard and jumped out and watched as the car gained momentum and then crashed through the guard rail, over the edge of the ravine and tumbling end over end into the river below as it exploded into a fiery mass of crumpled metal.

The car sunk slowly down into the dark murky depths along with the memories he hoped to wipe from his mind.

But the dirt of those bygone days wouldn't wash away so easily and it was funny how the abused so easily became the abuser. He wasn't sure when or how it happened,

133

but perhaps it was the power he'd realized when he took on Jonas's mantra: 'Because I can'.

The power those words meant were like a drug flowing through his mind and poisoning his soul with every passing day.

And as the years had gone by, something made him decide to go to law school. After all, Jonas had been rich and provided them a good lifestyle, hadn't he? And just because his mother was a fucking bitch who'd allowed Jonas to physically and mentally abuse him for years, that didn't mean all women were like that.

And yet, every time he looked at the face of his last three girlfriends, all he could see was the face of dear old mom there...laughing as Jonas had violated him over and over again. He couldn't make her pay anymore, but he certainly had made them pay before they became just like her. Dead!

They had been nothing more than worthless bitches living off his money...not worthy of the title of wife or mother. Scheharazade was no different. She'd married him thinking he was going to advance her writing career, and then had the nerve to defy him just for him showing her a little discipline. She'd run off and was already likely shacked up with that piece of shit carny who'd been with her the night she filed that police report.

His mind snapped back to the present.

Whoever this Z was, he was going to get rid of him. It would only add to the excitement if she actually were having an affair with this cretin and particularly if she had feelings for him. Perhaps it was time for another 'barbeque by the river'.

He stood up and walked over to a picture hanging on the wall and carefully took it down from its hanger, exposing the the safe on the wall behind it, where he kept his favorite pictures. The ones of mother...and Jonas...and his lovers. Their dead, cold eyes staring up at the camera in the

134

moonlight before he'd sent them back into the earth where they belonged.

He pulled out the folders he had there...each labeled with their names, and rifled through the pictures. The last folder at the back was empty. It was labeled 'Scheharazade'. He longed for the day when he could add her pictures to his ever growing 'album'.

He smiled and put the folders back in the safe, carefully closing and locking it and then hanging the picture on the wall that covered it.

He headed upstairs to lie down. His head was still throbbing. Maybe a nap would bring relief...and he could dream for now of what he'd make into reality very soon.

Abdul watched from his side of the mirror as the human had spoken on the phone and was intrigued by the conversation he heard.

This Derek Worley, whose home he had come into was some kind of criminal and he definitely had plans for the demise of his wife. He had a dark side...and the more Abdul watched and listened, the more he liked what he saw and heard.

He couldn't help but wonder who this 'magician' named 'Z' was that Derek had traced to his wife...surely he was some pathetic human who practiced the usual parlor tricks that passed for magic.

He had little interest in such ridiculousness...his main and only concern was finding Azizi. He had no idea where to begin, but he needed to get out of this place and go out into the world to start his search.

He materialized and stepped out of the mirror into the living room, breathing the air into his human lungs and reveling again in the feel of his body once more. It was absolutely intoxicating! No wonder Azizi had broken The Law to do this over and over again.

He walked across the room, getting the feel of the motion of his legs, and as he passed by the coffee table, an image sitting on the computer screen caught his eye.

It was a carnival flyer for the one Derek Worley had been discussing on the phone. He looked down and shook his head in disbelief …there was a carnival emblem along with the image of a tent that said 'Smoke & MirrorZ', and standing in front was the man called 'Z.

It was none other than Azizi.

He leaned in and did a double take to make sure as a smile spread across his face and his thoughts began to race at breakneck speed.

So…Azizi was pretending to be a carnival magician. How utterly pathetic! Not that it really mattered.

He looked over to the end table beside the couch and happened to notice a picture of Derek's wife sitting there…and for a moment his breath caught in his now human throat.

Never since he'd laid eyes on Soheila had he seen a woman who stirred his senses such as this. He picked up the picture, running his fingers along the image of her face.

So…she was keeping company with Azizi. An immediate twinge of jealous hatred streaked through his veins. He didn't even know the woman, but the mere idea that Azizi might have her was enough.

His mind began to put together an idea…one that perhaps would benefit both he and his 'host'…this Derek Worley who was still apparently completely unaware that he'd called forth a Jinn, who technically was bound to serve at his beck and call.

As it stood now, he was simply there sort of stuck in limbo. Perhaps he could offer to help this Derek find his wife, Derek would remain oblivious to the fact he was a Jinn and owed him three wishes. They could both benefit from he situation, and he wouldn't be under any obligation to serve the human.

136

He would have his revenge on Azizi…drain him of his power and send him into an eternal state of limbo from which he would never return, and perhaps if this Derek were so inclined he would be willing instead of killing the woman, to sell her to him. Or maybe he would simply get rid of Derek along with Azizi without giving it another thought. He liked the sound of that plan…but making Derek think that he was on board to help him track down his wife would certainly help things along for now until he had whatever information he needed.

He stared at the woman's picture again entranced by the long raven curls that hung loose around her shoulders, and hazel green eyes that seemed as windows to a soul of passion and imagination. Another full body picture was all he needed to know that she was as beautiful in form as she was in face.

His mind roiled with fantasies in which he changed her and took her back to the Jinn realm where he would keep her captive as his mate.

As mere human, whose physical make-up had been changed so that powerful heat energy of the Jinn realm would not destroy her, she would likely be quite fearful and lost in a strange world where she was only one of a handful of her kind. Perhaps she might even become fond of him over time after realizing he was her only means of survival.

The picture of her naked, wrapped in silken sheets filled his mind and stirred his male body. He smiled.

He looked at the location of the carnival and focused his mind on dematerializing and reappearing there. His body began to thin and turn back to mist…and then all of a sudden…it stopped. What was going on?

He suddenly realized that he was not actually really free. He was only here because Derek Worley had summoned him…and he could not simply go do as he wished. Even though Derek had not actually ordered him to serve…he still had been called forth and the only way he was going to be able to leave this place was if Derek wished it.

137

It seemed he was not going to have any choice in the matter. He was going to have to grant those three wishes. He somehow was going to have to make sure one of them was getting to where the woman and Azizi were.

This adventure in revenge had just gotten a bit more challenging.

CHAPTER ELEVEN

"Okay…so we need to teach you how to fight."

A few more days had gone by, and Z eyed Scheri as she stood across from him with her arms folded across her chest. It was late morning and they'd come out here after coffee and breakfast to the dirt lot where the trailers stood in neat rows.

As long as she was with him, he knew that he could protect her. But there were going to be times when she wasn't and after she'd left this place, she was going to need some skills to fight back somewhere down the line.

She sighed. "So far Derek has never showed up to haul me off without a gun. So trying to teach me to kick his ass or any of his buddies isn't going to do me much good."

"I didn't say I was going to teach you to fight fair…I just said I was going to teach you to fight. And you're going to learn how to shoot a gun too."

"I already bought a gun and learned how to shoot it…sort of. But the last time he had me tracked down the guy he sent broke in while I was asleep. He somehow disarmed the alarm in the place I was staying and I grabbed the gun to shoot him, but he was just too big and too fast. He got it away from me and that was the end of it." She shook her head. "If I could have been just a few seconds faster maybe he wouldn't have gotten me. I wish I could have a next time with that bastard. I really do."

"Your wish is my command," he said under his breath. Funny how that phrase had been feeling so right lately, whenever he was with her. "Come here. This isn't just about Derek. We have to make sure what happened out behind the tent never happens again."

She walked over to where he stood and he turned her back around to face him and then hooked one arm up underneath her body and pretended to have a gun to her head with the other.

She could feel his lips as they brushed the back of her neck and liked the way his arm felt around her. She closed her eyes, fighting back the feeling.

"Do you feel where my arm is here? Well most women would grab this arm to try to move it so you doing that wouldn't raise any red flags with him. He would expect it as you raised your hands up. But what he wouldn't expect is for you to reach back and with just two fingers you can take him down."

Her brows knit together. "How?"

"Just reach a little higher and turn your hand around keeping your fingers firm. Hit him with your fingertips right in the Adam's Apple. The pain from so little force in such a small area is excruciating….disabling. And in that short moment when he is gasping for air and blinded with pain, you can disarm him if you know the right moves. Now sometimes this won't work if the guy is built like the Terminator and has that level of pain threshold, but for the average-sized attacker, like those scumbags outside the tent, this does increase your chances of getting away."

He turned her back around to face him and then showed her what he was talking about with his fingers, as he very lightly tapped her in the throat.

She reached up, marveling at how so little force had actually caused a little bit of pain. If someone were to even poke you in the throat with any more force than that, it would be completely disabling.

He then proceeded to show her a couple of moves which involved pressure points to the neck, wrist and other areas of the body from which one could easily disable someone quickly, even if they had a weapon.

He'd picked up many fighting techniques over the centuries and decades. He could pretty much dematerialize if he needed to during a fight or skirmish, but particularly in past centuries when one would be accused of witchcraft, he'd only done it as a last resort, because once that particular power was seen, there was no going back...and he'd be forced to lose his home and move on. Not only that, since his power had been so limited, at least up until now, he couldn't travel across space and reappear any further than within eyeshot of where he was at the time he would dematerialize. He simply couldn't have humans seeing him disappear and reappear like that...unless of course it was a modern day magic show where 'illusions' could explain away most anything.

If it was a public fight or barroom brawl where anyone was watching...and he'd been in plenty of those, he usually ended up taking a few hits as well, and would walk away with a few scrapes and bruises that healed much faster than would be expected since his body didn't age or decay at the same rate as a normal human being.

They practiced what he showed her over and over until he was confident...and more importantly that she was...that she could execute the moves.

As they were finishing up, he laid a hand to her shoulder and for a second he felt as though someone had laid a white-hot brand to his hand and jolted electricity up his arm.

Images flooded into his mind...vague and disjointed, of a dark place, and the feeling of being tied and gagged. He could smell gasoline for an instant and he drew back from her as though he'd been burned.

He'd picked up a lot of pictures...the many beatings she'd taken but he'd never seen this before and the images had been so fleeting it had been hard to catch it all....but it was there.

She noted how he'd drawn his hand back from her so suddenly.

"Is something wrong?"

"No…it was nothing. Sometimes I just see some of what he did to you. I block it out and once I've seen it, it fades away to some degree. Sometimes more comes into view though."

He looked down at his hand. What he'd just felt wasn't…normal. Well, nothing he ever felt was normal, but this was not normal for him.

The searing white-hot jolt he'd felt surge through him had caused pain, and then for a few moments it was as though he were in another realm. His mind wasn't here…and yet it was. It was the strangest damned thing he'd ever felt.

What the *hell* was that?

Her voice dragged him out of his stupor and back to the present.

"I guess I don't have to tell you how disturbing it is having someone who can just invade my privacy…to see my thoughts, every time they touch my hand."

"I don't see your thoughts. I already told you that. I see pictures of your life."

"Same thing!"

"No, it's not. I wish I could describe it to you. But I can't. It's not what you think."

"And are you ever going to describe to me how you do the mirror illusion? I think I've got it figured out, but it would be nice to get a confirmation."

"Nope."

"Nope what? You're not telling or I don't have it figured out."

"Both." He smiled and looked over at her as they walked towards Louie's.

"What are you doing? I thought we were going back to your place?"

"Nah. Let's go see what Lou's doing this morning."

They walked up the steps to Louie's trailer and he knocked on the door. Louie answered a few minutes later looking a little bleary-eyed standing there in a plaid bathrobe and a pair of socks.

"Hey buddy, what'r you doin' here so damned early?"

He motioned for them to come in.

"Jesus my head feels like a bowling ball...I drank a couple too many beers last night after you took off."

Louie padded over to his kitchen and put a pot of coffee on to brew as Z and Scheri plunked down on his couch.

"Hey Lou...you been to the shooting range lately?"

"Nah, not in a long time. Why?"

"We need to take her over there and get some practice."

"Hey, I don't blame ya after what happened a couple of nights ago." He sniffed and wiped his nose as he nodded to Scheri.

"You got a piece already? If not I know where to get you top of the line for a good price."

"Um...Louie, thank you but Z's teaching me some self-defense moves right now. Maybe when I get some money saved I'd think about that, but not right now. I'm a carny right now. Translation: I'm broke." She laughed.

"Ain't we all! So, how bout we say this one's on me?" Lou smiled.

"And how are you supposed to afford it?"

"I don't ask where my buddy who sells 'em gets 'em, but he gets 'em cheap. And that's all I know." He winked.

Z stood up and walked to the kitchen where Louie was standing by the coffee pot. He patted his shoulder and poured a cup of coffee.

"I need a favor."

"Whatcha need?" Lou grabbed a pack of cigarettes off the counter and lit one up blowing a thin trail of smoke out over his shaved head.

"You still have friends upstate right? Ones who might be able to get information on someone if you asked them to?"

"Yeah...it's been awhile, but I got a couple of buddies who owe me favors. I kept them from having to do time more than once. What do you wanna know?"

"Whatever you can find on Derek Worley. Attorney...in Evanston. I want to know any and every piece of dirt you can find on this asshole. And someone needs to watch him. See what he's up to at all times."

Scheri stood up. "What do you think you're doing?"

"Look, he somehow manages to track you down...he's got someone watching you. Or at least he did. Well, now we're going to turn the tide and have him watched. You said you wanted to take him down...it's time for the predator to become the prey."

What he was really hoping was that he could slip out and see if it was possible for him to teleport himself up there and see what this guy was up to. He would take no greater pleasure in knocking the shit out of him the good old-fashioned human way, but he also knew that wouldn't solve anything except the personal satisfaction of giving him back what he'd dished out. The better way to get rid of him would be to find the dirt on this guy...dig up his crimes and expose him. Let him get locked up for the rest of his life and be done with it. If he could teleport up there a few times to keep an eye on him...maybe go look around his apartment and gather up some information himself, that would be a start. The question was, whether his powers were strong enough to do it.

Having Louie get someone on it would serve as a good cover story and back-up plan in the event he wasn't able to dematerialize and rematerialize there. He also knew that he couldn't stay up there for 24/7 surveillance even if he was able to teleport, so he was going to need help anyway.

"What if he figures out what's going on?" She seemed a little uneasy.

"Why would he suspect anyone is tailing him? And even if he did, anyone Louie puts on it isn't going to be leaving any kind of trail that leads back here."

Her brows knit together. "I guess you're right...but I'm still a little nervous about it."

"He's not gonna know."

He walked over to the door and as she stood up he motioned for her to stay put.

"I'm going to go out for a little bit...you should stay here with Lou til I get back. Maybe go work the concession for a couple of hours if you wanna make a few bucks? Or just go do some writing if you want to be by yourself. But after what happened the other night, I'm a little sketchy about that til we get you completely up to speed on the self-defense moves."

"Where are you going?"

"I have to go test something out and see if it works."

He sounded vague, figuring she would assume it was for the next show.

She nodded. "When will you be back?"

"When I'm done figuring out whether what I want to do works or not."

"Can't I help you with it...or just sit and watch?"

He smiled. "Not this time. Remember..."

She rolled her eyes and cut him off before he could finish. "Yeah, I know...first rule of magic. Jesus, I'm sick and tired of hearing it."

Louie laughed. "Hey, honey, I'm right there witcha. I been hearing it for years."

Z waved him off and stepped out of the trailer door and walked down the steps, heading over to his own trailer to pick up his mirror.

Scheri watched intently through the window as he came back out of the trailer and headed down the steps with the mirror wrapped in a canvas cloth and held tightly under one arm. He headed across the lot toward the Smoke & MirrorZ tent.

What was he up to?

.

CHAPTER TWELVE

Z walked over to the Smoke & MirrorZ tent where he planned to head back into the 'dressing room' area off-stage and see if it was possible for him to teleport himself to another location.

When he'd first arrived here in the human realm he'd been able to do it, but it was very short-lived. As soon as the pollution of this matter-heavy atomic world had its way with his energy, and his power began to wane, so did that ability along with it. He'd brought his mirror with him, because now that he was no longer alone in the trailer, he didn't want to risk leaving it in anyone's presence...not even Scheri.

He'd taken the mirror from the old magician whose magic had helped open the portal which he came through all those countless decades ago, and he usually kept it close by for safety reasons.

He didn't bother to turn on the lights when he'd come in...other than the small lamp plugged in back in the dressing room.

He hadn't tried this in such a long time because he knew it didn't work...the last time had been a complete failure. He was able to teleport over very short distances, like from where he was now out to the stage, or maybe just outside the tent, but to go any further wasn't something he was counting on. He still had to give it a shot.

He decided to try teleporting from the stage to the lot out behind his trailer, a couple hundred yards away. He closed his eyes and began to concentrate and as he felt his energy begin to disintegrate, molecule by molecule he focused on the location he wanted to re-appear. Usually he did this going into his mirror, which was not nearly as difficult because he was simply converting his energy back to its native state.

In this case he had to take the matter of his body apart, traveling over distance….through the seemingly endless void of space, which isn't really empty at all, and then reassemble everything in the correct order in the new location.

For a Jinn in their native state and in their own realm of less solidity, this would be such a simple matter…but in human form, polluted by the material universe? It wasn't so simple at all. He knew that at full power, and especially if his powers were somehow increased beyond that of a normal Jinn space and distance would no longer be applicable. But he would also need to somehow learn to bend space at the same time he was manipulating the matter that his human form was composed of. Kind of like what humans called 'traveling through a wormhole' but not exactly.

In the state he'd been in since coming here, those things were so far out of the scope of possibility it wasn't even funny. Just being able to teleport further than a few yards was a big step.

He dematerialized and after a seemingly endless amount of time, which in reality was only a few seconds, he reappeared. But not in the lot by the trailer as he'd envisioned. Instead he found himself in the Porta Toilet out behind the back gates.

"Shit," he said, looking around, and realizing how appropriate a term it seemed right now given the way it smelled in this small, blue sewer he was now sitting in.

He closed his eyes again and focused on ending up in the lot by the trailer. And to his surprise when he opened them that's exactly where he was.

Okay. So he'd discovered that he could go about half the distance he envisioned.

He closed his eyes again and envisioned himself back at the stage and within a few seconds found himself standing by the dumpster outside one of the games tents.

He sighed heavily. Great...smells nearly as good as the 'House of Shits and Grins' I just left!

He looked at the logo on the side that said, 'Top O' The Heap Waste Services'. It was a perfect moniker to go along with the nauseating smell of rotten food and god only knows what. But what really mattered was that he'd gone half the distance he envisioned, twice in a row. It wasn't much, but it was indeed a small confirmation that his powers had increased at least a little.

Ah, well...outhouse or garbage dump...I'm going places! He almost laughed out loud as he walked back across the rest of the lot to the tent and went inside.

He was surprised to find Scheri standing there when he arrived.

"Where were you? And why are all the lights out? I thought you came over here to try out some new illusion or something."

"And I thought you were going to stay with Lou or go write."

She shrugged. "I just wanted to come see what you were doing. I thought maybe I could help."

"I stepped out to go grab something...but I forgot what I wanted. Never mind."

He was messing up by the second and she looked at him like he was nuts.

"So, why don't you tell me about your family? Do you ever visit your mom or dad?"

He groaned inwardly. Why was she bringing this family crap up again now? He hadn't had time to think up anything in depth to tell her other than the vague information he already had, and what he really wanted to do right now was to just keep pushing to see how far he could go if he dematerialized.

"My mom...she pretty much raised me as a single mother because my father left us when I was just a baby."

"That's so sad…how could he have abandoned you like that?"

"He just…did. I lived. She lived. No, not happily ever after, but hey, I'm here."

"And I'm glad you are."

She stared at the mirror standing in the middle of the floor still covered with the cloth he'd wrapped it in.

"I know your secret you know. You are projecting some kind of movie image that looks you're stepping in and out of it."

"Is that right?" He smiled.

"Yep."

"Well I guess you've just got me all figured out then."

"Not yet, but I will soon enough."

She turned and started to walk out of the back flap of the tent. "I'm going to go work with Louie during lunch hour and then maybe go write for awhile. I guess I'll see you when you come back over to the trailer."

He nodded. "I'll see you then."

She walked out and he peeked make sure she was on her way over to Louie's cart before heading back into the dressing room area.

He closed his eyes and began to concentrate, focusing all his attention on appearing out by the trailers again. He began to dematerialize, but to his dismay, discovered that he was unable to go all the way. He looked down as it was happening and could see himself, see-through and not quite solid…and then a few seconds later he rematerialized still standing where he was.

He sighed. He'd drained his power down transporting himself twice in a row over that much distance. He'd never tried that before, and now he was gonna be up shit's creek if his power didn't come back by the time it was ready for tonight's show because he wouldn't be levitating any chairs or taking any magic carpet rides if it didn't.

He looked over at his mirror, wondering if he could still step in and out of it. If he went back to the other side into the in-between-area it would help regenerate some of his native energy, and maybe bring him back up to at least his 'normal' level.

He reached forward, and closed his eyes, focusing on the other side and felt his energy change as the glassy surface turned to mist and he stepped forward through the portal into the ethereal place on the other side.

Scheri gasped and covered her mouth at what she just witnessed from just off stage.

Z had just...disintegrated. Then he'd reappeared and then stepped into the mirror.

She'd gotten half way across the lot, and then decided to turn around and come back here to let him know that she would be at the trailer instead of with Lou and had walked in to this.

She shook her head in disbelief, struggling against the urge to run, and fascinated at the same time.

How the hell was he doing it? The mirror wasn't on stage. There were no lights. No projectors, no anything...at least not that she could see from where she was. And how had he just...disintegrated like that?

She took a deep breath trying to calm her nerves. There had to be an explanation.

"Z? Are you in here?"

She walked into the dressing area expecting him to walk out from somewhere announcing that the illusion worked and showing her some kind of special machine that would create a holographic-like, see-through image or something. It was pretty advanced, but it would be the only explanation she could come up with for what she'd just seen.

She looked around but there was no one...nothing but silence and a thin trail of mist coming from the bottom of the mirror.

She reached forward running her hands through it, and noted the chill as it touched her skin. She also felt something else; a presence. Strange but it felt like...him. She pulled back from the mirror looking more than a little disturbed. Maybe he was outside?

Z watched from the other side of the mirror realizing what had just happened as she'd walked into the dressing area and started looking around. He wondered how much she'd seen, but he could tell from the look on her face, she'd seen more than he'd ever want her to. Shit. Now what?

Well, in order to make things look 'legit' he was going to have to try to rematerialize just outside the tent and meet her there as she came out and act like what she'd seen was his 'new illusion'. There was a chance it would drain his power back down, completely screwing him over for tonight but it was a chance he was going to have to take.

He'd wait til the last minute, until she walked outside so he would have as much time to regenerate in here as possible before trying it. There was a good chance she wouldn't buy it, but it was all he had so he was gonna have to think fast on his feet so he could answer her questions. The 'first rule of magic' crap wasn't going to fly with her for much longer.

She looked around and then when he saw her head toward the back exit he focused everything he had on rematerializing just outside the back of the tent.

To his relief, he felt his energy begin to solidify and take human form again and a moment later he appeared...but not where he'd hoped. He was back at the scenic Top o' the Heap.

He sighed in frustration. *Christ, here we go again. My favorite landing pad.*

He took off running and a minute later was around the far side of the tent. He slowed his pace and caught his breath as he rounded the corner to meet her.

"Hey! I thought you went to Lou's. I was just trying a new illusion. Disappear in the mist inside and slip out the back, Jack." He tried to sound relaxed and casual but he could tell he wasn't doing such a great job of it.

Her brows knit together. "Uh-huh. Well I was just in there calling to you. Didn't you hear me?"

"Um. Well, no. I was into what I was doing I guess."

She stared at him for a long moment. "I saw what you did. That is just creepy. I mean it scared the bejeezus out of me kind of creepy. The only reason I'm not running is because you saved my life last night…and somehow I'm hoping there's some kind of explanation. And it had better be good."

"Well….it's pretty technical. Kind of hard to explain. I use a smoke machine and the right lights. What you're seeing is a reflection from one larger mirror into the smaller one. I have one turned at certain angle and then I step behind it and from a certain position and distance the reflection looks like I'm going in."

She looked at him like he was out of his mind, and he was pretty sure there as a little of the 'Herb' look thrown in for good measure.

"I know what I saw and it wasn't that. *What* the hell was that?!"

"I told you. Take it or leave it."

"You're still pulling this 'first rule of magic' stuff on me. Okay, fine. Keep your secrets. But that? It's just freakin' scary. I'm beginning to think you are some kind of alien or something. The only other time I freaked out and thought something like that was when I saw David Blaine levitate in the street one time. It looked so real, I actually thought for a moment maybe he was some kind of supernatural being."

He laughed but didn't reply.

"I'm going to figure it out, you know. I ended up looking up on line to see how David did it. We can't have a relationship with all these secrets."

She blushed when she realized how it sounded.

"Not a relationship….I mean magician and assistant."

"I know what you mean," he said quietly.

"How am I supposed to work with you if you can't trust me enough to tell me?"

"You're right. If and when the time is right, well…then you'll find out."

She sighed. "And when is that going to be."

"I didn't say when. I said, 'if'. And if it's right, you'll just know. And so will I."

She seemed annoyed but didn't ask any more questions. He was relieved because he was running out of plausible answers.

Damn. He really needed to dig up the dirt on Derek Worley and help her get on with her life. There was a reason why he'd never allowed any humans to get close to him.

Then again…maybe the time was right after all. Not to reveal everything, but maybe to teach her a few human illusions he used on stage that he used to enhance his show. It would keep her busy and take her attention off anything else she saw that seemed 'off', plus help make things seem more plausible when he did offer up explanations for the unexplainable. Once she saw what were illusions with real techniques, maybe she'd focus on those and stop asking too many questions about anything else and he could work on finding out how far he could push his powers in peace.

He walked over and flipped on the lights.

"What are you doing?"

"The time is right."

Her eyes lit up for just a moment. "Are you serious?"

"Yep. Now get over here and I'll show you a few tricks of the hand. But the mirror is still off limits and so is levitation. Got it?"

She nodded.

"Good. That's for later on after you've proven yourself for awhile."

154

What it really meant was he needed more time to figure out what the hell to tell her about the mirror or how he got things to 'float' and hopefully she'd be long gone on her way before it came up again.

He pulled up a chair and table and spent the next hour or so showing her a few illusions that were simple and yet powerful....pouring salt into his hand, and making it disappear into thin air, only to appear again a few minutes later as he held out his hand and poured a thin trail back out onto the table. Tossing money against a window and having it appear on the opposite side of the glass.

She watched in fascination and then when he explained how each illusion was done she laughed out loud with childlike wonder.

"You wanna help me do this on stage? You can bring out the table and any props I need....you can pick out the audience members who come up too."

She nodded.

He smiled. "Maybe if you watch and learn you can do this too."

"So I guess then this makes me your apprentice?"

"I dunno. Are you staying?"

"Well let's see....you're a former drug dealer, your best buddy next door is an ex-con, you just scared the living you-know-what out of me doing something I have no way of explaining. Hmm....move on and stay on the run, or take my chances with the riff-raff who offered me a job, saved my life and who...makes me smile. I think I'll go with the riff-raff for 200 Alex Trebeck."

"Riff-raff? Is that even a word?"

"Yeah. I heard my mother say it a few times."

"That can't be good."

"No...it's not." She laughed out loud.

"What happened to you sitting in my kitchen this morning thinking I'm the good guy?"

"Who said I thought you were the good guy?" She raised a brow playfully.

"Thank God. My reputation is still intact."

He shut off the lights and opened the back flap.

"C'mon. Let's get out of here and go help Lou."

"You? Helping Louie make cheese steaks?"

"Yeah. Why not? I've helped him a lot of times."

She shook her head. "This I gotta see. I can't picture you in an apron. Do you wear a hair net too?"

"It's a fashion statement. Just like dancing in chiffon."

She laughed as she followed him out and they walked across the lot to spend the afternoons helping at Louie's concession.

An hour later he took off his apron and stepped outside the concession to cool off and take a bag of trash to the dumpster across the lot.

He slowed his pace as he was coming back, watching her as she stood behind the counter, smiling and laughing as she chopped onions or peppers.

She had opened up in the short time she was here…and who would have known that beautiful smile and easy demeanor was hiding behind the angry façade she had when she's first arrived.

Her expression changed and she turned and opened the door of the concession stand and a moment later bent down to pick up something. She stood back up and there was a very small grey kitten in her hands. Probably one of the strays that hung out by the dumpsters looking for scraps.

She snuggled its little body up against her face and took it in side showing it to Louie who immediately walked over and picked up a piece of wax paper and put a few pieces of steak on it.

She said something and Louie busted out laughing. For a split second he almost felt jealous….the intimacy of that moment between them. It was selfish but he couldn't help it. He was feeling more for this girl than he should be. And yet, he wanted to feel it. For the first time, he wanted to feel something other than the fleeting pleasures of the moment.

And yet, his time with her was fleeting and would soon be over.

He pushed the thought aside. He'd known what he was getting into the moment he'd offered her a job and invited her into his life.

Okay....that was a lie. He hadn't banked on any of it, including the way he felt every time he thought of her taking off and leaving all of this behind. Of leaving him behind.

He opened the door and walked back inside the concession, looking down at the tiny visitor on the floor hungrily lapping at its lunch. It was so tiny, an fragile...skinny. Looked like it needed a friend. The same way she had when she'd come here.

The little cat finished its meal and then began washing its face with its tiny paw as she scooped him up in her hands and nestled him under her chin.

"Can we bring him home with us?"

"He's a stray...he could have rabies or something."

She held him up and nuzzled his nose, his little yellow eyes filled with wonder and curiosity

"Somehow I don't think so. Louie does he look rabid to you."

Lou chuckled. "Absolutely. Look at the foam all over those huge fangs of his."

Z knew there was no arguing. Not with her...not with himself. The way she glowed when smiled at him like that he doubted he'd have been able to say no if she asked him to bring home a pet kangaroo.

He sighed in resignation.

"Yeah. You can bring him....or her home."

She squealed just a little and kissed the kitten on the nose before turning it over to see rif it was a he or a she.

"Well damn Z, you've always been the ladies man. So now it looks you have more than one puss...." Louie coughed, remembering he was in mixed company. "Never mind!" He laughed out loud as Scheri shot him a warning glare.

She looked back down at the kitten.

"It's a him."

"Whatcha gonna name him?" said Louie.

She shrugged. "I dunno...how about George?"

"George? Why George?" Z asked as Louie looked on in amusement.

"He's my little George of the Jungle. Just look at him. He's a grey tiger. Fierce and ferocious."

Z laughed as he walked over and gently stroked the kitten's tiny head. It had been a long time since he'd had one...and he had to admit he missed it. He just hadn't had the heart after the last one he'd owned died. He'd loved that cat and didn't want to go through giving his heart over to loving a pet again and then having it pass.

He'd gone through it one too many times since he'd come here to this realm. Just one more reminder of why getting too close to humans wasn't a good idea either...because they would either die, or he'd have to leave them at some point to protect his secret.

"Come on, and let's take him home. I have to go pick up some cat food and a box for him," she said as she walked out the door of the concession.

He stared over at her as they walked across the lot and she nuzzled the kitten, realizing that he'd do just about anything to be close to her...whether it was offering her protection or letting her bring home a cat.

So much for good ideas.

158

CHAPTER THIRTEEN

Z walked out to shake hands with the crowd at the end of the night's show. He looked back over his shoulder at her before he'd stepped out, half expecting that she might decide to come out with him but she just smiled and nodded for him to go and he knew she'd be here waiting when he was finished. Then he would shut down, turn off the lights, and they'd walk together back to the trailer that was no longer his alone. He'd grown fond of their little 'routine' and it felt so normal...so right, that he found he was having trouble remembering what it was like before she came here. Or maybe he just didn't want to.

Nearly six weeks had passed since she'd arrived. Their tenure in this town had been extended because numbers were up and ticket sales were more than good. His power had increased incrementally with the passing days, and although it wasn't nearly what it was in his native state or what it had been when he'd first come here before his essence had become polluted with the matter of the material world, it had indeed expanded and now allowed for a much greater manipulation of the matter of this universe.

What fascinated him was that he had less attention on that fact these days than the anticipation of the time that he would spend alone with her sharing dinner and talking when they got back to his place after the show every night.

What was supposed to be him taking her in for a night or two had somehow turned into her staying at his place. He'd thought of seeing if she could stay with someone else, but somehow he just never got around to making it happen...or maybe he just didn't want to.

His mother had said something about certain Jinn having a 'twin soul' in the human or other plane to which they were assigned, and he was beginning to wonder if this was one of those cases. Was it even possible? For most of his existence he'd scoffed at the supposed legends she had told him, denying much of it other than whatever traits served his own whims. And he had never wanted to hear much of anything about his father's side. But something had happened since she came here…to his powers…to him personally.

He'd slipped out many times during the days to practice in the privacy of the tent and test his abilities…to see exactly what he could and could not do.

So far he was now able to make objects materialize here on this side of the mirror and they held together with perfect polarity instead of later disintegrating. His ability to read minds had increased tenfold and now he could see pretty much everything about a person within less than a minute of touching their skin. He had also successfully traveled over longer and longer distances. He hadn't been able to teleport himself up to where Derek was so he could have a look at what the guy was up to, but Lou had put a couple of his people on it.

This guy was good…better than he'd anticipated at covering his tracks, because they couldn't find anything on him. Not one shred of illegal activity. He knew the only way they were going to get something on him was if his powers somehow grew strong enough so that he cold teleport up there and watch this guy, unseen in his own apartment and figure out some way to get his activities recorded.

That aside, just as his power had grown; so had hers, right along side of him. Not magic powers…but then again, perhaps the healing of the human spirit held a magic all its own too.

She had gained not just a sense of confidence in being on stage with him, but most importantly in her growing confidence that she was safe and that she might have a hope of living with some sense of normalcy again.

No one had come looking for her so far and she'd seemed a bit more relaxed. It had helped no doubt, that he'd insisted that she stay at his place, though he couldn't say he

160

was in any state of relaxation watching her every night cooking dinner, walking around in her pajamas...and drinking coffee with him in his kitchen every morning , as though they were a couple. Except they weren't a couple and he had to remind himself of that fact constantly as desire coursed through his veins like a raging river.

He hadn't been with a woman since she'd come here...and what surprised him the most about the whole thing was that he hadn't wanted to...other than that second night when he'd almost taken off with the party girls. Night after night had gone by, and after every show, there was always the usual parade of willing women waiting to meet him. He'd gotten angry with himself a couple of times over his foolishness and had planned to head over to Marlena's a couple of times, but for some reason he stopped himself before he made it out the door. There was just something about the intrigue of wanting Scheharazade Bloom...of having her right here within arm's length and yet so far out of reach.

The way she'd look at him sometimes, with him always on the verge...wondering if the moment would ever come where he could sweep her up in his arms and carry her to his bed to play out the many fantasies that flashed through his mind as if on a movie screen, day and night had made for a few more than satisfying solo 'relief' sessions in the shower.

It was probably the worst when she would come out to lie on the couch to watch t.v. late at night and especially when she would borrow one of his shirts to wear as a bathrobe...the way it would lay against the curve of her thighs when she walked drove him out of his mind. Or when her face would light up when he would come in the door...the way she playfully argued with him over almost anything just because she could sense he enjoyed it. He got the most pleasure though in watching her as she'd sit at his computer, writing…in her pajamas and reading glasses with her hair up, and those stray curls that wound around the nape of her neck.

A few times she'd let him read what she'd written…and once or twice she'd opened up to him and played the game he'd suggested of telling him stories, there on the spot. She was good at it…and if she could just get herself free from that asshole she was married to, and go on, maybe someday she could still achieve her dream of becoming a successful author.

She was a woman of depth and intellect….all she needed now was the confidence to go forward and not allow fear to keep her from going after the things in life she wanted, or from doing whatever was necessary to take down Derek Worley so he could never hurt her, or anyone else again.

His mind flashed back over the countless times she'd walked in the room or the way she would snuggle that little cat he hadn't wanted, but who somehow always ended up in his bed at night, and somehow…his human heart skipped a beat just knowing she was there.

And then there was that time when he'd had her up against the wall of the tent before he'd taken her over to work with Louie. It seemed like an eternity ago…and yet it had only been a couple of months. In that short time, he'd gotten to know everything about her…and not just from the pictures that he'd picked up every time he touched her, either. He'd learned that by not looking at too much of her pictures, he could then experience the newness of each new thing she shared about herself, from her *own* perspective.

He thought he'd experienced pretty much everything since he'd come here to the human realm…but she'd proven him wrong on many accounts, especially when it came to emotion. He'd seen many things over the years…interacted with many people, and yet never allowed himself to get close to any of them. Not until now. Not until her.

She'd stayed on far longer than either of them expected and she'd gotten pretty damned good at everything he'd taught her on stage too. She knew a few of his illusions now well enough to do them herself.

But the time had come for the carnival to move on to the next town.

And now, the reality had hit them both that this was the last weekend here and the time had come for her to make some hard decisions too....where she would go, and what she would do from this point forward. She'd been thinking about it in recent days, but it was always on the backburner, amid the nightly shows, and the easy camaraderie they'd come to know sharing close quarters.

There was no more pushing the issue to the side for later. She'd saved up plenty of money to last a little while, since he'd let her stay with him for free other than whatever groceries she insisted on paying for herself despite his protests.

And there was no mistaking the attraction between them. But he had somehow politely kept his distance physically and emotionally so that she could start fresh wherever she went, hopefully with some small reassurance that not all men were like the one who'd abused her. He'd given up awhile ago trying to figure out why he gave a damn, but he did, and he'd stopped fighting it.

He knew he should be glad that it was time for her to take steps toward a new life and make the decision where she would go next, because he wasn't sure how much longer he could endure the torture of keeping his distance. And yet, he was fast becoming aware that he wasn't sure how he was going to take it when she was gone.

There would be a void in his show, in his life...and in his heart.

He quickly finished up as the crowd thinned out and the tent emptied and walked back stage to where she was standing. "Ready?"

She nodded, and he noted her sad expression.

He laughed, trying to lighten the mood.

163

"Damn…did you miss me that much? I was only gone for what? Ten minutes."

She forced a smile. "Well your ego certainly hasn't gotten any smaller since I came here."

He walked over and tipped her chin up to look at him. "Just for the record, in that ten minutes, I missed *you*. And as for my ego…well, having a woman as beautiful as you by my side on stage every night, I think maybe it gives me a few bragging rights."

She smiled fighting back the tears that threatened to spill from her lashes.

He knew he shouldn't do it, but he could no more stop it than he could stop breathing as he reached forward and traced the curve of her mouth with the pad of his thumb and without another word he moved in and replaced it with his lips. Softly at first and then with more urgency as he realized that she wasn't backing away.

He'd been fighting this for days now….weeks, in fact, and now here it was; the softness of her body against him, the taste of those sweet lips and an avalanche of pent up frustration, crashing over him like the tide rolling into the shore.

Her arms wound around his neck and her fingers laced through the length of his hair as his tongue danced against hers…soft like velvet and sweet like honey. He showered soft kisses down along her jaw-line and then meandered downward as he trailed a damp path along the skin on the side of her neck to the hollow of her collarbone. She dragged in a deep breath as goosebumps broke out all over her body.

His hands traced the curve of her back as he pulled her body closer to his so he could feel her heart beating against his own. Reality set in a moment later and he pulled back from her for just a moment and shook his head.

"I'm sorry. I shouldn't have done that, I know."

"I wanted you to," she said quietly. "I never thought I could say those words to a man again. But...." Her voice trailed off.

He leaned in and pressed his forehead to hers, as he brushed the curls back from her face with his hands and softly kissed her lips again.

"I think maybe I'd better stay over at Lou's tonight. Because if I come back the trailer with you...I can't promise you I'll be able to stay away from you. I already just broke your trust."

"I'm not asking you to stay away from me."

He smiled. "Remember...sometimes the things we don't ask for are the things we need the most. The last thing you need right now is me messing up your head in these last couple of days while you're here and keeping you from making the right decisions about your life." He reached forward and touched her bottom lip with his forefinger.

She laid a hand to the side of his face, stroking the razor stubble on his cheek.

"You haven't broken my trust. Not even a little. And I think you need to let me be the judge of what I do and don't need. When I came here, Derek had nearly broken me."

She paused and laughed a little. "And yeah, I was a complete bitch to you because I just had to have this wall up at all times so no one could get anywhere near me. And yet...you saw through all that. You gave me the space I needed so I could start gluing myself back together. You didn't do it for me. You let me do it myself at my own pace. You gave me a job and a safe place to stay so I could heal enough to find my way back to me. Not the scared, beaten down me, but the me I used to be before I married him. I needed that more than anything. And if there's any one person on earth right now that I'm willing to take a chance on trusting....it's you."

The words felt like a ton of bricks crashing down on his soul as he stood there staring into her eyes with a look of trust shining from a place where there had been none.

She thought she knew him. But what did she know? The smattering of lies he'd told her about a fake family that didn't exist from somewhere 'out west'? The life of lies he'd built for himself here at this carnival, plying his trade every night for audiences who knew nothing of him either?

She believed he'd seen through something when he met her…but the truth was he hadn't seen through anything at all. He'd just seen an angry human female, of which he was hesitant to have anything to do with other than the fact he'd felt some kind of jolt to his power and wanted to know what the hell was going on.

"C'mon, we can talk more on the walk."

"What? You think you're going to talk me into changing my mind about you on the way home?"

He looked over at her. She had said the word 'home'…and what was the most strange about it was how right it felt hearing her say it. He'd never considered this place or his trailer 'home' in all the years he'd been here. And yet hearing her say the words made him acutely aware of the fact that for the first time he did feel like he had one.

He picked up his mirror under one arm and took her hand in his as they walked out of the back flap entrance of the tent and headed across the lot.

A few minutes later they got to the trailer and he quickly unlocked the door and flipped on the light.

They walked inside and he put the mirror down in the middle of the living room floor and headed back to his room to grab a change of clothes so he could slip next door to Lou's to spend the night. Strange, but out of the entire time she'd been here this was the first night he'd be sleeping somewhere else.

She stopped him and turned him around to face her.

"Please don't go," she said quietly.

166

He sighed. She wasn't making this very easy…he was trying to do the right thing. Something that up until she'd come along, was completely foreign to him.

He stared at her for a long moment weighing what to do. His head was telling him to get the hell out while he still had enough of good sense to do it…but his body and his heart were screaming something else entirely.

She leaned in and took his face in her hands and kissed his lips very softly. "Please?"

He knew it was his undoing as "Your wish is my command" escaped his lips before he could stop himself.

And then without another word pulled her body in next to him and enveloped her lips with his, nearly dragging the breath from her body as his velvety soft tongue played against hers with an urgency that spoke of the weeks of longing he'd endured.

She kissed him back with equal fervor as his fingers traced a path down the curve of her neck and drifted to the soft crease of her cleavage, peeking out from the top of the pretty harem girl outfit she still had on from the show. Her arms had found their way around his neck and her fingers delved deeply into the raven depths of his long hair…and then splayed out across the broad width of his well-muscled shoulders.

She melted against him and he knew that all the magic he wanted to work on every square inch of her body…tasting, touching, exploring and inviting an explosion of the senses, wasn't going to happen standing here in the living room. He swept her up into his arms to carry her to his bed.

"Are you sure?"

She nodded.

All the nights he'd fantasized about this…bringing her back here wrapped up in chiffon and brocade, and then removing it like wrapping paper from a gift, here it was happening in the flesh.

167

He kicked open the door of the bedroom and set her gently down on the edge of the bed. He knelt down between her legs and kissed the soft skin above her cleavage, working his way back up to her lips as he moved his body up and lifted her up so he could lay her back on the silky damask bedspread.

She could feel his heart beating against hers as he gently pulled aside the veil that draped from her hair down under her chin. He kissed the side of her face and then began working a slow, sensuous path with his lips and tongue down the soft skin of her neck to where the tops of her breasts peeked out from the bra top, heavily laden with gold coins and a silky drape that hung down across her bare midriff.

He cupped one of her breasts in his hand and trailed a wet path down the soft skin of her chest to her cleavage, and then gently pulled the top of her bra down to expose the rosy tipped confection waiting there. Damn but she tasted so sweet, and the feel of her soft curves beneath his hands as they traced every contour was driving him out of his mind. How the hell was he supposed to resist? He tasted the rosy bud sitting there in front of his lips and felt her fingers work their way into the depths of his hair, guiding him along.

He pulled back from her for a moment and the smiled as he lifted the veil from her midriff slowly and began kissing a wet trail down across her stomach toward her navel and below.

She dragged in a breath as she felt the softness of his tongue against her skin and then just before he got to the sweet, warm place he sought, he abruptly…stopped.

He pulled himself back up the length of her body and picked her up dragging her further up on his pillows. He laid her back and then slid between her legs balancing his weight on one elbow as he traced the curve of her face with his finger and then kissed her softly.

He sat there staring at her for a long moment.

"Is something wrong?"

168

"Yeah. It is. You shouldn't be here with me."

"Why would you say that? I want to be here."

"Scheharazade, you don't really even know me. I'm just some guy who took you in when you needed a friend and you're falling for something that's not real."

She reached up and stroked the side of his face.

"You're real. Well...when you're not disappearing on me or stepping into mirrors." She laughed.

"I'm serious." He shook his head. "None of this is reality. It's all smoke and mirrors. You haven't even re-built your life yet. Yeah, we could do this...and then what? How are you going to feel about it when you wake up tomorrow...when you leave?"

What he was more concerned with was how was *he* going to feel about it when she left...but he didn't really want to admit that to himself, much less her.

"I don't want to take advantage of you. It's important that the next time you do this to be with a man who really does care about you...and doesn't treat you like he did. I care about you and I would never hurt you, but I know I can't be that guy."

His voice was thick with emotion as he spoke and he was finding that it had taken every bit of his inner strength to force himself to say the words that his head was telling him he had to say, but his heart was begging him to hold inside.

Her eyes grew misty. "What if I want to rebuild a life with you in it somehow?"

He pushed her hair back from her face and lifted away the single tear that fell down her cheek with his forefinger. He brought it to his lips and sucked it off the end.

"Whatever life you end up with, it can't be me. You don't belong with some lame-assed carny. You're a writer and you may have a real career out there waiting for you."

No sooner had the tear touched his tongue than a searing jolt of electricity surged through his veins, nearly blinding him with intensity. He gasped for a second and drew

169

in a ragged breath as a picture as clear as a movie screen appeared in his mind.

It was her…she was bound and gagged, stripped naked and tied to a chair as her captor paced around the chair. It was Derek Worley…and standing behind him was someone else. He couldn't make out the features because he was in the shadows but the other figure was clearly male.

Another vision quickly came into view. One in which Derek slapped her hard in the face and he suddenly felt a stabbing pain deep in his chest. He was struggling for air as Derek's face faded away and a second later the images began to fade away to black as he was jolted back to reality.

What the hell was that?

He stared down at her and a look of concern crossed her features as she sat up beneath him, pushing him back off her and laying him back on the pillows.

"Are you okay? You…looked like you were going to pass out for a second or something."

He nodded, still dazed from the rush in his mind.

"I just saw something. It was disturbing…I can't believe some of the shit he's done to you."

"What did you see?"

"Never mind, but if I had that son-of-a-bitch here right now…." His voice trailed off.

She sighed, remembering the night Derek had knocked her nearly unconscious and made her drink whatever he'd put in that glass…and she'd woken up wondering what had happened. Maybe he could see some of what she couldn't?

"Did you see me drinking something strange? Or me laying on the floor in the middle of the room? Was there someone else there? Because there was this night that he knocked me so hard I thought I was going to do die…and then he made me drink something that tasted like blood. I thought for a few moments I saw someone else but I just can't remember what happened. I'm pretty sure he allowed one of his friends to…you know. I couldn't stop them."

A tear slipped down her cheek and he pulled her to his chest, resting his chin on the top of her head.

"Now you see why I told you that I wasn't sure we should be doing this. You're not healed from what happened to you….at least emotionally. And when you finally are and you're ready, it shouldn't be with some guy who's not going to be around as a part of your life. It needs to be with someone who loves you and who's going to be everything he wasn't."

She looked up at him. "You're everything he's not."

"I appreciate the sentiment but I'm not who you think I am. Illusions are deceptive in magic…and in life."

"Well, who are you, then? So far, all I see is a man who's got a good heart, who cares for other people…who works hard, who shows compassion."

His conscience quickly added, *'and who's not really a 'man' at all, who only approached you in the first place to see why his power increased…and who can't tell you the truth about anything. Ever.'*

"When I look at you, I see a woman with her whole life ahead of her, whose story hasn't been written yet…and who deserves to spend it with someone who's got a lot more to offer than I do."

He stared at her for a moment longer and for a split second he could have sworn his heart whispered, *'and who I'm falling in love with,'* but he quickly tossed that one out to the wind. It meant nothing but trouble.

She dragged in a deep breath.

"I've been thinking maybe I should stay on for awhile. I could move on to the next town with the carnival. It'll give me time to save up more money and decide where to go permanently. And maybe we'll get lucky and dig up some dirt on Derek." She paused for a moment. "Unless you don't want me around?"

171

"It's not about whether I want you around."

"Well, what's the problem then?"

"The problem is that I most certainly want you around...too much."

She wrapped her arms around his neck. "Well I don't have a problem with that."

"Yeah....but I do."

"Why? Why are you so afraid to let yourself feel? I'm the one here who should be way more afraid of something like that than you! Look what happened the last time I let myself care about someone."

"My point exactly. I can't allow this to happen. Because in the end, I'm just gonna end up hurting you the way he did."

"How can you say that?"

"Because it's the truth. You said I was the one person you'd be willing to take a chance on trusting...so trust me on that one.

He got up from the bed and headed out into the hallway.

"Where are you going?"

"Out."

"When will you be back?"

"Whenever I feel like it."

His tone was almost icy.

She stared at him for a moment trying to figure out why he was being so distant and cold.

"Did I do something wrong? Why are you being this way all of a sudden?"

"This is the way I've always been. You've just never seen it; and thus my point. You don't really know me...you can never really know me. You're welcome to stay as long as you need to, but that's as far as this can go."

Her eyes welled up with tears as he walked out without another word.

He slammed the trailer door behind him dragging the night air into his lungs.

What had he just done? The right thing? It sure as hell didn't feel right. What would feel right would be to walk back in that door and tell her he didn't mean it. To tell her how he really felt about her and lay her back in his bed, tasting, touching, exploring every square inch of her until they were damp with sweat and smiling in the afterglow of the magic he'd worked on her body and the tide of unspoken emotions that washed over their souls.

But he knew that with the morning light would also come the reality that once they shared their bodies, it would open the door to acknowledging that there was something more. And then, there would then be no turning back...not only for her. But just as much for him. Hell, at this point he was loathe to admit, he was probably already there, and he hadn't even been in bed with her!

He needed a drink...and a couple of women for the night. This whole thing had gone way too far and he had to turn things around before it was too late. She could never know the real him and he'd been foolish to allow her to get too close. What was much worse was that he'd allowed himself to do the same.

Now the only option was to let her see the life he was used to living....crawling the streets at night, sleeping with whoever he pleased when he pleased. Then maybe she would realize that she needed to move on and get out of here without looking back. Maybe if she stayed off the radar for awhile longer, Derek Worley would just give up and leave her alone. After all, he hadn't come looking so far. Maybe he'd moved on by now.

He headed out into the lot and closed his eyes. The Mix was just a few miles up the road and with some luck, maybe Blondie and her friend would be there ready for some fun and games. A moment later he dematerialized and within seconds he found himself in the parking lot of the club.

173

He walked inside and as the thud of the music began to inundate his senses, he walked up to the bar and ordered a drink.

He scanned the club and didn't see the fair haired fantasy girl anywhere, but noted a tall brunette standing nearby giving him an approving look.

He walked over to where she stood.

She smiled. "So...I haven't seen you here before. My name's Lonette."

"Well, I haven't seen you here before either...but I guess that doesn't really matter because we see each other now."

They proceeded to share a drink and light conversation, which he didn't pay much attention to because the whole time he couldn't stop picturing the look on Scheri's face as he'd walked out of the room. Or the first smile she ever gave him...and even the 'Herb' look, which she would certainly be giving him right now if she saw him sitting here with this woman he barely knew trying to pick her up and get laid for the night....just like 'Herb' would.

He almost laughed out loud because right now he was no better than that, and any 'look' she would be giving him, he deserved.

He shook his head trying to focus on the task at hand, and was disgusted when he realized that it was a 'task' at all! Here he was in his usual element....loud music: check, booze: check, hot and ready woman: check, and plenty of other opportunities if this didn't work out. This should not be a 'task'. And yet...it was. He didn't want to be here. He didn't want this brunette, or anyone else.

There was only one woman he wanted to make boring conversation...or interesting conversation, or *any* conversation with right now. And that was Scheharazade Bloom. And in fact, forget the conversation! All he wanted was to feel her soft curves against him and taste those lips of hers that he'd been fantasizing about for weeks. To touch her skin…to see her smile…to see that look in her eyes when he walked in the room. He knew exactly where he wanted and needed to be right now. It was back home.

"Listen…Lonette. It's been nice getting to know you a little but I have to go."

"But I thought….." her voice dropped off as she looked at him, puzzled.

"Yeah. Me too. But I was wrong."

He got up and dropped a few bucks on the bar and walked out, closing his eyes almost the moment he hit the parking lot.

He began to dematerialize almost instantly, but a moment later he wasn't back at the lot by the trailer. In fact he was a couple miles away.

Shit. What happened? Then it dawned on him. His power always waned a bit after drinking alcohol…and even though he'd had a substantial increase to his power in recent weeks, that was probably his undoing right now. The more his human body senses were dulled the less he was able to focus his energy. That was why he never drank before his shows.

He started walking at first and then took off in a light jog down the street heading south in the direction of the carnival on the other side of town. Maybe if he got his blood pumping and the alcohol level in his blood decreased his power would go back up.

He was right, because about five minutes later he closed his eyes again and focused his thoughts and a few seconds later, he rematerialized outside his trailer.

He caught his breath and composed himself trying to figure out what he was going to say when he got inside.

He'd been a complete and total fool, and now all he could hope is that if he went in there on bended knee, maybe she would forgive him.

He didn't know how he was going to deal with all of it…his own emotions, the fact that he'd fallen for her…which he was now having to admit to himself as well. And as for the truth of who he really was? That was a hurdle he couldn't even fathom.

Could he allow her to live a lie?

Maybe he wouldn't have to. There had to be some way. And if there was he was going to find it.

Z walked up the steps and opened the front door, half expecting her to be standing in the living room.

What he saw instead caused his heart to stop beating for just a moment.

"Hello Azizi…."

There, standing in the middle of his living room was Derek Worley…accompanied by none other than Abdul al Leil.

CHAPTER FOURTEEN

Derek had been sitting in his living room planning his next move, when out of nowhere he'd seen motion in the mirror hanging on his wall....the one he'd used for his rituals.

A thin trail of smoke had emerged, and he'd gone over to investigate. He remembered the ritual he'd performed a couple of weeks back and now wondered if it had actually worked. He pulled out one of his books and there was little mention of something coming out of a mirror.

What the hell was this thing?

He'd stepped around and around the mirror and then a thought occurred to him. This sort of reminded him of all things of Snow White...a child's cartoon movie of all things. But there'd been an entity in the wicked queen's mirror and it looked somewhat like...a genie.

He didn't know anything about that aspect of magic but he quickly got on-line and began doing his research.

Everything seemed to line up.

He'd purchased this old mirror....it could be a portal of some kind. There were legends of Jinn coming through after being called forth. Had he accidentally done that when he'd called on the supposed dark entities in his ritual?

He scanned through page after page of information on The Jinn and then typed in 'how to make a genie obey.'

Several different sites and pages with suggestions, personal opinions and so on had come up, but there was one site that looked a bit more 'authentic' than the others, and there it had said something about rules.

It said, 'The person calling forth a Jinn must own the portal or the trap the Jinn was held in.'

Well, if this were the case, that was certainly no problem. He owned the mirror.

'The master must also call forth the Jinn and acknowledge that they knew the Jinn was there, and then

177

harness their power. And just like in all the story books, three wishes would be granted….but there were also rules to the wishes. One could not wish to be a God or Angel, as no power given to any entity could grant such a thing that would change the entire universe. One could also not wish death on a living thing as it was only the right of God to do that. And one could not wish for infinite wishes…although you could apparently wish for the Jinn to serve you for life in which they would be relegated to being exactly that…a maid or manservant. And one must never, ever wish for a Jinn's freedom once trapped because in that case, the story books were right and the master would then become the servant. Love was also not something that one could control by any form of magic, Jinn or otherwise.

He'd marveled at the very idea that such a thing could exist, and yet, since there were occult entities, why couldn't there also be such beings of legend as a genie?

He lit the candles and first cleared the air of all other energies, and then declared his ownership of the mirror before him just to be certain. Then he read the ancient words that were to be spoken to call forth and take command of a genie. He stood there looking skeptical of the whole thing…it seemed ridiculous and a bit too 'Disney' compared to the gothic cool of reading the Necronomicon or The Book of the Law.

But, nonetheless, a few moments later a thin trail of smoke emerged from the mirror and out stepped a Jinn, who announced that his name was Abdul al Leil.

He marveled at what he'd just witnessed and then sat down to digest the enormity of it. Could this be real? He now had three wishes? Three wishes that could bring him power beyond imagination, money beyond his wildest dreams….and revenge.

"My name is Abdul, and I am now at your command for three wishes. I have been watching you. Do you wish me to take you to her?" Abdul said grudgingly.

He looked positively hateful in that moment and he could tell the Jinn was pissed beyond words that he'd been trapped. Oh, this was just too good for words.

He smiled.

"I don't need you to take me to my wife...I already have someone on that who knows exactly where she is. However, if you're interested in helping me absorb her life's energy when I slit her throat, then maybe we can talk business."

"You know I cannot help you take her life, nor can I help you absorb any energy associated with her murder. My powers will not function in that capacity."

He'd stared at him for a moment and then walked over to the bar to pour himself a drink.

"Yeah. I know...I read the website."

He almost laughed at the comment because of how ridiculous it sounded, but damn if it wasn't the truth! He hadn't gotten the information from some dusty and revered tome on a bookshelf....he'd just looked it up on line.

He quickly guzzled down a shot and poured another.

He was going to have to think very carefully about this....about every word that came out of his mouth now, because if he slipped up and accidentally said, "I wish I had an ice cream cone", with this genie creature hanging around, there went one of his wishes.

He started to tell this Abdul character to get out of his sight and go back into the mirror, but he realized that sounded an awful lot like a command and he wondered if it would count.

"So, if I tell you to get out of here right now and leave me alone, is that using one of my 'wishes'? Is that a command?"

Abdul smiled smugly. "I am only under obligation to grant you three wishes, not to answer your questions...unless you would like to command me and wish me to do so?" He raised a brow.

So....this Jinn was a douchebag. Fair enough. He was going to have to think carefully on what to do and how to handle this.

His mind began playing out scenarios beyond anyone's wildest dreams of personal gain.

Handling wifey was going to be another ballgame altogether since it was apparently against the rules for a Jinn to cause death to a human. There was certainly no rule about him transporting his wife to him was there? Then again if he was bringing her here to kill her then that would be leading her to her death. He wanted to ask, but knew that Abdul's surly 'answer' would be no answer at all.

For now, his focus needed to be on power and money...how and where to get into the most of each.

He poured a couple more shots into his glass and drank them down as Abdul watched in silence.

"What the fuck are you staring at? So now I'm stuck with you hanging around watching me?"

Abdul said nothing.

"Well then...let's just get this part over with quickly as far as power and control goes. I want to have complete and total control over all governments in the entire world...I want to own the world."

"Is this your wish?"

Derek thought about it for a moment.

He would be the ruler of every nation...of every citizen. He would be the law. No one could counter his word....there was no law he could not bend, break or change to suit his own whims because he would make the law.

He could control populations like a herd of cows or an ant farm...scrambling along on their busy path every endless, useless day of their lives. It sounded like utter utopia. To have the freedom to dominate at will....to watch anyone he didn't like suffer or die a miserable death at his whim?

He smiled. "Yes, as a matter of fact it is!"

Abdul nodded. "Your wish is my command."

Derek stood there in awe at how utterly, cartoonish and ridiculous it sounded. And yet…he also couldn't help looking around the room because something incredible was about to happen. He would be sitting in the president's office, or some new 'world union' government office as the world around him faded away and was replaced by the new.

He stood there. Waiting….and waiting…and waiting.

He turned around giving Abdul a sour look.

"I thought you said I would be the ruler of the world?"

"You are," said Abdul quietly.

"Well, why am I still here? Can I just pick up the phone and whoever I call, they'll know who I am and do as I say?"

"You didn't say which world you wished to rule…only that you wished to have complete and total control over all governments in the entire world."

"What the fuck are you talking about?"

"Exactly what I said. You did not specify which world you wanted to control. So…you now control every government and every nation in a very tiny planet that is not visible to the human eye. It is in another dimension. The people there…well, they will probably view you as their unseen, unheard ruler and perhaps a false god who they will pray to every day in good faith. Would you like me to transport you there?"

Derek started toward Abdul. "You son-of-a-bitch. That's cheating."

Abdul smiled smugly. "It is not cheating…I am a Jinn. I gave you *exactly* what you asked for."

Derek's mouth tightened and the muscle in his jaw ticked. "Maybe you are just full of shit and have no power to grant me anything."

"Oh, I can assure you, I most certainly have the power to grant you exactly what you ask for. Perhaps you simply do not know the Jinn."

181

Abdul smiled because this lowly human obviously knew little about the fact that most Jinn when ordered to grant wishes would do anything to bend, twist or change the wish into something else. Perhaps it was their tendency to want to cause trouble and rattle cages…but that was always the way it went down. This time was no different…he had gotten what he wished for.

Derek sat there trying to figure out how to get this creature to prove what he said was true. If he really was able to grant wishes, then he would be wasting another wish ordering him to prove that he had powers. If he did nothing and then made another wish, the Jinn may try to pull another stunt on him.

He was going to have to take his time and do some more reading to understand how this shit worked.

Abdul watched as Derek's expression changed from pure, unadulterated anger to a more thoughtful one.

So….the human was now thinking things through more carefully and taking his sweet-ass time. But then maybe that was a good thing because once he made his three wishes, then his tenure here was over, and his energy would be dragged back to the Jinn realm, like it or not. Then the only way back here would be to be called forth again…because he sure as hell hadn't come here on his own this time around. It had been an accident…and how often did something like that happen? Granted he'd wanted to come and had been looking for a way here…but it was still an accident.

He supposed he should be glad to just give Derek Worley whatever he wanted and then be sent back to the Jinn realm and be done with it because this place pretty much was worthless, other than the few pleasures of a human body's five senses. That grew boring within days and his power was already starting to grow weaker than usual for some reason…he was pretty sure it was some strange side-effect of this place. Or maybe just from being in a state of limbo, where he wasn't actually serving his master nor was he free either.

He'd have happily gone back to the Jinn realm already, but once he'd gotten here,he was unable to go back until he'd granted the wishes.

At first he hadn't wanted to be in anyone's servitude, and so had avoided having Derek find out who he really was, by staying out of sight and spending much time on the other side, but once he saw how crappy this realm really was? He wanted nothing more than to go back.

But now there was something here in this realm that he wanted more than he'd ever wanted revenge on Azizi….her name was Scheharazade Bloom. And if she were living with or having an affair with Azizi, as Derek suspected, his revenge and his desire were all tied up in one neat package, because once he stole her away, it would be a worse hell than draining Azizi's power and sending him off into oblivion.

If he were ever going to be able to get to Scheri Bloom, he was going to have to find some way to trick this human. The fairytales said that if the human gave a Jinn their freedom they would become a Jinn and have to serve. That premise was exactly that; a fairy tale. There was no way for a human to become a true Jinn because the human soul even if separate from the human form is made from a different kind of energy than the Jinn. They could however, be forced to take on the position of a servant for life.

If he could somehow fool this human into that, he could be free of his command, steal the woman, change her body's energy and take her back to the Jinn realm. If he was lucky and she were now Azizi's woman, there would be no need for any further revenge.

The longer Derek took to make his decisions the more time he would have to think. He had two wishes left, and after he was given exactly what he asked for this time, he would not be making the same mistake twice.

Maybe it was a good idea if he went back into the mirror to allow Derek time to ponder…and himself the time he needed to plot his way out of this mess he'd gotten himself into.

"I'm going back to the other side. When you're ready to make one of your wishes, call me out."

Abdul then dematerialized, leaving Derek alone in the room.

A short time later, Derek called him forth.

Abdul materialized and quickly took form, standing in the middle of his living room.

"I've decided what I want from you, genie."

"And what would that be?" Abdul said, curious to see what the human would ask for this time. He had no doubt it would have something to do with money or power.

"I changed my mind about you taking me to my wife. I want you to take me to the exact location where my wife, Scheharazade Bloom is right now…the one Scheharazade Bloom who I am married to, and to the exact location she is here on planet earth in this dimension and in this timeline, right now on this date, and at this exact time."

He said the words very carefully, making sure he stated exactly where he wanted to go and who he wanted to be taken to…even stating her name so there could be no twisting the words and making sure he repeated a few things, redundant or not.

Abdul raised a brow. "Is that your wish?"

Derek smiled. "I intend to make absolutely certain you can't bend my wish into something else this time…and I intend to make sure she is…unharmed wherever she is right now."

"You do realize that if you are asking me to help you bring her back here so that you may murder her, I cannot do that."

"That is not what I asked, genie. I simply asked you to take me to the exact location where she is right now."

184

Abdul shot him a skeptical look.

Derek said nothing. There was no way he was going to risk losing his wife now that he had the perfect way to get to her right here and now. Once he was there and he secured her so she could be brought back here, then he would make his final wish...one that included money or power. He craved those things yes, in fact he craved many things. But not as much as he craved the feel of her throat beneath is fingers as he watched the life leave her body.

He wasn't sure how he would make it happen, but he most certainly would. And for now, as long as he wasn't asking the Jinn to help him bring her back here to kill her, then technically he wasn't breaking any Laws that would prevent the wish from taking place.

Abdul nodded and they began to dematerialize. A few seconds later they materialized in the living room belonging to Azizi ab'd al Jadu.

Scheri heard noise and wondered if Z had come back from wherever he'd gone and walked out to discover Derek standing in the living room with some other man.

She quickly darted back down the hall, to get the gun Louie had picked up for her. She'd spent hours at the shooting range and knew this time around she wouldn't miss the mark if she could just get to it. She made it down the hall to the door and just as she was about to scramble through, Derek caught her. She turned around and punched him hard, bloodying his nose and then put her finger into his eye socket like Z had taught her.

He screamed in pain and then punched her hard in the jaw. It dazed her for the split second he needed to get another grip on her, dragging her down to the floor. She kicked at him but he was on her in a second.

"You little fucking bitch. I see someone's been teaching you how to fight back. Hope you enjoyed it because as you can see it didn't do you one bit of good."

She remembered the throat jab move that Z had taught her and as Derek grabbed ahold of her she jabbed at his throat and hit the mark. As Derek was gasping for air she kicked him hard and struggled to get out from under his weight, but somehow with an almost inhuman strength he managed to drag her back despite the blinding pain and without warning he jabbed a needle into her thigh pushing the plunger as she screamed.

Her vision began to dim and her arm fell back as she tried to reach out to hit him again, and her eyes rolled back in her head as everything went dark.

He stood up catching his breath and wiping the sweat from his brow and the trickle of blood from his nose. He struggled to regain his composure because his throat was on fire felt as though there was a lump of stone sitting where his Adam's apple was. Damn…the little bitch had put up quite a fight! This Z…or someone she knew here had been teaching her well. He picked her up and carried her to the kitchen, tied her to a chair and taped her mouth shut. If for any reason she woke up he certainly couldn't have her screaming and bringing the neighbors over snooping around.

Abdul looked on in disapproval.

"You may not kill this woman…my power will not allow you to. It is The Law," Abdul said matter-of-factly.

He looked over at Scheharazade Bloom keeping an even expression despite the fact his human body heart was pounding in his temples. She was more beautiful in person than in her pictures. He wasn't sure how, but he was going to think of some way to get her away from Derek and have her to himself.

Derek shot him a look of disgust.

"Do you see me killing or harming her?"

"Why did you tie her? We could simply leave."

"Maybe I'm not ready to leave yet. Maybe there's some bargaining to do."

A moment later, they heard noise outside the door and it opened, and in walked Z.

Derek quickly pulled out a knife and held it to Scheri's throat as Abdul looked on. He knew that Derek would not be able to push the knife into her throat, because he had transported him here…and then it would technically be so that he could commit murder. However, if Derek took her away from here, without his assistance, which he was guessing he was planning to do…then he wasn't so sure if that rule would still hold true.

Z had come through the door and his heart skipped a beat when he saw them standing there, greeting him with a 'Hello, Azizi' as if they were old friends.

His expression changed from shock to anger very quickly. And his blood chilled in his veins when he looked over toward his kitchen and saw her…stripped nearly naked and tied to a chair, her mouth duct taped and Derek held a knife to her throat. She was unconscious and the realization hit him of the picture he'd picked up when he'd tasted her tear on his finger just a couple hours ago: it hadn't been a scene from her past. He'd seen her *future*. Apparently this was a new development.

"What did you do to her and what do you want," he said with a business-like cool that belied the inner terror he felt knowing that knife was only a few centimeters and one good push away from severing Scheri's carotid artery.

And it was more a statement than a question because he knew that if Derek Worley was here with Abdul it meant that he knew more than he would prefer.

"Well, let's see, Z….that is the name you go by these days, am I right? What do I want? I'd say you're probably the man to make that happen. My wish is your command." He smiled sarcastically.

"What are you talking about?" Z's gaze never left Abdul and he wondered how much he'd told Derek.

"Well, your friend here tells me that maybe you're not exactly who you're pretending to be here at this carnival. Am I right?"

Z laughed. "Look ass-wipe, I don't know who you think I am or what you think you're getting but you leave her out of it." He nodded toward Scheri.

"As of right now she is none of your business. She's not part of any bargaining rights, genie," Derek said nonchalantly

"Bargaining rights? For what? Look, whatever this guy told you, he's playing you. You come breaking into my place ranting some shit about genies and I haven't got a clue what you're talking about."

He looked over at Abdul and wondered how long he'd been here and if he himself had lost his own power or if Derek had already trapped him.

"What about you, Abdul? Are you serving this piece of shit? Do you have any idea some of the things he's done?"

Abdul kept an even expression as Derek taunted Z.

"Obviously, you two are the best of friends, and I'm sorry to have to break up this little party but it's time for me to take my wife home. Perhaps I'm in the market for another genie as well?"

Abdul he realized that his moment had come while Derek had his attention on Azizi..

He stepped over to where Derek held the knife to Scheri's throat. He knocked Derek aside and laid a hand to her shoulder, admiring how beautiful she looked with all those black curls tousled around her shoulders and gently framing her face.

There was no turning back now. He was leaving and taking the woman with him and Derek was not coming with them.

Derek couldn't stop him...if he commanded him to stop then he would be using up his last wish, and he just had a feeling Derek didn't have the balls to do that. He might order him to bring her back later but he doubted it. Not when the promise of being a billionaire or having some form of control was sitting in the palm of his hand.

He began to dematerialize with the woman as a look of hatred and surprise crossed Derek's face.

A moment later, they disappeared into thin air.

CHAPTER FIFTEEN

"You son-of-a-bitch! Where did he take her?" Z's voice dripped with all the anger and venom he felt.

Derek's mind was racing a mile a minute. Where had Abdul taken her? He knew he certainly couldn't go far. He was still under his command and owed him a wish. His guess was that he'd gone back to his place.

"I have no clue, genie. He took her without my consent."

Z lunged at Derek and hit him so hard he toppled back against the back wall of the trailer.

Derek quickly stood up and looked over at the mirror standing in the middle of the living room. It must be this genie's portal. If he could get to it and get out the door fast enough, he would then own the mirror and own the Jinn. Three more wishes.

He started toward it, but Z already knew what he was thinking and headed him off. He grabbed him in a headlock and hauled him towards the door of the trailer and threw him down the steps, out into the lot.

Shit. Now what? Abdul had taken Scheri and he had no clue where he'd gone with her. If Derek was still owed a wish...he couldn't go back to the Jinn realm yet, so then he must've gone back to where his portal was, which would be in Derek's possession.

But where was Derek's place? He closed his eyes...he could see it clearly in his mind, but was having trouble knowing exactly where it was in the city. Dammit. There were city streets flashing through his mind...he could see the building but then it faded away quickly.

Derek would be on his way there as soon as he could get himself to a car rental place or on a plane. It was only a matter of hours.

He had to think.

Suddenly he raced down the hallway to his room where several boxes of her things were stacked neatly in a corner. There had to be something in there with her old address. A bill...an old piece of mail. Anything. Maybe it had a clear picture or something where he could look up the address and get a real fix on it.

His powers had increased in recent weeks, and now they were about to be put to the ultimate test. He was going to have to find some way to have enough to get to her before Derek did.

He tore open one of the boxes and found it full of clothes, and another with shoes. The third box down had several photo albums and a stack of envelopes held with a rubber band.

He flipped through them and soon found an old letter from her former employer's office with a formal job offer. At the top was her old address.

He tore it off and put it in his pocket, and grabbed his mirror. He'd never tried to dematerialize the portal with him and wondered if it would damage or degrade it in some way. No way to know...but he wasn't leaving it here, just in case Derek or one of his buddies came back here looking for it.

He closed his eyes envisioning the place where she was, but it wasn't there anymore. Where the hell had she been taken? He could feel her now...it was strange, but something had happened when he tasted that tear. He could see things more clearly; past, present and future.

He also realized that he wasn't going very far until the rest of the alcohol in his system had worn off. He hadn't even been able to transport himself from The Mix back home just a little while ago, much less transport himself and his mirror all the way out of state.

He closed his eyes again trying to pick up her essence and sense her again. She was in a strange place right now and something had drastically changed. It wasn't Derek's apartment. It wasn't clear or...solid.

His mind raced for a moment and then he felt something inside of him. He could feel her soul there...and he could sense that she had been changed somehow. Her energy had been transformed and didn't feel the same. A moment later, he realized that Abdul had taken her into his own portal with him.

Shit! He had to get to Derek's place now because if Abdul tried to take her all the way through to the Jinn realm, she would most certainly die. Human energy was not the same as the fire of a Jinn...and according to the legends he'd never believed in but was now being forced to, the rare human who'd ever come over had only been able to do so because their energy had been merged with their twin soul from that realm.

Abdul most certainly was not Scheharazade Bloom's twin soul...and in fact probably just the opposite.

He closed his eyes and focused on Derek's apartment. Just focusing wasn't going to be enough to go that far. He needed to remember....to look back at how he'd come here when he'd had all of his power. He focused on seeing the space between spaces...in between atoms and instead of just trying to dematerialize and transport all of his heavy energy, he refocused on bending space, so he could separate the solid parts enough so he could walk through it and simply appear where he needed to go.

He'd been living in this place so long...and become so polluted with the solidity of the material world that he'd forgotten all about this special talent he possessed. It was both rehabilitating and liberating to know that freedom once more.

And in that moment it occurred to him that maybe he'd only lost his powers because although he 'knew' it, he hadn't *really* acknowledged the fact that this world was no more than a distraction set up to make anyone here forget who they really are. They take on the body they dwell in, and they are continuously distracted by all the sensations it creates and all the myriad of sensations that this place itself encompasses.

True power in every capacity, could only come when one were free from those distractions. Perhaps that freedom was closer than he thought. This was a start.

He freed his mind from his body, focused on bending space and second later, he appeared in Derek's apartment. It looked exactly as he'd seen in his mind and in the pictures he'd picked up from hers.

Scheri and Abdul were nowhere in sight, and neither was Derek. It would take him hours to get back here no doubt. He saw the mirror hanging on the wall, and immediately knew it was Abdul's portal. Scheri was just behind the glass ...so close and yet so far.

"Abdul! I know you have her in there."

He paused for a moment waiting for a reply he knew wasn't coming.

"If you try to take her all the way over to our realm, you *will* kill her. You know that...right? You can't do it because her energy will be burned away."

Silence.

"Answer me, God dammit!"

Still nothing.

From inside the mirror Abdul watched as Azizi paced back and forth standing there. Was he speaking the truth? He looked over at the woman who was now laying on the bed he'd created here in the 'in-between-area' on the other side of his mirror. Damn but he wanted nothing more than to take her over to the other side, but if Azizi was correct it would burn away her energy and destroy her.

As long as she was in here, Azizi couldn't get to her because this portal was his alone. Derek would be back at some point as well, and if he ordered him to bring the woman back through as a wish, he would have no choice in the matter. He appeared to be at an impasse.

"Abdul. Listen to me."

He couldn't believe what he was about to say, but he also knew that Scheri was in grave danger.

"I know you hate me…and quite frankly I've hated you for a long time too. But, you have to listen to me now. If you take her to the other side, it will kill her. And when Derek gets back here, if you bring her back through here and he gets his hands on her, you know what is eventually going to happen. Maybe he can't kill her right now because it's part of the whole three wishes bullshit….but what else can he do to her? Do you have any idea the beatings she's taken from him? Can you just let that happen? And what about later, after you're gone and he's had his three wishes. You *are* going to be sent back once that last wish takes place. Once you're gone, your magic has no bearing anymore and he will kill her or have someone else do it. So if you do what you are planning…or if Derek gets her, either way she dies."

A moment later Abdul stepped through the glass.

"Why should I believe you?"

"Didn't you see it when you touched her?"

"I didn't see anything. Except what I envisioned with her lying in my bed."

Z dragged in a deep breath, controlling his emotions. Maybe Abdul couldn't see her pictures the way he could. And the thought of him touching her sent fire raging through his human veins. But right now, he needed to keep it together because he somehow had to get through to him and get him to allow him to take her out of here.

"You have to let me take her out of here."

He stared at Azizi hating him in that moment because he knew he was right. He'd watched Derek Worley for days and knew he was planning to kill the woman.

"It's only a matter of time before he gets here. And you know damned well he's going to command you to bring her back through."

"How can you be so sure? Derek Worley wants power and money more than anything else."

194

"Maybe so…but he wants her dead just as much. I've seen it," Z said quietly.

His mind ran back over the image he'd seen in the bedroom when he'd felt as though the life was draining from his body. He'd later realized that what he was feeling and seeing in his vision was from her perspective…it was what *she* would be feeling very soon if they didn't stop Derek.

"I am aware that he wants her dead. And I informed him that my power and his wishes can be no part of that. So now what? You're proposing that I just give her to you?"

"Yeah, actually…I am. Bring her through. Let me take her out of here, and you go back inside. When Derek gets here he's going to believe that you have her in there with you. When he calls you out, don't say anything. When he commands you to bring her through…well, you can't because she's not there. And guess what? You don't have to tell him where she is…unless he's willing to waste his last wish commanding you to tell him.

"What if he commands me to bring him to her, as he did before?"

"You have to resist…you know he is going to kill her, so you can resist. You can't use your power to grant him any wish that will cause the murder of another."

"He'll promise not to kill her…that's what he did before."

Z sighed. He had to think of a loophole.

"Well, if he does it again, I'll be there with her, and I'll transport her out of there. He'll have used all three wishes, she and I disappear off the grid again, and he's done."

Abdul stared at him in silence.

"Why should I give her to you?"

"I love her."

There. He'd said it. He hadn't even slept with her and yet he just knew instinctively that it was the truth. He didn't need to share in the senses of their bodies to know that he loved her. And in that moment a realization hit him. Love was something that didn't have anything at all to do with the material world...or this place or how we share in the pleasures of our bodies. Real love was something ethereal. Spiritual.

Maybe that was what had really drawn him to her in the first place and why his powers had begun to increase. The power of love and its companion compassion had worked a magic all their own. They were emotions of the spirit that flowed through us like a river heading out to the larger seas. And this realm was sort of like a dam...holding back that flow as it polluted the senses, trapped the spirit in a body and acted as a barrier between our souls and real, pure love.

Somewhere along the line the dam had broken...and he'd fallen in love....with a human.

Abdul's mouth drew into a tight line.

He didn't want to give her up ...but then again he had no wish to commit murder either. His only wish in coming here had been to get revenge on Azizi. And yet, it seemed that Aziz's own private hell in this place...stuck here with no powers, unable to return to the Jinn realm because he would be destroyed had been revenge enough. And in fact, one that had caused him to change.

He remembered back over time what a selfish, impetuous youth Azizi had been. No care for anyone but himself...perhaps this place had changed him for the better and after coming here, he realized his jealousy had been for nothing, because there was nothing in this realm that held any meaning for a Jinn!

He finally grudgingly nodded in agreement, because he realized that no matter what he did, he couldn't keep Scheharazade Bloom. She belonged here in her own world...and if there was anyone she did belong with, it was Azizi ab'd al Jadu.

And if nothing else, maybe when he returned to his own realm if he told Soheila what had happened, and that he'd helped her son...perhaps it might stir some feelings that were not there before.

He dematerialized and went through the glass and a moment later, came back through the mirror with Scheri in his arms, still asleep from whatever Derek had injected her with. She stirred just a little as Abdul handed her to Z and her eyes opened for a second. She looked dazed and then drifted back off.

Z looked down at her. "When I met her, the only reason I gave her the time of day was because when I touched her, something happened and I started to get back some of my powers. But since I've gotten to know her...something else happened and I would do anything to protect her."

Abdul nodded still feeling jealous that Azizi had apparently found his twin soul in this realm. "You better go now. Leave the rest to me."

"Thank you."

"Until we meet again...' said Abdul as he dematerialized and retreated back into the mirror to wait for Derek to get back here.

Z picked up his own mirror under one arm while carefully standing Scheri on her feet and supporting her with the other, and then closed his eyes, forgetting all about the distractions of the material world, the nuisance and bulk of his human body...and hers. He could see every particle each of them was made of and that of his mirror, as he focused nothing but pure subatomic energy on bending space and moving matter out of the way so he could walk directly through the self-made 'portal' to his destination.

A moment later they dematerialized and then reappeared in the living room of his trailer back at the carnival.

They would be safe here for now, because Derek was on his way back home and by the time he got there, Abdul distracted him and then he finally found out he no longer had

Scheri, the carnival would have moved from this place to another.

Once Derek blew his last wish ordering Abdul to tell him where she was then he would no longer have the option of instant transport. And if he showed up here, he would be ready and waiting. If Derek wanted power and money, they could still hide out and stay off the grid to avoid being found..someway or another.

He set the mirror down behind the woven wicker screen that stood by the bookshelf, locked the doors and then carried her back to his bed where laid her down gently, covering her with a blanket. He removed his shoes and crawled underneath beside her, pulling her body close to his, drinking in the scent of her hair on his pillow.

He wouldn't be sleeping, but he would be watching and waiting with her here wrapped in the protectiveness of his arms as he came up with a plan to put an end to Derek Worley's mission once and for all.

CHAPTER SIXTEEN

Scheri opened her eyes, struggling to focus and blink away her blurry vision. Her head as hurting and the room began to spin as she started to roll over.

Where was she? As her vision cleared she realized that she was lying in bed in Z's room...and he was lying there next to her, propped up on one elbow.

He brushed a strand of hair back from her face and kissed the end of her nose.

"Hey," he said softly.

She tried to sit up but he quickly held her back.

"No...don't do that yet. You've been drugged and you're still dizzy." He slid closer to her laying her back down against the pillow.

"What happened?"

"Derek broke in here while I was gone...remember?"

She struggled to regain her bearings. "Yeah. I was trying to get the gun and I jabbed him in the throat like you taught me. But it didn't stop him. He stuck me in the leg with a needle and that's all I remember."

"I came in after that...and well, maybe we'll just wait until you feel better to go over everything else."

"What did he do?"

"Not much. But you had a little trip."

"What kind of trip?" Her brows knit together.

"Shhh." He put a finger to her lips and then replaced it with his lips, kissing her softly. "We'll talk about it later."

She nodded. "I thought you didn't want to be here with me. You said you were going out and you didn't know when you'd be back...and all his other stuff you said about me not knowing you. And that I belonged with some other guy who'll be better than Derek."

"I was an idiot," he said quietly. "And if you'll forgive me, I promise you I'll do all I can to be that guy."

199

"Really? Well, you took off and look what happened. Maybe you were right and I don't know you."

He sighed. "Yes. You do."

"Then why did you say what you said and take off like that?"

"Because I was a complete and total fool and I didn't want to admit how I feel about you."

"And how is that?"

"I think I'm falling in love with you."

She stared at him for a moment.

"Well, after what you said...how do I know if I'm falling in love with you or some illusion I've created in my own head?"

"You don't. But I am asking you to give me a chance to let you fall in love with me. The real me."

"And who is that?"

He kissed her forehead. "You'll see soon enough. Right now you need to rest, and we can talk about it in the morning. Are you thirsty or do you want anything to eat?"

"Yeah...I feel like I could drink a gallon of water right now."

"Your wish is my command," he said quietly and he got up and went to the kitchen and brought back a bottle of water.

"You've been saying that a lot lately."

"It just seems...fitting."

"Well, dear God if I could have three wishes, I think I'd be living in a big house in Bimini or something." She laughed and then cringed at the pain that shot through her eyes and forehead.

"If you could have three wishes...what would you wish for...seriously."

"I don't know. I can't really think very straight right now."

"Well, when you feel better I'll ask you again."

She looked at him like he was nuts. "Okaaaay."

200

After a while he fixed her some soup and when her head had cleared a little more he helped her to the shower.

Her legs were still a little shaky from being drugged as she walked in his bathroom and as the steam filled the air she turned around to face him.

"If I could have three wishes, one of them would be that somehow someone would find evidence against him and he would get locked up for the rest of his life."

"Don't let go of that wish. Just remember it and keep it in mind, because you just never know when your wishes may come true."

She stared at him for a moment.

"Did you mean what you said earlier? About asking me for a chance to show me the real you?"

He nodded.

She smiled and raised a brow playfully.

"How much of you?"

He moved in closer to her and traced the curve of her cheek with his finger. "As much of me as you want to see."

"Then maybe you can start right now. My second wish would be that I could see all of you." Her eyes traveled up and down the length of him.

He looked a little surprised. "Right now?"

She nodded.

"Are you sure you're up to that? Your legs are still shaky."

She nodded. "Well, if you come close enough to help hold me up, the more I can see."

He smiled. 'Your wish is my command."

He stepped closer to her and slowly pulled his shirt up over his head, his gaze never leaving hers.

She drank in every inch of lean torso, six pack and shoulders thick with muscle as he stood there just inches away. The dragon tattoo danced on his bicep as he tossed the shirt off to the side on the bathroom floor.

He reached out and her breath caught in her throat as he picked her up and walked toward the shower with her in his arms. Her hands found their way up across his shoulders and wound around his neck and as he set her down on the floor he moved in capturing her lips with his.

He gently tasted her bottom lip before he deepened the kiss and his tongue moved with hers, in a slow, sensuous dance.

He pulled her in closer to him as his hands traveled the length of her back down along the curve of her hips and then back up as he helped her undress slowly...seductively. He kissed his way down along the soft skin of her neck and down to the tops of her breasts, into the crease of her cleavage, and finally over to the soft peaks, tasting each one as her fingers wound into length of his hair.

He kissed his way down further, across her smooth midriff working his way lower and lower until he found the soft, wet place he sought. She lifted one leg, putting her foot up on the ledge of the tub to give him better access as he kneeled down to do the job right. She was sweet to taste and damp to the touch...and he took his time bringing her to the edge.

She felt as though she were drowning in a raging torrent of pleasure with every stroke of his hands and his mouth. And when she was ready to tumble over the edge of the falls....he pulled back and kissed his way back up across her stomach, higher and higher to her neck and then her lips.

She could taste her own scent on him as he kissed her deeply and she found it arousing.

"I've been wanting you like this for...what seems like a long time. I know it's not. But then maybe it is," he said quietly.

She looked puzzled.

"Never mind. All that matters is that we're here now. And I hope you'll let me be him."

"Who? What are you talking about?" She laughed.

" I told you that you belonged with someone who'll love you like he didn't and who'll be around for you. I hope you'll let me be that man."

He pulled her hands up to his lips, kissing the inside of each one of her wrists and then taking one of her forefingers into his mouth and sucking on it. He took her hand and moved her wet finger down between her legs, urging her on.

"I like to watch," he whispered against the skin on the side of her neck.

She smiled and obliged him putting on quite the show as she gently stroked the little bead nestled there, occasionally delving into her own wetness and putting her fingers to his lips.

He was rock hard by then, and quickly slid out of his pants as he knelt back down between her legs to indulge in the glistening sweetness she'd let him sample from her fingers. He took his time, savoring the taste and smell of her. He'd been without a woman for a long time and he wasn't going to let this go by too quickly for either of them. He slid one finger in and began gliding it gently in and out in a smooth rhythm with his tongue.

He pulled back for a few moments teasing her..he didn't want it to end too quickly. He leaned in and kissed her deeply, gently running his hands along her hips and backside before sliding back down her midriff and continuing the sensuous dance his tongue had been playing a few moments early.

The sensations built as she leaned her head back and threaded her fingers through his long black hair. He could feel her body thrumming in tune with every stroke until she exploded into a million shards of pleasure.

He stood back up and as the steamy mist surrounded him, she pushed him back against the wall and slid down his body, tasting the rock hard pebbles of his nipples as she moved downward…then licking along the rippled muscles of his abdomen, and finally reaching her destination.

He was hard as a rock and glistening wet with the drops of his excitement. She took a tentative taste first, and then covered him with the velvety soft wetness of her lips and tongue, salty and sweet at the same time.

He dragged in a ragged breath as she stroked him, softer and then with more urgency until his blood was about to boil over, every muscle in his body taut like a drumhead.

He stopped her before he exploded and instead opened up the shower curtain and picked her up and stepped into the warm spray. He set her down and then poured a generous amount of liquid soap into his hands, lathering up and then stroking up and down her body….across the peaks of her breasts and back down between her legs.

He pulled her to him and kissed her again, feeling the slippery softness of her body against his and then kissed down the side of her neck.

"I'm not taking this all the way just yet, because I want to carry you to my bed and just lay you back and enjoy every inch of you. I've dreamed of being able to hold you like this since pretty much the moment we met."

She smiled playfully. "You didn't like me when we met, remember?"

"If my memory serves me correctly, it was the other way around. Hopefully you won't call security on me for what I'm about to do."

She wrapped her arms around his neck. "I might call security if you make me wait til we get to the bed. I want you….now."

She pushed his back against the tiled shower wall and as he reached over head to grab the showerhead behind him, she lifted her leg and slowly pushed his shaft inside her and began sliding up and down on him. She moved slowly as she reached between her legs and began stroking herself.

A few moments later, he traded places with her and leaned her back against the shower wall and braced himself on his arms as he began to move with her...faster and more urgently.

She wrapped one leg around his waist, feeling the muscles of his butt moving against her calf muscle, as he reached down with one arm to help support her weight.

The warm water sluiced down the muscles of his chest and his tight abs and she could feel it dripping down between her legs, spraying against her little hotspot as she watched the erotic scene.

He leaned in and kissed the side of her neck, licking the water from the erogenous zone that ran from the back of her ear downward, as her fingers dug into the muscles of his back and shoulders.

He grabbed her butt cheeks and pulled her in closer, burying his face in the side of her neck as the warm shower of water trailed down his wide back.

He pulled back from her and as his gaze met hers, the golden flecks in his eyes seemed to take motion for a split second.

"You own me, Scheharazade," he said quietly. He leaned in and kissed her lips.

A moment later she began to boil over in white hot eruption of sensation. She dragged in a few ragged breaths as wave after wave of pleasure rolled from her heat up through her belly and goosebumps broke out all over her body.

As soon as he felt her muscles contracting around him he exploded into her, driving in deep and hard. A surge of white hot energy flowed through his veins that almost knocked him to his knees, but he kept his footing and held her fast where she stood. He caught his breath for a moment as he buried his face in the side of her neck, kissing her skin softly and hugging her tight to him.

He pulled back from her for a second and as he looked into her eyes, he noticed the golden flecks, so like his own, for the first time. And for a split second it was as though he were looking into a mirror. He wasn't just seeing her pictures now, he was feeling her. Twin souls…that for a moment in time had merged through the joining of their bodies.

She stared at him looking puzzled as she felt a strange hum in her chest for a moment and for a split second she could have sworn she saw some strange pictures…of him. A strange, unfamiliar place that seemed almost ethereal. And of him burning away to some sort of energy form. It was indescribable.

"Did you….?" She looked a little confused. "What was that?"

He smiled. "It was me. The real me."

She reached forward and touched his face as water dripped from the end of his nose.

He reached behind her and shut off the water, took her hand and led her out of the shower stall and grabbed a thick towel from the shelf and wrapped it around her.

He grabbed one and toweled off, then wrapped it around his waist, and then grabbed her hand and led her out to the bedroom. He plunked down on the edge of the bed and motioned for her to sit beside him.

"My name is Azizi ab'd al Jadu. I am…a Jinn. Well. Mostly. I'm half Angel too…though I can't say I've ever been all too happy about that part."

She smiled. "Okay, magic man. But don't you have to wait a few minutes before we play the next game?" She raised a brow and nodded toward the shower.

He reached out and laid a hand on her thigh.

"You said you wanted to know the real me."

She laughed. "Yeah. I do. But not just the role playing stuff."

"I'm serious."

Her expression changed from playful to concerned.

"You're telling me you're a Jinn…a genie?"

"Yeah."

She sighed. He was so smart...and handsome. And up until now he'd never shown any signs of mental illness. Was he delusional? This couldn't be happening.

"Please tell me that you're just playing a joke on me...you know, Ashton's going to jump out and say, 'You're punk'd' and we're going to start laughing and all that."

"Scheri. You know what you saw in the tent. You were scared. You told me so yourself."

Her mind traveled back to that moment when she'd seen him disappear into thin air. And then of course there was the 'mirror trick' every night on stage. And all the other unexplainable things she'd seen....as well as all the things he'd known about her from the moment he touched her skin that first time.

She drew in a deep breath, trying to calm herself.

"Z. This is....scary. Scarier than what I thought I saw in the tent. Do you have some kind of issues you haven't told me about?"

"There are no issues. Remember you asked me how you could work with me if I didn't trust you enough to share my secrets with you. Well...I'm trying to share them now. If you'll let me."

Her brows knit together with worry.

"Okay. So...you're trying to tell me that you're a...genie. Like in Aladdin." She drew in a deep breath. "And my name just happens to be Scheharazade....like in Arabian Nights. And you just happened to decide to do some show that has that theme. Oh, god...." She shook her head and a laughed. More out of nervousness than irony. What had she gotten herself into? She'd gone from a violent psycho husband into the arms of a delusional one. He wasn't violent and he had a kind heart, but he was still mentally ill and needed help.

She stood up and started toward the closet to get some clothes.

207

"Where are you going?"

"I have to get out of here and think for awhile."

"You don't believe me?"

She sighed heavily.

"Z..." she shook her head and her voice trailed off.

She stared at him for a moment wanting desperately to believe him. She remembered the moment when she'd been standing in front of his mirror thinking how otherworldly it had felt just being near it....she'd seen things with her own two eyes over and over that didn't add up. And yet, now, in present time, when presented with this explanation...that certainly would explain everything, and yet that defied everything the real world was supposed to be, she didn't know what to think.

She'd always been the kid who believed in fairies...the one who got made fun of because she believed she could disappear and be invisible to everyone around her. The one who believed she could make objects move with her mind. Maybe that's what had driven her to want to be a writer in the first place. Because it was the one place where those fantasies could come to life and become reality on the pages. When she'd been a little girl, she'd believed in magic, but she'd soon learned that no matter how much she wanted those games to be real, they were make-believe.

And now here was someone telling her that such things might not be so make-believe after all. Maybe she was just as delusional as he was for even standing here questioning it!

He stood up and walked over to where she was and took her hand in his. He kissed her lips softly, knowing that what he was about to do could scare her and drive her away from him forever. But the time had come for her to know the truth.

If he was going to love, it was going to be honest...and she had to be able to love him for exactly who and what he was.

He closed his eyes and focused on bending space and converting their energy. For some reason what had once been difficult, now seemed virtually effortless, and a moment later, they rematerialized on the stage in the Smoke & MirrorZ tent.

She looked around her and gasped and then covered her mouth to stifle her scream as she backed away from him.

"What are you?"

He reached out to try to calm her. "I told you. I'm a Jinn."

"That's not possible."

"Yes. It is."

He stepped closer to her.

"Don't touch me!" she said, backing away further.

"Scheri…you don't have to be afraid of me. Ever."

Her posture softened a bit and he cautiously moved closer and she allowed him to touch her again.

"Let me take us back to the trailer. Okay?"

She looked absolutely petrified, but nodded in agreement. He wrapped his arms around her, closed his eyes and a split second later, they were back in his bedroom.

"Now…do you believe what I've said?"

She plunked down on the edge of the bed, staring up at him, trying to digest what had just happened. Her stomach was in knots and she felt like she was going to pass out. The unexplained things that she'd seen now were explained in full…frighteningly so.

She drew in a calming breath and then spoke, trying to maintain her composure. He was some kind of what? Creature? Spirit?

"You're not human, then."

"I am in a human body right now…but I am not human when I am in my native state."

"How did you get here….on earth, I mean."

"An old magician helped open the portal I came through. It was a long time ago."

"How long?"

"Centuries."

She looked away from him trying to decide whether to sit there, or get up and run...even though she was pretty sure he wouldn't chase her if she did.

"So you said I went on a little 'trip' earlier? What did you mean? Does Derek know about you?"

He nodded. "Yeah, unfortunately he does. And he hooked up with one of my worst enemies from back home. His name is Abdul and fortunately for you...although I can't believe I'm saying that...Abdul had his eye on stealing you for himself. He took you into his portal while you were drugged and I convinced him to bring you back out of there and let you go. A Jinn's magic can't be used to cause death to another, and he knew that no matter what Derek said he was planning something of that nature. Abdul realized it and let me take you home with me."

Her eyes widened. "So I was inside this guy's mirror and I'm guessing that Derek probably took off for home to try to go get me back from this Abdul?"

"Yeah."

"And now Derek's after you too. What are you going to do if Derek comes back after us?"

"I don't doubt that he will. But I'll be ready for him. He knows I'm not going to let him take you."

She started shaking all over...this was completely insane and just as frightening. Like something out of a bad sci-fi movie come to life.

She sighed. "Okay I guess I have to try to digest all of this. So, how did you end up here at this carnival?"

"I needed something to do. My powers...they haven't worked right since I got here. They had dwindled away to a few tricks that work well for magic shows...back days gone by I entertained kings, or traveled with gypsies. And that's about it. This place is different than my world and it somehow polluted my energy with all the physical distractions here."

210

He sat down next to her. "That is until you came. When I touched you, I could see everything that had happened to you. And you said I saw through all your anger and pain to who you really were. And now I'm about to be honest with you…and you can leave here if you want when you know the truth. But when I met you, I touched you and something happened. My powers started to increase, and that was the only reason I chased you down outside the tent that day when we met. I didn't know at the time what would happen…but something did since then."

"So the only reason you helped me was because you thought it was going to fix your powers?"

'Yeah."

She looked distant for a moment and he took her hand in his.

"That was only for a few days. As soon as I started to get to know you and actually the moment I saw what he'd done to you, I actually did want to help you. I didn't know why at the time but I do now."

"And why is that?"

"I believe we're meant to be together. Legends say that every Jinn has a twin soul out there somewhere…usually in the human world. I think that's why my powers increased…it's because when we're together, and especially now after what we just did, I could feel you flowing through me. Look at me and tell me you didn't feel it too."

She wrapped her arms around her body as if trying to get warm…or maybe protect herself from her feelings. From him.

"I don't know what to think of all of this. I'm scared. This is like something from an episode of a sci-fi series or something. I've always wanted to believe in the supernatural…but this is nuts! This just can't be real!"

"Forget what you know, and listen to the little girl in your heart. The one who believed she could make objects move with her mind." He raised a brow.

211

She gasped...though she shouldn't be surprised he'd seen the pictures from her childhood.

"You wanted the truth...and I gave you the truth," he said quietly.

"Well I sure as hell wasn't banking on something like this!"

"Neither was I. I've never felt this way. Hell...I've never allowed myself to get close to anyone like this."

"You've been here all this time and never loved anyone before?"

"Nope."

"How could you live like that? Don't you get lonely?"

"Always surrounded by people...always alone. Because no one could ever know the truth about me. Not until now."

"So...Louie doesn't know? He seems pretty close to you."

He shook his head. "Nope."

"Why did you tell me? You've only known me for not even a couple of months now."

"You said you wanted to rebuild your life with me in it....unless you changed your mind. If there's any hope of that, there can't be any first rule of magic between us. No secrets."

He reached over to touch her and she flinched a little.

He took her hand in his and kissed her wrist.

"Scheri, I'm still the man you just made some pretty incredible love with in that shower."

"Love?"

"Yeah." He took a deep breath. "I've fallen in...pretty hard as a matter of fact."

She shook her head and turned away from him struggling to hold back the tears that threatened.

"What are you...are you a man?"

"When I'm in human form."

"What are you when you're not?"

"My energy comes from a kind that's not visible to the human eye...and it's very hot. Like a smokeless fire. There are different types of Jinn. I am Ifrit."

"Do you live here all the time...why don't you go back to your own world? You said your powers faded away in this place."

"I can't go back there."

"Why"

"Because there are some who want to destroy me for breaking their Law. Abdul was one of them, but I think he's changed his tune now that he's come here and see that it's not the playground he thought it was. I came here of my own free will. I wasn't called to serve. And for whatever reason that pissed them off. And don't even get me started on my father's kind."

Her brows crinkled. "Your father's kind? Who are they?"

"My mother is Ifrit Jinn...and my father is an Angel."

She looked even more stunned if that was possible as she struggled to accept what he was saying and not write him off as a complete lunatic, despite the fact he had already proven to her that not all magic is illusion.

"So where do you go when you go into your mirror."

"It's kind of an in-between-worlds place."

He sighed and slid off the bed, kneeling down in front of her.

"Can you take there. Can you show it to me?"

"Yeah."

"Really?"

She had that expression many people have when they are about to get on a rollercoaster for the first time. Fear mixed with anxiety and adrenaline rush.

"There's going to be a million questions you'll want answered....hell, I think you've covered about half of that in the last ten minutes." He laughed lightly. "And you're going to want me to show you things too. And I promise I will. But not all of it tonight."

He slid in closer and traced the curve of her cheek with his finger and then took her face in his hands, kissing her lips very softly.

"You still have decisions to make about your life. But I swear, I'm not letting anything happen to you, even if you don't want me."

"Well I think after all of this, you have some decisions to make yourself. You can't just stay here working this carnival now that he knows where you are...and who you are."

He smiled. "Well the carnival moves out tomorrow. They're going about 100 miles from here. We could take a chance and stay on. He may not find us if he comes looking. Not unless he blows his last wish commanding Abdul to bring him to you. Either way, I guess we're both up the creek. It's easier to row when two people share the load. Let me share yours. I won't let him near you...I promised you the day I met you that I'd keep you safe. And that still holds true no matter what."

He slid upward pulling her with him and laid her back on the bed, being careful not to put too much of his weight on her. He didn't say a word...just stared down at her.

"Z. I'm afraid...I mean, you're not human. You're like some other species or something."

He busted out laughing and rolled over on his back.

She looked over at him annoyed by his amusement at her statement.

"What!? I'm serious, dammit!"

He reached over and pulled her down on top of him.

"Scheri, I'm human...almost. I have a human body. It doesn't age like yours I guess because I don't age. My energy is immortal and pretty much indestructible except by Jinn magic. And even then it can be disbursed but not completely destroyed."

"Isn't that what the human soul is supposed to be like?"

He nodded. "Yeah. I suppose it is."

"Then why do we age?"

"I don't know. I'm a Jinn not a science professor."

"Can I see what you look like when you're not human?"

"No. Jinn energy isn't visible to the human eye. The only way you can see us is if we materialize and take human form. But if you could see me in my native state, I would like like what you see now."

"What about if you take me to where you're from? Could I see you then?"

"No. It would destroy you…at least according to the legends. Your energy is different than mine and it would burn it away. There's some who've said that they can bring their twin soul over but I wouldn't want to take that chance."

"But you said you could take me to the other side of your mirror."

"The other side of the portal isn't the Jinn realm. It's an in-between area that's neither here nor there. I have to change you to take you there, but it's not the same as going all the way to the other side."

"So how is this supposed to work between us?"

He smiled. "Well…you saw how it works. In there." He nodded toward the shower. "And we've been making this work with you living with me for weeks now, right?"

"Well if you don't age and I do, how can it even if I did admit that I love you too. You're not going to want to be with me when I'm an old lady and you're still young and looking like this."

"You love me?" He feigned surprise.

"Stop pretending you don't know."

He smiled. He knew…he'd known for a while exactly how she felt. But it was good to hear her finally say it.

"Say it again."

"No." Her voice was firm.

"You told me that you didn't think you could ever want to be with a man again, or trust them either. I know you trust me. And I know you love me too….even if you hadn't said it."

She started to roll off him.

"This is just too much. I don't know how to handle this. A few weeks ago…hell, forget that; a few hours ago, I would never have believed something like this could exist!"

He held her against him and forced her to look at him.

"But it does exist."

He brushed the hair back from her face.

"Stay with me. I know you're afraid right now…but if you just give me a chance, I'll be that guy we were talking about. The one who'll love you right."

She hesitated and then finally gave into her urge to wrap her arms around his neck.

"I don't know how we'll do this…but you're right about how I feel about you."

He smiled.

"We'll find a way to make this work. I promise. But there's a few new rules of magic between us. First rule: no secrets. Second rule: whatever happens, you own me…heart, body and mind. My power seems to be working pretty well…and I'm taking care of that first wish you made. The evidence you asked for is about to turn up.

"How can you do that? So far nobody's been able to get anything on him."

"The evidence they're looking for hasn't happened yet, but it will. And as far as the wish itself, a Jinn doesn't always have to be commanded in order to grant wishes. If we're not owned and under anyone's command we can

216

choose to grant wishes if we want to. You said you wanted him taken down. Well he's going to be. He won't be back here."

"Is there a third rule? Or is that it."

He smiled and trailed his finger down the length of her nose.

"Yeah. You have to lay in my arms like this every night for the rest of your life. And if you want to lather, rinse and repeat what we just did in the shower every so often, that's perfectly acceptable."

She smiled and then laughed.

"See..I knew it."

"Knew what?"

"That I could get you to smile."

She rolled her eyes. "I've heard that line somewhere before. You need a new one."

"Hey if ain't broke, don't fix it."

She pulled his face closer to hers and kissed his lips.

"Thank you."

"For what?"

"For helping to fix me…and for saving my life. You said your father was an Angel. Maybe you're more like him than you think."

"Don't say that. I will never be like him or any of his kind. He left my mother and me to go off on some 'higher mission'. What could possibly be a higher mission than the woman you love and the child she bore you?"

She stared at him for a long moment. "What's your mother like? You said she was a Jinn…like you?"

He nodded. "She came here too at one time. She'd fallen in love a with a human." He smiled. "And she made a mistake. She'd lost her powers too because of this place. And he…my father…came here when her lover was killed in an accident. He saw her there and felt sorry for her I guess. He took her under his wing…literally, and they fell in love."

"Sounds sort of familiar, hmm? Him taking in a human who needed someone?" She raised a brow.

"He was kicked out of The Order for falling in love with her. And then I don't know what happened…but he restored her powers and sent us back to the Jinn realm. I guess he won his favor back with them and went back to work. Leaving us behind. He told her something like, 'Someday you'll understand.'"

"And did she?"

"She never stopped defending him. And I don't think she ever stopped loving him either."

"What about you?"

"I've never loved him or understood him. I never asked for him to be my father."

"I remember someone once told me, 'Sometimes the things we don't ask for are the things we need the most.'"

He smiled and traced the curve of her cheek with his finger.

She looked thoughtful for a moment. "You know, come to think of it…we have something in common. My father left me too, just like yours. Except he wasn't the good guy on some noble misson; he just took off, and left my mother never to be seen or heard of again."

"We have many things in common," he said quietly. "More than you know."

She smiled. "Thank you again for saving my life. More than once."

"You saved mine somewhere along the way. It was the least I could do."

He pulled down the towel that was wrapped around her and tossed his own to the side as he slid her up further on the bed, laying her back on his pillows.

He began kissing a path down her throat toward the crease of her cleavage.

"Now what?"

218

"I dunno. The night's still young. Make a wish," he said suggestively.

She smiled as he slid down her body and kissed a wet trail up the inside of her thigh.

CHAPTER SEVENTEEN

It was the crack of dawn.

Derek Worley got out of the rental car he'd just driven into the parking garage of his apartment complex and slammed the door. He walked toward the elevator, got in and headed up to his floor.

He unlocked the door, tossed the keys down and walked over to where the mirror hung on his wall. He was so livid he wanted to smash it into a million pieces but instinctively knew that if he did the Jinn would not or could not grant him his last wish. And he intended to have it come hell or high water.

He poured a drink and plunked down on the couch. He'd had a long night of driving time getting here to think on the matter.

Money, power, immortality perhaps? Although he wondered about that one since the 'rules' clearly stated that one couldn't wish to elevate themselves to a status of a God.

Utter and complete control of an entire world or a planet of living human beings would likely fall under that category as well...perhaps that was why the Jinn had twisted his wish when he'd wished it before.

What if he could be the richest man in the world? Surely then he could buy off nearly anyone in any government he wanted. And at some point he could have the little bitch taken down. If he wasn't able to kill her, well...maybe he could at least have her locked up and spend the rest of her life in prison. Plenty of torture to go along with that. Maybe that was even better than taking her life.

He envisioned it. It was nice, but still there was some unseen, primal urge within him that craved the feel of her throat beneath his fingers and the gurgle of her last breaths escaping her lips while he watched.

His mind traveled back in time to those moments when his last girlfriend Susan had begged for her life. She was tied up, just like mother had been, and locked in the trunk of his car.

Her lips stained with blood…her cheeks rouged with the red welts he'd slapped there. Her eyes blackened with the shadows of the bruises he'd put there…and her 'perfume' the gasoline he'd doused her with for the fire he would be lighting up in her honor. She looked so beautiful lying there. He was quite the make-up artist indeed!

But the most rewarding moment of the whole thing hadn't been the look in her eyes, the tortures he'd inflicted or even raping her while she were gagged and bound. It was that moment of utter and complete power and domination, when her last breath escaped her body and he felt it leave her.

They'd been down by his favorite spot by the river near an old gnarled tree and as the moonlight glinted off the water he'd felt her body go limp beneath his own hands. No amount of money or earthly power could compare, actually. Because in that moment he was a God…he had the power to take life. What else could compare with that?

"Abdul…bring her out here."

There was nothing but silence.

"I will wish it if that's what I have to do."

No answer.

Derek became more agitated. It seemed that there was no way Abdul was going to bring her out and he wasn't coming out unless a wish was made.

What he needed was more wishes. And yet, he knew he couldn't wish for more wishes or infinite wishes. These rules were stifling and this Jinn seemed fairly worthless.

And then it dawned on him.

"Abdul, I know what I want to wish for."

Abdul stepped from the mirror.

"I need more wishes."

"You know I cannot grant you that."

"No, you can't. But I have an idea who can."

He stopped for a moment to think very carefully on how he worded his next wish so the Jinn couldn't twist it into anything other than what it was.

"I want you to bring me the mirror…to this place, in my apartment, right here on planet earth, in this timeline, in present time….the tall free standing mirror that is the portal of the Jinn named Azizi ab'd al Jadu who is living as a carnival magician."

Abdul looked distressed but knew he couldn't avoid granting the wish. He could already feel his power gathering of its own accord, de-materializing the mirror.

Derek smiled. "You thought perhaps you could outsmart me taking her away? Well think again. You can't bring her to me for the reasons I want her here, and neither can he. But if I bring him here, then if she's in there with you he can make her materialize here. If she's not, and you've hidden her away somewhere, I know somehow she will know I have him, and she'll come after him in some noble sacrifice trying to save him. So…I'll have my wishes, he will be unable to save her because I will command him, and she will be here of her own free will."

A moment later Z's mirror appeared in Derek's living room and as it did, Abdul began to dematerialize as he was drawn back through the mirror to the realm of the Jinn. His tenure here was over and there was nothing more he could do.

Z opened his eyes as the first pale fingers of dawn spread out across the sky and a thin trail of sunlight peeked through a crack in the drapes of his bedroom.

He looked down at Scheri, beautiful…naked and asleep with her hair splayed out across his pillow like a thick black cape of silky curls.

He could scarcely believe that she was really here...and yet the taste and feel of every curve of her body was a fresh reminder that she was.

Since she'd come here, something profound had happened to him. And it wasn't just that he'd fallen in love with a human. It was something else.

He looked down at the dragon on his arm remembering the hatred he'd felt when he picked it out. She'd asked him if he understood his father, and looking at her laying there, and everything that had happened over the course of the last several weeks, he realized that maybe he sort of did. Because he knew he would do anything to protect her. Even if it meant placing himself in danger.

Love was something that wasn't under our control...and when we love, neither is our urge to help and preserve life. Maybe his father's inherent need to help others was so strong that it surpassed even his own needs...a force so powerful that he'd left behind the woman and child he'd loved. Maybe his father had somehow known that his son would come to this conclusion someday, and if he'd have been around maybe that wouldn't have happened.

He didn't know, but he knew that maybe the time had come to fully let go of all the discord in his heart over it, and focus on the things that really mattered. The things that had changed his life in the past weeks.

She rolled over and opened her eyes to find him staring down at her.

"Hey," she said softly. She reached up and laid her hand to the side of his face. "Did you sleep?"

"Not much. I wanted to keep watch."

She sat up on one elbow. "You can't just endlessly go without sleep."

"I'll do whatever I have to."

She kissed him softly and slid out of bed and go to the bathroom to wash her face and brush her teeth. She

223

returned a moment later and started toward the closet when she noticed a strange light coming from the living room.

"Z…come here." She nodded toward the hall.

He stood up and walked down the hall and looked around the corner. A flash of light went off and a puff of steamy mist came from behind the wicker screen and he instantaneously knew what had happened.

He turned to Scheri. "Son of a bitch! He made a wish and Abdul had to do it. He's got my mirror. We've only got a few moments, so listen to me carefully. Listen to what's in your heart because I'll be there. Take the gun Louie got you and bring it with you to his place, and when the time comes you need to be strong. I want you to destroy my mirror. He can't make any wishes if I'm not there to grant them."

Her eyes welled up with tears. "I can't. I'll destroy you."

He took her hands in his and kissed her fingers before pulling her in for one last kiss.

"He can't order me to do anything that will result in your murder. And now is the chance you've been waiting for to take him down. You have to be brave though, and face your greatest fear. And you have to destroy the mirror the moment you walk in the door. Once he makes his third wish, I'm getting sent back anyway. If I'm going to get taken away from you, I'd rather have it be on your terms than his, and I'd rather have it mean something."

She shook her head as tears began to run down her face grabbing on to him and burying her face in his chest.

He began to hear some strange words in his head…like someone yelling from a distance and a second later he dematerialized before her eyes and disappeared into thin air.

She panicked for a moment dragging in a few deep breaths, and feeling as though she would pass out.

What was she going to do? Derek had stolen the mirror and now commanded Z. He would be forced to give him three wishes. She closed her eyes and she could hear him there inside her somehow. Calming her...reassuring her.

She drew in a deep breath, focused her resolve and ran back to the bedroom where she threw on some clothes, grabbed the gun out of the closet, and tossed a few things she might need in her handbag.

She ran over to Louie's and knocked on his door.

'Hey, doll! Come on in...whatcha need?"

"Listen, Lou...I have to go out for awhile. Can you babysit with George?"

He looked confused. "Yeah...but ain't you gonna be back before we finish packing everything up later today? Some of us'll be heading out first thing in the morning and then the rest of us whenever we finish getting loaded up."

"Well I hope we'll be back before then. But just in case, please take care of George."

Lou looked a little distressed.

"Is something wrong? You in trouble?"

She wanted to pour out the whole story...and ask for Lou's help, but she knew it would sound completely insane and she might end up getting 'help' alright. Mental help.

She couldn't tell Lou. This was something she and Z were going to have to handle themselves.

She smiled. "No Lou...everything's fine. Z and I are just headed out to the lake for the afternoon. I'm meeting him there now...he's surprising me with something romantic I think."

Lou smiled and nodded. "Wining and dining. Damn. That ain't like him, but then again I ain't never seen him the way he is around you."

He reached forward and took little George from her hands snuggling him under the day old growth of beard on his chin.

"I'll take good care of him til you get back...even if you stay an extra day. I'll hang out and wait so we can ride out of town together."

She hugged Louie and kissed George on the top of his little head. "Thanks, Louie."

She dragged in a deep breath as she turned and headed out the door and off to the nearest car rental place a few blocks up the road.

CHAPTER EIGHTEEN

Z materialized in Derek Worley's living room to find him laid out on his couch with his feet propped up on his coffee table, with a brandy snifter in hand, acting as though it was no more than a casual Sunday afternoon cocktail hour.

He looked up when Z popped in and nodded for him to have a seat. Z stood where he was and Derek shrugged.

"You want to stand, genie? Fine with me. You can't stop what's about to happen." He smiled.

"Well?" said Z.

"Well what?"

"You brought me here...you know the game. Your wish is my command."

"I'm not making any wishes. Not yet anyway."

Z stared at him in silence. What the hell was he up to? Derek seemed to know exactly what he was thinking.

"She's already on her way, you know. And guess what? Since you didn't bring her here, your 'Law' holds no bearing whatsoever!" He smiled smugly and took a large sip of his drink.

"What about your wishes?"

"That can wait until after I'm finished with her. And if I don't use any wishes up, then you're pretty much stuck here my friend...at my whim until after it's all done. And I'd even be willing to use up one wish to make you sit here and watch. In fact, I think that would make this little game all the more interesting. Oh and don't bother with the physical violence because I'll just wish you into your mirror until I call you. And remember, you can't kill me anyway...I own you now."

Z struggled to maintain his composure.

He had a plan and he already knew Scheri was on her way here. In fact he was banking on it. Now all he could do at this point was hope that his theories were correct. They weren't based on any empirical data...just a hunch. A gut feeling....and something he hadn't ever thought of much during all the time he'd held onto his vendetta against his father and all of his kind: faith.

He kept an even expression and said nothing. It was important that Derek couldn't read into anything he said, or any motions he made right now. Time was on his side, because every moment that passed was one moment closer to when Sheri got here. He could see her future now and he knew that if he played his cards right that future held great promise. Part of that promise was her coming here now and facing her fears. The other part was knowing that she had the courage to take down Derek Worley. Even if it meant that he had to sacrifice himself in the process.

It was late afternoon when she drove into town.

Her hands were shaking as she drove past every familiar landmark...the newsstand sitting on the corner, and her favorite bar and grill in the downtown district.

She pulled into the parking lot. She typed in the code to open the gate and pulled into one of the parking spaces in the garage. She'd gotten a no contract cell a few weeks ago, but hadn't had any reason to use it yet. It seemed strange that the first time would be to call the police. She pulled it out of her purse, trying to decide what she should tell them.

"911. Would you like to report an emergency?"

She stalled for a moment. What was going to happen when she got up there? Was Z already granting Derek his wishes?

"Hello? Would you like to report an emergency?"

She was jolted back to the moment.

"Um...yeah. I'm at Hallendale Apartments, Unit 813. I need help. My...boyfriend has threatened to hurt me and I don't know what to do. I'm hiding right now. In the bedroom but he's threatening to break down the door and if he does I don't know what he'll do to me."

"Ma'am, stay where you are and remain calm. We'll get someone over there as soon as possible."

She hung up, dragged in a deep breath and headed for elevator.

The elevator opened and she walked down the hallway as the memories flooded through her mind. How many times she'd walked these halls. How often she'd felt as though they were her prison of no escape.

How many times she'd walked past Mrs. Shafer in 812, smiling and pretending everything was fine, even though her arm felt as though it had been dislocated after Derek had grabbed her and dragged her on the floor from the kitchen to the bedroom, kicking her so hard in the ribs she thought he'd broken a couple.

She swallowed hard as she knocked on the door.

She heard the buzzer...he didn't' even bother to ask who was there because he knew she'd come.

She drew the gun and walked in the door to see Derek sitting there waiting for her. Z was standing close by next to the mirror which was standing near the bar on the far wall.

He laughed out loud when he saw the gun.

"Well, that wasn't exactly the greeting I was expecting from you...but then I forgot your lover over here has been teaching you a few things."

"Shut up, Derek."

"What else has he been teaching you?" His voice was taunting.

"Maybe everything you couldn't," Z shot back.

Derek stared at her with a smug look. "Well, what are you waiting for? Go ahead and shoot."

Her hands began to shake remembering what Z had said about destroying the mirror so Derek couldn't make any wishes.

"Scheri...remember what I told you," Z said.

Derek turned around and looked at him.

"Oh, we have a plan there do we big man?" He laughed out loud. "Well don't bank on it. She doesn't have the guts to shoot me. And whatever you thought you taught her about fighting back didn't do her much good last night, now did it?"

Scheri looked over at Z and a tear slid down her face. He nodded, and she could hear him in her mind as he said, "Don't wait. Have faith."

She aimed the gun at the mirror and pulled the trigger as it exploded into a million pieces all over the floor. Z began to fade and his energy dissipated into tiny shards of light before floating off into every direction. He was gone.

Derek looked over in disbelief.

"You fucking bitch. What have you done?"

She stared at him as her eyes welled over with tears at the realization that Z was really gone. Her hands wavered and she almost lowered the gun as the unspeakable grief hit her. And in that split second, when her guard was down, Derek lunged.

He knocked the gun from her hands and punched her. She laid there dazed as he straddled her body, his fingers tight around her throat.

She kicked him as hard as she could and punched him so hard, she bloodied his nose. She scrambled to reach the gun and managed to get it as she struggled with him on the floor and as he tried to fight it away from her she fired at him, but it missed, and only nicked him in the shoulder.

He roared with pain as the bullet grazed across his skin, with searing white hot heat.

He restrained her wrist and managed to get the gun from her hand and toss it as far across the room as he could. She bit him and jabbed at his throat but now that she'd done it once before he was half expecting it and dodged the move.

Oh, how he wanted to choke the life out of this bitch right here and now, but that would be way too easy. She

230

needed to suffer just like mother had suffered. Just like the others before her.

He hit her again, hard enough to knock her out, and then made sure no one was out in the hallway. He stood and wiped the blood from his nose and winced as he reached up to staunch the blood pouring from his shoulder.

She'd actually hurt him. The genie had taught her all too well.

He had to get out of here now, because someone likely heard the gunshots and called the police. They wouldn't know it came from his place, but even so, they couldn't just come barging in without a warrant. By the time he came back they'd have brushed it off as a false alarm, be long gone and he could clean up the mess later when he returned.

He walked out and checked the hallway before dragging her out and into the stairwell. There would be far less chance of anyone seeing him carrying her out if he took her down the eight flights of stairs than in the elevator. It was getting close to dark now anyway, so it would be easy at this point to drive out to the edge of town, have his way with her and then bury her in the muck by the river, just as he'd done with her predecessor.

He peeked out into the garage and saw no one, duct taping her mouth and hands before dumping her into the trunk. The gas can was already in the back and all ready to go. He pulled out and headed up the street toward the edge of town, just before the police car rounded the corner and pulled into Hallendale Apartment complex.

Z could feel his energy floating off into what seemed like a billion different directions. His conscience was still intact and yet it felt almost distant and unorganized and he struggled to maintain directing it.

231

He was still him…but not him. He was floating in some kind of endless void of heat energy with no matter, no space, no time as visions of his past, present and future all melded into one. He was consciousness without thought. And in that moment when he became aware of who he was thought became reality and his energy began to reassemble.

Perhaps his whole mission on earth had been his own way of finding himself…of discovering his desire and his inherent nature to want to help. His selfish Jinn side would certainly have prevented that and he would have needed a clever way to lead him to this place where he now was. Living as a human…experiencing all of humanities flaws, emotions, frustrations, and the hurts that lead them to compassion. He had needed those lessons. And so he had gotten them.

He was not the Jinn he'd been pretending to be for so long. He had more Angel in him than he'd ever wanted to admit and his gut feeling had been correct. It was called faith.

An image appeared to him out of nowhere standing there in front of him. It was a man who looked remarkably like himself…with long dark hair and golden flecked eyes. It was uncanny; almost like looking into a mirror.

He he knew instinctively it was the Angel named Morad. The father he'd never known, the one he'd hated for so long.

"I know who you are," he said quietly.

"Then you know why I'm here," the man replied.

"Why did you come here now…after all this? Don't you think it's a little late?"

"I came to let you know that you have a place among us. You were willing to sacrifice yourself for her. I'm here if you need me."

"Where were you for all the time that I already needed you?"

"You know, I loved your mother just the way you love Schehrazade."

"Then why did you leave."

"Why are you leaving *her*?"

"Because it's for the best."

"Is it now?" said Morad, raising a brow. "Did it occur to you that maybe I left for the same reasons?"

Azizi looked away from him.

"You should have been here."

"And would you have made the same decisions if I had been? Perhaps my not being there is the very reason you're standing here talking to me right now."

Z looked at him with surprise.

"So you knew that this would happen all along?"

"Not necessarily. It's only one of many timelines. But it was always a probability I was willing to take a chance on."

"So now what? What do I do?"

"Do what's in your heart," Morad said as he began to fade away and disappear.

Z felt overcome with emotion at meeting the father he'd never known, and finding out that maybe he hadn't left for any of the reasons he'd assumed...and he could sense that he would be seeing him again. What was even stranger was that he wanted to.

Now here he was doing exactly as Morad had said...he was following his heart.

He could still feel Scheri there strong and true. She was in trouble, just as he'd known she would be, and she needed him now more than she ever had.

He focused his energy to Derek's apartment, and it was quite remarkable how now that he was in this altered form, or rather had acknowledged who he really was, he no longer had to bend space or do any of the other arduous manipulations of matter to transport himself. He could simply think...and thought became direct motion and creation.

When he arrived there he could see the police outside the apartment knocking on the door. They had probable cause

233

to break in, but he decided to help them. The door suddenly cracked open of its own accord, and as they walked in and saw the broken mirror on the floor, drops of blood on the carpet and evidence of a scuffle, the picture covering Derek's safe suddenly fell exposing the door of the safe, partly cracked open.

They quickly taped off the area, got a warrant and as Officer Roberto Bullara looked through Derek's 'album of conquests' they realized that based on the blood and signs of a struggle she may have been taken against her will and could be running out of time even as they spoke.

"This can't be happening. I mean this is Derek Worley for Christ's sake! I sit in court with this guy day after day. I've seen him bring cases to court put some of the worst behind bars. I've had dinner and drinks with him and his wife at charity auctions...well, I mean before she left. He said she'd left because she ran off with some guy. I don't know why she came here today...but whatever it was, it set him off. Someone else called in a few minutes after she did. They heard the gunshots."

He sighed and shook his head disgusted and saddened beyond words that someone he thought he knew so well, was apparently from what the evidence was suggesting, a serial killer.

He went back through the stack and called his partner over. "Look at this. He's taken all these pictures of his vics, and then has this shot. What is this? Moonlight on the water? There's no dead body. Just the scenery....like he's taking pictures on vacation after he kills someone."

His partner nodded. "I recognize that tree. That's the old hanging tree down by the river on the east side by the bridge. I wonder if that's where he buries them."

Bullara's expression turned more serious than it already was. "She called for help. Somehow he must've hauled her out of here in the time it took us to get here. Send someone over there to that area immediately. And let's pray we're not too late."

CHAPTER NINETEEN

Scheri opened her eyes. Her vision was blurry and she could smell gasoline. She could only see out of one eye, because the other one was swollen partially shut where Derek had punched her.

She was in the dark and could feel the bumpy motion beneath her, and she instinctively knew she was in the trunk of his car.

Her head hurt so bad she could barely think and her mouth was taped and her hands bound behind her. A tear slipped down her cheek when she realized what dire straits she was in.

Z had told her she was going to have to face her greatest fear to take Derek down. She'd done everything he'd asked her to do...she'd destroyed the mirror, losing him in the process. She'd called for help but no one had gotten there in time. Now here she was, about to face death at the hands of her abuser. Maybe Z had been wrong. Or maybe he had issues and had simply abandoned her the same way his father had abandoned him and his mother. He had told her he was always with her...and yet, here she was alone in her darkest moment.

She struggled against her bonds but they were too tight. She could tell it was duct tape. It was pitch black and the way she was laying it was fairly impossible to feel around for a sharp edge to try to cut it through. She was going to have to lay here until the car stopped and Derek came to pull her out. She could only hope that he wouldn't shoot her while she was in the trunk. At least if he pulled her out, she might have a chance to kick him...head-butt him and run...anything to try to escape.

The car came to a sudden stop and a few moments later Derek opened the trunk.

He pulled her out and threw her on the ground.

"I guess you thought you did something really smart shooting out the mirror. You think that just because I didn't get to command that Jinn that you somehow could stop me? Look at you. Here you are…on the ground. About to die."

He knelt down over her taunting her some more as he opened his gas can and sprinkled gas over her.

"Let's see the charges are: failing to obey. Didn't your marriage vows say the word 'obey'? Domestic violence. Kicking and punching your husband." He paused and wiped the trickle of blood away from his nose. "Oh, and let's not forget adultery. I know you slept with him. And since I'm both the prosecution and the defense, why don't you speak up and defend yourself." He laughed. "What? Nothing to say? Well, for lack of testimony and since I'm also judge and jury, I find you guilty as charged. Your sentence? Death of course. I'd say a barbeque is in order. But not before the appetizer. We need to tenderize the meat a little.

He stood up and reached in the back of the trunk, pulling out a pair of pliers.

He looked down at his arm where she'd scratched him the night before when he and Abdul had broken into Azizi's trailer. "Let's see…the Bible says, an eye for an eye and that it's better to pluck out your eye if it doesn't see clearly. It seems you have a penchant for scratching. So, maybe we should remove those offending fingernails for a start."

Scheri closed her eyes. She would not scream. She would not give him the satisfaction.

She braced herself for the unbearable pain and a second later she felt a presence and heard a familiar voice.

"The Bible was not written by God…it was written by man. If you want to know what God says, perhaps you should try listening."

Derek turned around to see Azizi ab'd al Jadu standing behind him.

"What are you doing here? Did you get sent back to grant the wishes you thought you could get out of? I've studied up on your kind and you are liable for any wishes not granted. You are a Jinn and you are still under my command by the very fact you came back here."

"Maybe if I was simply a Jinn that would be true. But I am also half Angel, and I serve no one. And when I do serve it is in the interest of protecting the higher power of life."

He looked over at Scheri. "You're not going to hurt her, Derek."

"Try and stop me."

Z walked over and stood in front of Derek and with a single thought the pliers were ripped from his fingers and lay half buried in the muddy soil several feet away. Derek tried to move but found himself unable to…bound by some unseen force of energy as Z reached down and pulled the tape from Scheri's mouth.

He smoothed her hair back from her face and kissed her softly. "I'm not going to undo your bonds because it's important that they find you here just like this with him. They already found the evidence they need in his apartment and I promise I'm close by and you're safe. He can't hurt you anymore. Your first wish is about to be granted."

A moment later they heard the sirens heading in their direction.

Derek turned to her. "You fucking bitch. I'll kill you."

"Well…I think maybe where you're going, you're going to have to wait a long time to do that, asshole."

Z put the tape back on her mouth and then disappeared before their eyes.

The force holding Derek held him fast until the moment the police officers approached with their flashlights in hand, appalled by the sight before them and then suddenly let him go. He stood and started to run, grabbing the gun from the seat of the car.

Officer Roberto Bullara pulled up and walked up to the scene.

"Derek...listen let's talk. We can get you some help. You know how this works.

"Fuck you, Rob. I'm not going in."

"Why would you do this, Derek?"

Derek looked a bit detached for a moment...as if out of touch with reality. Mother was there. No more than a ghost and yet so real; taunting him...along side of Jonas. And so was his last girlfriend, Susan.

He smiled because only one answer came to mind.

"Because I can."

He wasn't going to spend the rest of his life in prison...and at this point he was fucked. There was no way he was going to let them take him away. His career, his life was now ruined and not worth living anyway. So may as well go down in blaze of glory. He pulled his lighter from his pocket, and pushed the button and in that second that it touched the gasoline that had splattered on his clothes when he'd doused Scheri, his body became engulfed in flames and he raised the gun to his head and pulled the trigger.

It was not the ending he'd planned on, and yet somehow he'd known it was one possible one from the moment he'd put his mother and Jonas at the bottom of this river all those years ago. Perhaps he had the power of God after all. He'd been in control of taking their lives...and now he was in control of taking his own.

Scheri looked on in horror and turned her face away as the police unbound her and helped her to her feet.

They drove her to the police station where she answered their questions about what had just happened and about the year of abuse she'd taken before she'd run. It was both emotional and cleansing finally being able to tell someone what he'd done and most of all...knowing they would believe her.

Later that evening as she stood in the shower of her hotel room she realized that Z had kept his promise about that 'first wish' she'd made last night...and even the first time she'd ever said something like that sitting in his kitchen weeks ago when he'd told her he was going to help her get her life back. Derek had been taken down and her life could go back to normal again.

Maybe she could get herself an apartment here in the city...go back to her old job, and publish the short stories she'd been writing back at the trailer.

She turned off the shower and walked out into the room and sat down on the edge of the bed, wondering where he was, and whether he'd be back.

"Z...can you hear me?"

There was no answer...only the silence of the room.

She thought of driving back to the trailer tonight to see if he was there but she instinctively knew he wouldn't be. There was nothing to go back to, except little George. She would drive back to get him in the morning and she supposed if Z didn't show up she was going to have to come up with something to tell Louie and everyone else who knew him.

She slid up into the bed and covered up, as the tears began to flow into the pillow. A few moments later, her eye swollen and sore, and her body as bruised and tired as it had been when she'd first run, she fell asleep.

Z watched unseen from the corner of her room. The pull to go to her when she'd called him was almost too strong to fight back against and yet he had to. At least until he could reign in the emotions he was somehow able to feel even being outside of a human body and in the space between spaces outside human perceptions.

In the short time he'd been here, The Order of Angels had come to visit him. And since he'd acknowledged his power as one of them, it meant that his term on earth serving this human was nearly over. He'd fallen in love as a

240

man...learned compassion and a wealth of other lessons while living as a Jinn. And now he was something more. He was still part Jinn but he was also an Angel. And with that greater power also came greater responsibility and selflessness.

His love for Scheharazade Bloom couldn't be matched. She had saved him as much as he'd saved her, but now that he'd changed form he knew that he would be called to serve others and there would be little time for personal relationships. She deserved to be with a human...one of her own kind who would love her the way Derek hadn't....and the way he did now. He knew he had to let her go and he had to gather enough strength to do it.

He watched her there, looking just as she had in his own bed with her long hair spread out around her head. He pictured how beautiful her body was....naked and wet as it had been in his arms. The way her sweet lips tasted every time she kissed him. The feel of her hand when she'd lay it on the side of his face. And the first 'Herb' look she'd ever given him.

They were memories he would carry with him for the rest of his long existence right alongside of the love in his heart. The love she'd helped put there. He would always be there watching over her, so near and yet so far away. The same way she'd been for all those long days that he'd watched over her and admired her when she was staying with him at the trailer. Funny how his human life seemed to be a reflection of his life as both Jinn..and what would come as one of the Angels.

She wouldn't understand and he knew how much it was going to hurt her, when he told her. But it had to happen. He was going to have to at least say goodbye to Louie too.

Damn, he was going to miss Lou's smiling face...his off-color jokes and Betty Boop bobbing to the Hawaiian music outside his door at the tiki bar.

He materialized in her room, and walked toward the bed where she lay sleeping, slipping out of his shirt and under the blanket next to her. He kissed her swollen eye and it immediately began to heal…the purple bruising diminishing and the bloody spot on her lip began to heal over too.

He reached down and traced the raw spots on her wrists with his finger, taking care not to wake her up, and they too began to diminish and heal over.

God she looked more beautiful to him right now than she ever had. Maybe it was because he was seeing her with new eyes…with a new outlook. Or maybe it was because he treasured every second with her now more than he ever had.

He may not be able to share her life, but at least he could share one last night sleeping with her in his arms.

A moment later she stirred in her sleep and rolled over. She opened her eyes and discovered him there next to her and she quickly sat up and threw her arms around him.

"I thought you were never coming back."

He smiled. "I told you…I'm always with you."

She reached up and touched her face and looked a little shocked when she realized her eye was seeing normally and the swelling was gone.

"What happened?"

"I healed you."

"How did you do that? Can genies heal people?"

"No…but Angels can. And as a matter of fact, I need to stop by and see Louie. He doesn't know it but his lung…never mind. But he needs to stop smoking now before it's too late."

She stared at him for a moment.

"I thought you hated them and didn't want to have anything to do with them."

"I did hate them…at least I thought I did. Maybe that was just a cover-up or something. I don't know. But something changed and I met him."

"Who?"

242

"My father. His name is Morad."

"Was he what you thought he'd be?"

Z shook his head. "No. As a matter of fact he wasn't. I understand now why he did the things he did. And I forgive him."

"So now what? Where do we go from here."

"Where do you want to go?"

"Well, I have to go get George in the morning and bring him back here. Unless we're going to stay at the trailer?"

She smiled.

His expression stayed even and she wondered why he wasn't smiling back.

"I can't go back with you Scherharazade."

"Why?"

"Because there are others who are going to need my help. And you should be free to spend your life with someone... a human. One who'll love you the way I've said they should all along."

"But I love *you*."

"I know. And I love you too. I always will...maybe I always have and I just didn't know it and needed some way to express it and that's why I came here in the first place."

"How can you just leave...didn't you say that's what your father did to your mother? All this time you've expressed so much hatred for what he did. Now...how can you?"

"I understand now exactly what he did....the sacrifice he made."

"Will I ever see you again?"

"I'll always be close by."

She started to cry and as the tears dripped down her nose he reached over and wiped it away with his finger touching the salty dampness to his lips.

He leaned over and pressed his lips to hers, softly at first and then with more urgency. And as she wound her fingers into his hair and dug her fingers into the muscles of his shoulders, he realized that if he was going to say goodbye, he was going to do it right.

He kissed a wet trail down the side of her neck to her cleavage and across the soft tops of her breasts, opening up the top of her shirt and exposing the pink tips dragging each one into his mouth before kissing a path down across her abdomen taking his time, until he reached the soft, wet place he sought. He could feel her moving with every stroke of his lips and tongue as he tasted and teased her until she was begging him for release. But he stopped and didn't give it to her because he wanted to wait…he wanted to look into her eyes and tell her everything he may never get to say again, as their bodies and spirits came together as one.

She sat up and started to push him back against the pillows to return the favor, but he stopped her and instead rolled her underneath him. He wanted to be inside of her this time….to move with her. To bring their souls together through the union of their bodies.

He looked down at her lying there beneath him and he didn't know how he was going to bear leaving her to live the life she was destined, or to bear the thought of her lying in another man's arms like this.

He moved inside of her.

She started to say something but he kissed her lips.

"Shhh. You don't need to speak. I can feel everything you want to say."

He wasn't lying.

He could feel the love she felt for him right now, flowing through every square atom of her being. It was pure and it made him love her even more.

"I love you Scheharazade Bloom. You think I saved you…but you're the one who saved me. From myself. From this place."

He kissed her deeply and began to move with more intensity as she wrapped her legs around his hips, and pulled him deeper, as if to bring his very essence inside of her with his body.

Her arms wound around his neck tighter and she could feel the heat building to an eruption of both physical sensation and emotional outpouring.

A few minutes later her body responded in the only way it could as wave after wave of intense pleasure rolled through her and for a few seconds she thought maybe she'd died in his arms as he came with her...in an avalanche of sensation.

She looked up at him and for a moment the golden flecks in his eyes seemed to take motion...just like before in the shower. Only this time, she too could feel his soul there inside of her. She could see what he was feeling and there was no doubt in that moment how much he loved her.

He buried his face in the side of her neck and then slid down along her body, laying his head against her breasts while she toyed with a lock of his hair.

"I wish we could stay this way forever."

He smiled. "No you don't...you have a life out there waiting for you. The one I promised we were going to get back for you."

"So you're not a Jinn anymore?"

"I am technically but I'm also changed. I don't live by Jinn Law anymore...not that I ever have."

She smiled. "Yeah. I'd say you're not much for following rules. But you don't grant wishes anymore now do you?"

"That's Jinn territory, not for the Angels."

"Well you're still half Jinn."

"I am."

"Well...you remember in the shower you asked me what my first wish was. And I told you I wanted to take Derek down. And you told me to hold on to that wish and believe it can come true."

He nodded. "Yeah. And it did."

245

"And my second wish was that I could see all of you. And well...I'd say you made sure I saw all of you right then and there."

She paused for a moment and smiled.

"But physical love aside, you've let me see all of you since then. The Jinn, the angel, the secrets. Everything. You made that wish come true too."

Her expression grew more serious. "So now I'm just asking, in theory, do I get a third wish?"

"Well if I was under your command and you owned me I suppose you could."

"You told me yesterday that I owned you, and that you're with me always."

He smiled. He'd said those words, and told her to hold onto them.

"You do. But I'm not the same anymore, and I can't stay with you. But if you could have a third wish, and I'm only asking *if*...what would it be?"

"I'd wish that we could be together and love each other the way we do right now, for the rest of my life...our lives."

She reached forward and brushed a lock of his hair back from his forehead. "I know you think I belong with someone human who could love me better than you, or who'd be there for me when you can't. But the fact is that I don't care if you're a Jinn, or an Angel with a mission, or a carny or a guy who works at a coffee shop. And you have lived as a human, so you are part human too. I just love you...the real you, with all my heart and I don't want to spend my life here on earth or anywhere else without you in it."

He stared at her for a moment and then leaned in and kissed her lips very softly.

He didn't say a word but he pulled her into his arms and held her there for a moment.

"I have to go now....but I'll always be with you. And now I have a wish."

"What is it?" she said trying to speak past the lump in her throat.

"Just promise me that when I whisper in your heart, you'll hear me."

Tears began to stream down her face and she hugged him tighter as a light began to surround them both and he began to dematerialize, finally disappearing from her grasp, leaving her alone where she sat.

"Your wish is my command," she said softly wiping the tears from the end of her nose as the emptiness she would now know without him engulfed her.

A moment later as she lay back on the pillows and closed her eyes, everything faded away to nothing and she heard a far-off noise that sounded almost like a buzzer. She felt as though she were being dragged through a long tunnel. There was no light at the end but she could feel her consciousness heading toward something at breakneck speed.

He was an Angel now. Was she dying? She'd heard of people who'd come back from near death experiences describing a tunnel and a buzzing sound and a light at the end of the tunnel. She struggled to see up ahead but nothing came into view.

The buzzing sound got louder and louder and a moment later reached a fever pitch.

CHAPTER TWENTY

Scheharazade Bloom sat up in bed with a start and reached over to shut off the loud buzz of her alarm that had decided to go off an hour later than it was supposed to.

She looked around the room, confused, trying to get her bearings and remember where she was. She wiped a tear from her eye that she'd cried only a minute ago in a dream in which the love of her life had just vanished from her arms after she'd made a wish. A wish that they could stay together somehow. It had seemed so real, she had to remind herself where she was for a moment.

She laid back against the pillows as the hazy fog cleared from her mind.

She was a writer and had been suffering from writer's block for weeks now. Maybe this dream was the answer to her problem....in fact right about now she wanted to skip going in for the job interview she had scheduled and instead sit down and start writing it into what might make a great book!

She looked over at the time....dammit!

She was late already and had only maybe twenty minutes to get ready. Her career goal was to be an author, but for now, working a real job was gonna have to do. The copywriter's job she'd applied for last week would definitely pay the bills better than the job she had now. So better get moving and make that interview.

Damn, but what a dream that had been! There had been some pretty scary and painful parts of it, but there'd also been some incredibly erotic and sensuous scenes too.

She hugged her arms around her body remembering the feel of the arms of the man she'd fallen in love with. His name was Azizi…and he was a Jinn.

A Jinn? Wait a minute.

She looked down at the book she'd been reading last night before falling asleep. It was a book called 'Legends and Myths' and the page she'd been reading before she dropped off said, 'The Jinn'.

She put on her reading glasses and looked down at the page. There in print it said:

'The word genius in the English language is derived from the word 'jinn' or 'jinni'. This came about because many thought that although the Jinn and particularly the Ifrit, were usually malevolent spirits who took pleasure in frightening humans, they were also sometimes attributed to wisdom and new ideas, often through *dreams* they would send to a human they had their eye on, or who may be their twin soul in the mirror dimension if the human world.'

Dreams?! Mirror dimension?

Goosebumps broke out all over her body as she read the words on the page. What an uncanny and downright eerie coincidence that she'd just read this passage before falling asleep last night and then had an extraordinary dream that could be quite a unique story idea that would get her published and out there as an author.

She shook off the feeling as she headed toward the shower, but then as she lathered her hair and rinsed the soap from her body, she felt aroused remembering the feel of the hands and lips of the tall, handsome Jinn from her dream named Azizi ab'd al Jadu. She closed her eyes and she could envision him standing there, naked, wet, tan and ripped with muscle...his long black hair dripping with water as he moved in toward her. So familiar and yet so...surreal.

She opened her eyes. *Damn, Scheri. Get a grip!*

She rinsed off before the urge to pleasure herself became too much...not that she wouldn't have enjoyed the release and needed it in fact. It had been a long time since she'd been with anyone...well not counting in that dream last night. But this morning she was already late for her interview and needed to get dressed and head out the door. At this point she didn't even have time for a cup of coffee!

She got out, threw on a nice outfit, dried her hair and did her make-up and then headed out the door.

Twenty minutes later as she stood in the elevator a group of four people came rushing up, yelling 'hold the door'.

They stepped in and as the elevator started up to the tenth floor she looked over and noticed a handsome, well-groomed man in a business suit staring at her.

He was well-built, with clear blue eyes and a smile that would stop traffic.

He looked familiar and as he moved closer she felt uneasy. He looked down to the piece of paper in her hand with 'Winston & Koener' written on it.

He smiled. "Do you work there?"

She shook her head. "No. Not yet...I'm applying for a copywriter's job there."

"Well good luck." He stuck out his hand to shake hers. "My name is Derek. Derek Worley."

And then it hit her. This man was the face of the criminal...the one who'd been her abuser in her dream.

Her eyes widened for a moment and she backed away slightly trying not to freak out.

"Are you okay? Miss...I didn't catch your name?"

She nodded. "Um. Yeah..I'm fine. My name is...Lily," she said politely, giving him a fake name.

"Well, Lily...maybe I'll be seeing you around," he said, before stepping out of the elevator on the eighth floor and heading over to the law office where he worked.

"No, you won't," she said under her breath as he walked away.

She dragged in a deep breath struggling to maintain her composure until everyone else was out of the elevator before she gasped and covered her mouth.

What the hell was going on?

That was the man from her dream! The one who'd beaten her...the one who'd murdered his mother and father. And who'd murdered his girlfriend before her....at least in the dream.

As it stood now, she didn't know the guy and planned to stay as far away from that office building as possible. There'd be no way he could track her down since she gave him a fake name.

She quickly pushed the button to take her back down to the ground floor. There was no way in hell she was going for that job interview!

She headed down the block trying to decide what to do, and figured maybe she should just go home and write the story she'd dreamed. Had it really been a dream? Was there a message in it?

She walked further down the block away from the office building and as she passed a little street side café and coffee shop, she noticed a television hanging up under the awning there and a news bulletin flashing on the screen along with Derek Worley's picture and a picture of a dark haired woman of about 25 years old.

She moved closer and her eyes widened as she listened to what the reporter was saying.

"The community is both shocked and angered as local attorney Derek P. Worley has been brought in on a suspected murder charge of Susan Miller, missing for the past three months. Ms. Miller's remains were unearthed yesterday at an undisclosed location near the water, and evidence was uncovered with her remains that led police to the apartment of Mr. Worley. Mr. Worley had no comment as he was taken into custody for questioning just moments ago in the downtown area....."

Scheri could hear police sirens in the distance as she looked up the street toward the Ashtonby Office complex she'd just come from only twenty or so minutes ago.

251

She plunked down hard on one of the café table chairs trying to compose herself and figure out if she was living in an episode of the Twilight Zone or if this was all really happening.

She looked around for a waitress so she could order a cup of coffee and noted a waiter was standing close by instead.

He turned around and started to walk toward her and then it hit her like a ton of bricks.

Her mind drifted back to the dream she'd been having. Just before she'd woke up she'd said to Z that she if she could have a wish, she'd wish that he could stay with her somehow in the human world and live the rest of their lives together. She loved him no matter whether he was a Jinn, or an Angel or a human, or a carny...*or a guy working in a coffee shop.*

Her eyes widened as he approached and she covered her mouth as tears began to well up in her eyes.

He walked up and smiled playfully.

"Can I help you, Miss"

He offered her his hand and when hers stopped shaking she placed it in his palm. He knelt down in front of her and lifted her fingers to his lips and kissed them softly.

"Is it really you? This...it just can't be happening. Am I losing my sanity?"

"Why don't you stand up and give me a kiss and find out?"

"I don't even know you!"

He stared at her for long moment and the words came to her in her mind. *"...I'll always be with you. Just promise me that when I whisper in your heart, you'll hear me."*

"You know me, Scheharazade."

He stood up and he pulled her into his arms with a very real familiarity, as her arms wound around his neck and she saw the golden flecks in his eyes. His lips caught hers, soft and velvety....sensuous and erotic just as she remembered from the dream. There was no doubt that this was Z's kiss.

He pulled her close to him and deepened the kiss, nearly dragging the air out of her lungs as a couple of annoyed onlookers whispered, 'Get a room, for God's sake!'

She finally pulled back from him and wiped the tears that were now spilling from her lashes in a steady stream. He reached up and lifted one from the end of her nose with the tip of his forefinger and brought it to his lips.

"I feel like I'm losing my sanity here. Am I still dreaming?"

He leaned in and whispered against her neck. "I figured I was batting one hundred with the other two wishes and I'd better not miss on this one."

"Did that really happen....I mean with Derek?"

"No. It didn't happen...at least not yet. But if you had gone into that office today for that job interview, and ended up taking that job and if you'd have shook hands with him and met him for dinner next week, like he was about to ask you, then that's exactly what would have happened."

"And what about the girl before me?"

"There was no way I could save her. I wish that I could have made that happen...but I don't have that connection with her. I had no way to get a message to her before it was too late. You are my twin soul, Scheharazade. But at least now justice is served. I promised you he would be taken down and he is."

"I still don't understand."

"Let's just keep it simple and say you lived it while you were asleep." He laughed. "It's hard to understand. I guess you'd better read that Legends & Myths book some more. The Jinn are legendary for bringing people ideas or wisdom or messages through dreams."

"Are you a Jinn or an Angel?"

"Both."

He paused for a moment looking toward the cash register at the heavy set man giving him a dirty look.

"Stay here and let me go get you a cup of coffee. I gotta keep up enough smoke and mirrors going so they think I'm actually working."

She smiled and then broke out in laugher as he walked away to go get the coffee.

A second later she heard a sound below her feet. It was a tiny, stray tiger kitten that had wandered in looking for scraps of food. She gasped and picked him up, nuzzling his tiny head, and whispered, "George!" in his ear.

Z came back a few moments later with not one but two cups of coffee. He took off his apron and sat down at the table across from her.

"What are you doing? Won't you get fired?"

"Nah. I just quit." He laughed. "I figure there's probably some better job for me. I heard there's a carnival in town."

She laughed out loud. "Are you serious?"

"Yeah. I hear they have great cheese steaks too. And they're looking for new entertainment. I have this idea...a magic act. I can be Aladdin and you can be Princess Jasmine. We can dress you up in harem pants and some veils. Whaddya think?"

"I am *not* taking off my clothes."

He raised a brow. "We'll see about that when we get home."

"And where exactly is that?"

"My home is where ever you are."

"Can you take me to where you're from? I want to see it."

"Yeah. Maybe later in the week. We'll have to find a babysitter for George though...unless you want to bring him with us."

"Really?"

"Yeah."

"But what about your realm burning up my energy? Isn't that what you said in the dream."

"We're twin souls. I'm an Angel and I can change your energy so you won't be harmed."

She dragged in a deep breath.

"Wow. This is...surreal. I have to get used to this."

He nodded. "I know. That's why I said we'd go later in the week."

"What about you not aging....how is this going to work?"

"However we want it to. I can look old if you want."

"Well...maybe we should wait a few years on that one."

He laughed as he stood up and threw down a couple of bucks on the table. They walked out onto the sidewalk as she carried little George in her arms.

She looked over at him as they walked along, admiring the way his hair fell around his shoulders and the shadow of razor stubble along his jaw line...so familiar and yet so new.

And she looked down at the dragon tattoo peeking out from under his shirt sleeve remembering the first time she'd seen it in the dream.

"Nice tat. Does it have any special meaning?" she said playfully.

He stopped walking for a second and looked over at her. "As a matter of fact it does. The dragon stands for knowledge, power...and *protection*. It's also a symbol of transformation and magic in many cultures."

She looked over at him with both wonder and admiration, because that was certainly a symbol of everything this man of her dreams was....literally.

'You know...it's really beautiful. And it's a shame that I can't see the whole thing."

She eyed him mischievously. "I know I said I wasn't taking off my clothes but when we get home if you take yours off first and show me more of it, I might reconsider."

He smiled, took her hand in his and brought her fingers to his lips as they kept walking.

"Your wish is my command."

CYNTHIA LUCAS

After reading countless romance novels, Cynthia Lucas decided to follow in the footsteps of her grandmother's love of writing and try her hand at writing her own.

Her newest release, SMOKE & MIRRORZ is the story of one down on his luck genie, one woman on the run for her life, a healthy serving of heated romance and fantasy, a dash of suspense and a liberal helping of redemption and second chances…her favorite recipe for a captivating page turner. And after numerous requests from her readers to appear on the cover of one her of her books, Ms. Lucas says she 'took the plunge at age 49, and if I was going to do it, there was no one else going on that cover with me, except the one and only Jimmy Thomas…the most published cover model in history.'

Her take on that one? 'LIVE your dreams!'

Ms. Lucas' first published novel, released in 2010 WHEN LIGHTNING STRIKES, weaves time-travel, swashbuckling and heated romance, and the premise that every action we take and the power of love can ripple through time like a drop of water in a pond into a captivating love and adventure story that leaves the reader turning page after page until the very end.

The book was a #1 Best Seller in Kindle Edition in October and November of 2012, and continues to be a Top 100 Best Seller in Time Travel Romance on Amazon.com. After numerous requests for a sequel, Ms. Lucas released QUICKSILVER MOON in the fall of 2012 to glowing reviews. That second book in this series has been nominated for and is a finalist for Best Time Travel in the 2012 RONE Awards.

Other titles by Ms. Lucas include, BLOOD FROM A STONE which was a Quarter Finalist in the 2013 Amazon Breakthrough Novel Awards, and has been nominated for Best Paranormal in the 2012 RONE Awards.

When not writing her stories, Cynthia, who is also an award-winning vocalist, songwriter and lyricist, entertaining tourists and locals alike with her band NORTH 2 SOUTH on many stages, both large and small near her home in Tampa Bay, where she resides with her husband of twenty-one years, their daughter and several pets, including exotic birds and various wildlife that she rehabs as a hobby.

21010440R00146

Made in the USA
Charleston, SC
02 August 2013